MASSACRE
THE HEBRAICA TRILOGY
BOOK TWO

CHRISTINE JORDAN

First published in 2023 by Bloodhound Books.

www.bloodhoundbooks.com

Print ISBN: 978-1-5040-8592-2

Also by Christine Jordan

The Hebraica Trilogy

Sacrifice

~

Writing as CJ Claxton

MisPer

CAST OF CHARACTERS

Gloucester

Moses le Riche: Wealthy Moneylender
Douce: Wife of Moses
Abraham: Son of Moses
Henne: Daughter of Moses
Vives of London: Husband of Henne
Benjamin: Son of Moses
Rachel: Wife of Benjamin
Justelin: Son of Moses

Zev: Silversmith
Arlette: Wife of Zev
Baruch: Son of Arlette
Rubin: Son of Zev

Elias de Glocestre: Moneylender
Mirabelle: Wife of Elias
Belia: Daughter of Elias
Isaac of Lincoln: Husband of Belia

Pucelle: Daughter of Belia
Bonanfaunt: Son of Elias
Genta: Wife of Bonanfaunt
Elias le Petit: Son of Bonanfaunt
Vives: Son of Bonanfaunt

Bellassez: Widow and Moneylender
Muriel: Daughter of Bellassez

Josce: Moneylender
Judea: Wife of Josce
Mannasser: Son of Josce

Abigail: Widow and Moneylender
Josce: Son of Abigail
Brunetta: Daughter of Abigail
Glorietta: Daughter of Abigail

Abbot Thomas Carbonel: St Peter's Abbey
William fitz Stephen: Sheriff of Gloucester (1175-1189)
William Marshal: Sheriff of Gloucester (1190-1195)

London

Isaac Gotsce
Abner Gotsce
Joya: Mother of Isaac and Abner
Jacob of Orléans: Learned Jewish Scholar
Benedict of York
Deudonne of Lincoln
Ranulf de Glanville: Justiciar

York

Josce of York; Wealthy Moneylender
Anna: Wife of Josce
Rabbi Elijah of York
Antera: Sister of Rabbi Elijah
Moses of Bristol
Yom Tov: Son of Moses of Bristol
Rabbi Yom-Tob of Joigny, France
John Marshal: Sheriff of York
Richard Malebysse
William Percy
Marmeduke Darell
Philippe de Fauconberg

France

King Henry II: King of England (1154–1189)
King Richard I: King of England (1189–1199)
Queen Eleanor: Mother of Richard I
Mercadier: Occitan Mercenary
Salvanhac: The King's physician
Pierre de Basile: Bowman

And the Lord saw that the wickedness of man had multiplied in the earth, and that every formation, or image, of the thought of his heart was only evil every day.

Onkelos Genesis 6:5

ONE

Baruch woke late with a headache. Too much ale the night before in his local tavern. He got out of bed, pissed in the *pot de chambre*, pulled on some breeches and sauntered over to the window. Jewry Street was busy with traders. One person stood out amongst the crowd. Brunetta. He watched her as she walked along the street towards the East Gate. She moved like the flowing branches of a willow tree, with the sensuality of a whore. Her long wavy hair, the colour of chestnuts, swung behind her to the rhythm of her hips. Baruch's loins twitched. He watched her until she passed through the East Gate and disappeared. A thought struck him. He pulled on his boots and a tunic and went downstairs. His mother, Arlette, and grandmother, Douce, were in the kitchen cooking. He slipped past them and went out.

Brunetta would not have got far. If he were quick, he could catch up to her. He was curious to see where she was going. Once through the gate, he crossed the wooden drawbridge. Looking left to right he spotted her walking along Shipsters Lane towards the river. *What is that little minx up to*, he thought.

He quickened his pace and once she was past Llanthony Quay he caught up to her.

'Good morning, Brunetta.'

She jumped and turned. Her cheeks were pink from walking in the heat of the sun.

'Oh, it's you,' she said. 'It's hardly morning. More like afternoon.'

'Don't you know it's dangerous to walk out alone?'

'Is it?' she said, giving him a coquettish smile.

'Of course. There are all sorts of vagabonds about.'

'Like you,' she said, her lips slightly apart.

'Like me,' he said, moving closer.

Brunetta stood her ground. Her amber eyes stared at him with a defiance he found beguiling. Baruch took it as an invitation. He tilted her chin upwards and planted a kiss on her lips. When she did not resist, he placed his arm around her tiny waist and pulled her to him. Her lips were soft and her body yielding. The aching in his loins intensified. He swept her up in his arms and carried her to a sheltered clump of bushes where he laid her down on the soft grass and knelt beside her. Without hesitation, he put his hand under her linen shift and traced his fingers along her soft inner thigh to that sweet spot. Brunetta moaned like a whore. Baruch fumbled with the cord around his waist, and with the hunger of a beast, entered her. Brunetta gave out a sharp cry. He ignored it. She tried to kiss him, but Baruch turned his face away. He pulled at her shift to expose her breasts, which to his surprise were large and firm. He grabbed one and squeezed hard, then bent down and bit her nipple. She cried out. Her cries intensified his pleasure.

It was over in minutes, brief, brutal and intensely erotic. He pulled out, extricated himself from her embrace and stood up. Brunetta's eyes were fixed upon him. He wiped the sweat from his forehead and swept his black straggly hair from his face, surprised at how easy she had been. He put down his wantonness to being still slightly drunk from the night before, but what was her excuse? She was staring at him, her thighs apart, looking like she wanted more. Baruch thought it best not to try his luck.

'See you around,' he said and walked away.

CHAPTER

TWO

Brunetta hurried home and changed. When she lifted her tunic, she noticed it was stained with blood. If her mother saw this she would know. She folded it up with some urgency in case anyone should come into the room and tucked it under her mattress till later. Now she sat at the dining table with her mother, Abigail, her brother, Josce, and her younger sister, Glorietta. Daydreaming. In her head she was reliving her encounter with Baruch, trying to work out how it had come about. Then she smiled. She knew how. He was attractive, and she had wanted him. His reputation in the community was legendary. A womaniser, a man of poor morals, a bad Jew. All qualities Brunetta found appealing. When she was a little girl, she would watch Baruch practise his sword-wielding skills in the synagogue courtyard. She knew then he was different from the other boys. Less devout. She remembered his kiss and a frisson of wickedness surged through her.

'She's doing that thing again, *ima*.'

'What thing?' said Abigail, turning her head to look at Brunetta. 'Stop mooning, girl.'

Her mother's sharp words broke her trail of thought. Her cheeks coloured as she realised everyone was looking at her. For a moment she worried that her mother could read her thoughts. She lowered her head and took a mouthful of food, eating without pleasure, the food tasteless in her mouth. Of course, her mother would not approve. That would be an understatement. Having been widowed for as long as Brunetta could remember, her mother had probably forgotten what it was like to lie with a man. And her brother, Josce? What would he do if he found out? He would be disgusted by her, enraged. He would probably try to defend her honour, but he was no match for Baruch.

Brunetta's mood sank into a pit of paranoid depression. Had either of them noticed her soiled tunic when she arrived home or the flush of her cheeks? Had the smell of sex been upon her? Was it still on her? Had they noticed something was different – that *she* was different? She searched their faces for a sign that they knew. Was that reproach she saw in her mother's expression? As she got older, prettier, her mother had become less kind, less loving. Why? Was she jealous of her? Surely not. She looked across at Josce. He was scowling at her. She looked across at Glorietta. She was eating her food with a healthy regard and oblivious to the undertones in the room. She suddenly felt unwelcome in her own home. Her eyes started to sting and mortified, she realised she was about to cry. She stood up.

'Please may I leave the table?' she said, fighting back the tears.

'Please yourself,' her mother replied.

Brunetta fled the room and went upstairs to her bedroom. She threw herself on the bed, and despite the smarting in her eyes would not let the tears fall. She was wrong. Her mother knew nothing. She was supremely indifferent to Brunetta.

Brunetta was unsure if her mother's indifference was worse than her hate. Hate was one side of a coin, the other love. Indifference was a place where love would never flourish. She shuddered and wiped the unwelcome tears from her face. She had to get out of this house, away from her mother. For a girl of her age, and in her community, there was only one way. She had to find a husband and get married.

Her thoughts turned back to Baruch. Would it happen again, she wondered? It was brief, intensely pleasurable, and sublimely improper. He had wanted her so much. It was empowering. Having so much power over a man. But then, afterwards, he had walked away. That part she had not liked. It left her feeling sullied somehow. And then he thanked her. That was odd too. As if they had just transacted a trade of sorts without the exchange of money. That made her feel worse. Demeaning. As if she were chattel.

She wondered whether Baruch would want to do it again with her. Could she arrange it so they would be alone again? It was tricky. Perhaps if she left the house at the same time as yesterday, he would be waiting for her? It was worth a try.

CHAPTER

THREE

Baruch made his way home after his conquest of Brunetta. It had been much easier than he thought it would be. He had no need to charm, cajole, coax. She was ready for it and for him. Her cry when he entered her was satisfying. She was a virgin; unlike the women he usually lay with. The whores in Three Cocks Lane. They had a smell about them. Fusty, like a well-ripened cheese. Brunetta smelled of lavender and roses.

When he arrived home, his family were gathered in the dining hall eating their evening meal. His father, Zev, raised an eyebrow when he saw him.

'To what do we owe this honour?' Zev asked.

'Leave him alone,' said Arlette. Then turning to Baruch, 'Are you hungry? There is plenty left.'

Baruch found that he was starving. As soon as he smelled his mother's cooking, his stomach rumbled. He crossed to his mother and gave her a kiss on the cheek, sitting down next to her.

'You're looking pleased with yourself. What've you been up to?' his younger brother, Rubin, asked.

'Gambling again, I shouldn't wonder,' Zev said.

'Have you been gambling, Baruch?' Arlette asked him.

'No, Mother, I have not.'

'Then let's say no more on the subject,' Arlette said, placing a piece of roast chicken on her son's platter.

When she had finished, she gave his hand a squeeze. Zev grunted into his glass of wine when he saw this.

Baruch ate hurriedly, stuffing his food into his mouth.

'Your mother taught you to eat properly. Mind you do,' his father reprimanded.

'Just let him eat in peace. You're always on at him.'

'And you're always sticking up for him.'

Rubin and his cousins, Henne, Benjamin his wife Rachel and Justelin, who had been sitting quietly at the table, looked up from their meal and gave each other a look. Baruch recognised the look. They were waiting for an argument to start. His grandmother, Douce, sat at the top of the table. She was in her forties now and had given birth to five children, four of which had survived. A few lines had appeared around her mouth, but she was still a very attractive woman. She had been quiet throughout, but now she placed her cup of wine on the table in a deliberate manner.

'Can we for once enjoy a meal without it turning into an argument?' she said, glaring at Zev, her tone sharp.

Zev appeared contrite. Baruch's mouth stretched into a smirk directed at his father. He looked across at Henne. A hint of a cheeky smile appeared on her lips. Sometimes, Baruch thought, she was the only person who truly understood him. Born on the same day, they were practically twins. Henne would always defend Baruch, even when Baruch's behaviour was indefensible. He fancied they might marry one day, but as Baruch grew older, they had grown further apart. His least favourite in the household was his cousin, Abraham. There was a year between them, but in terms of character, they were worlds apart. Growing up, Abraham had never been in trouble whereas Baruch had found it difficult to stay out of trouble. Baruch considered Abraham a dullard, boring and unimaginative. He despised him. He was the centre of his father's attention, schooled daily to step into his father's shoes. But he was not a patch on Moses. Rather, he lived in his father's shadow.

Both Moses and Abraham had gone to London for the coronation of the new king. Another bone of contention. Why wasn't he chosen? He was better company, better able to protect Moses on the journey there and back. Baruch finished his food and stood to leave.

'You're going?' his mother asked.

Baruch could see the sadness in her eyes. She was the one person in the whole world that he loved, if indeed he was capable of such an emotion. He hated disappointing her, but he knew that every day he *was* a disappointment to her.

'Do you want me to stay?'

Douce answered him. 'Of course. We don't see enough of you. Stay and have a cup of wine. Henne is going to play the kinnor for us.'

Henne had taught herself to play the old kinnor of her grandfather's. On hearing her mother's words, she walked over to the harp-like instrument and sat down to play. Baruch sat back down, listened and drank his wine. Henne was a competent player, but after the first few songs Baruch became bored. It wasn't exactly the sort of entertainment he was used to. He thought about the Lich Inn where his Christian friends would be drinking, telling bawdy tales, and Baruch smiled to himself. Then he looked at his mother. She was smiling, yet there was a sadness behind the smile as always. He wondered what deep secret she held.

9

CHAPTER

FOUR

M oses le Riche and his son, Abraham, were guests of the brothers Isaac and Abner Gotsce.

Moses had known Rubi Gotsce, their father, in the old country, Rouen. Rubi had settled in London whilst Moses had moved on to Gloucester. Rubi had done well in London, establishing the city's synagogue but, sadly, he had been dead some ten years.

Visiting London brought forth sad memories for Moses of the burial of his firstborn son, Samuel. Little Samuel had been on Moses' mind since his arrival. Whenever he had cause to visit London on business, he visited his son's grave. The unwanted image of the rabid dogs tearing at his son's flesh returned, even after all these years.

His last visit to London had been to see his business partner, the great Aaron of Lincoln but now, he too, had been dead these past three years. The occasion of his visit this time was the coronation of the new king, Richard. The new king's father, Henry, had died in France of a fever. Jews from all over England were to attend and offer their respects, bringing expensive gifts by way of thanks in the hope that the new king would continue the special relationship his forebears had established.

They sat around the long table in the great hall. A fire had been lit, to counter the early evening chill seeping through the thick stone walls of the Gotsce residence. A fine Normandy tapestry depicting a bucolic scene graced the wall opposite the fireplace. It fluttered occasionally in the cold draught animating the figures expertly sewn on the cloth.

'Do you think the new king will tolerate us as his father did?' Abraham asked.

'Do you mean will he stop burdening us of our unequal share of taxes? Will he stop accusing us of killing Christian boys? Will he stop attacking our homes, killing our people, putting them in the keep?' Isaac responded.

Without the sound counsel of his father, Isaac Gotsce had become an angry young man, full of naïve passion, who railed against injustices. Moses admired him for showing such passion but worried that the young man may find himself in trouble one day as a result. His brother was less vitriolic and more philosophic.

'No point in being angry, when there is nothing we can do about it.'

'It's not fair that our fortunes are tied so closely to who becomes king. Nothing should change but here we are worrying if the new king is to be good or bad for us Jews,' Isaac protested further.

Moses said: 'Well, it's not surprising that we are nervous about this new king. He conspired with Philippe Auguste against his own father, and we all know what Philippe did when he became king.'

The room fell silent and all but Abraham nodded their heads, knowingly.

'Am I the only one who doesn't know what happened?' Abraham asked.

Moses shook his head. Abraham was a dear son, but he had no head for holding on to facts. Abraham stared at his father, his dark eyes searching for understanding. Moses looked back at him. He was a young man now, full of ambition but without the skills to back it up. In appearance, he was a mirror image of his father: dark, curly hair, square jaw and as handsome as Moses was at the same age. But he lacked wisdom. It would come in time, Moses hoped.

'I see I have been remiss in educating you, my son. If the others don't object, I'll give you a quick, but seemingly necessary history lesson.'

'Go on then. Tell me.'

As there were no objections, Moses began.

'When Philippe Auguste came to power in 1179, he was only fifteen years of age, but he proved himself to be no friend of the Jew. He needed money and help to strengthen his hold on the throne and to fight the powerful feudal barons—'

'Where have I heard this before?' Isaac interrupted.

'He did this by confiscating the wealth of the Jews in his lands. Four months later, he imprisoned them all and only released them after they agreed to pay a heavy ransom—'

'Sounding familiar,' Isaac said, interrupting Moses' history lesson again.

'A year later, he annulled all loans made to Christians by Jews and took a comfortable twenty per cent for himself. Not content with that, the following year, he confiscated all their lands and buildings and drove them out of the lands he governed. And he was still only eighteen.'

'That doesn't bode well for us then, does it?' said Abraham in a desultory tone.

'This is why we are forming a delegation to the coronation...'

'You think that if we lavish him with rich presents, he will like us and not persecute us?' Isaac asked, snorting with derision.

Isaac's tone was sarcastic, deliberately simplifying the complex relationship the Jews had with the sovereign. He was verging on being seditious. Such talk could do no good. Moses had no stomach for it. They had had a relaxing Shabbat and, although it had ended with nightfall, Moses wanted to retain the harmony of the day. Since the troubles in Gloucester when the Jews had been accused of killing a young boy, his family had suffered so much, and as a consequence, he found his capacity for such talk greatly reduced.

'One thing's for certain,' he said to lift the mood. 'He'll tax us just the same.'

But his attempt failed. It seemed Isaac was hell bent at raising sedition.

'Yes, that's right, Moses. We must present him with gifts to show our fealty. What does he do in return? Tax us to the hilt.'

Whilst staying at the castle in Guildford in 1186 the late King Henry had levied a tax of 60,000 marks upon his subjects to prepare for the Third Crusade. This was to raise an army and take back the lands of Jerusalem that Saladin, the Muslim leader, had captured from the Christian Crusaders. Known as the Saladin tallage, it demanded one tenth of income and movable goods from everyone and proved highly unpopular.

'Yes, but he is also our biggest borrower of money. Where the king leads others will follow. All good for business,' Moses countered. But Moses was losing the argument. He turned to Jacob for help. 'What do you think, Jacob?'

Jacob of Orléans had been invited to join them this evening. He was a learned Jewish scholar who had studied under the great Rabbenu Tam of Troyes. His wisdom and knowledge made him a great scholar and his opinion at gatherings was always sought.

'The Jews have been massacred for centuries regardless of who is king or what country they live in or what tallage they burden us with. As you know, my great friend and teacher, Rabbenu Tam, bless his soul, suffered at the hands of those who call themselves Christians.'

Jacob launched into the story that he had no doubt told a hundred times, but all who sat around the table listened intently, whether they had heard it before or not.

'It was in the year 4907, more than forty years ago, and the second day of *Shavuot*, the revelation of the Torah on Mount Sinai to our people. The Crusaders forced their way into his town and pillaged and massacred many of the Jews. They broke into Rabbenu Tam's house, plundered all his wealth, and wounded him five times with their swords. But with *Hashem*'s grace he escaped, which was good fortune for me because I never would have met him.'

A wide grin appeared on Jacob's face.

'And for that we are very thankful,' Moses said, raising his cup of wine in the direction of Jacob.

'*L'chaim.*'

Moses emptied his cup and stood to leave. He easily tired these days and wanted to feel fresh in the morning for it was an important day and likely to be a long drawn-out affair.

'I bid you goodnight. I thank you all for your company, but I must retire to my bed. Let's hope tomorrow is a good day for all of us and we are received graciously by our new king.'

CHAPTER

FIVE

Moses arrived early and stood outside the abbey waiting for the delegation to arrive. He was accompanied by his son, Abraham, their guests from the night before, Isaac and his brother Abner, and Jacob of Orléans. Aaron of Oxford, Jurnet of Norwich, Rabbi Moses of Bristol, and his son Yom Tov were there. Benedict of York had travelled all the way from the North of England to be here today. Lastly, Moses spotted Deudonne with his older brother, Abraham, Aaron of Lincoln's sons. Moses had not seen Deudonne since the *brit* of his son Abraham, more than twenty years ago when his betrothal to Arlette was to prove short-lived. He looked more like his father than ever.

'I was sorry to hear of your father's passing, Deudonne. Please pass on my respects to your mother.'

'Thank you, Moses, you are most kind.'

Moses continued. 'This is my son, Abraham. You attended his *brit* all those years ago.'

'Ah yes, I remember,' Deudonne replied, appearing uncomfortable at the brief exchange, but shaking Abraham's hand all the same.

They stood in awkward silence for a few moments, then Deudonne asked after Isaac, his younger brother, now married to Mirabelle's daughter.

'My brother Isaac is well, I trust?'

Isaac, Deudonne's much younger brother, had married Belia, Mirabelle's daughter, fifteen years ago. Never one to miss an opportunity, Mirabelle had secured the family alliance that had been denied to Arlette.

'He seems to be, although we only see him at synagogue.'

Having exchanged a few more awkward pleasantries, they hurried inside to take their place in the nave of the abbey, now filling up with dignitaries. Moses recognised some of those present, mainly through his business dealings. Waiting patiently for her son was Queen Eleanor, recently released from her imprisonment, she stood with her ladies-in-waiting at the front of the altar. Next to her was Isabella of Gloucester, the wife of John, the Count of Mortain. Also there was Isabel de Clare, Countess of Pembroke and Striguil. She was the daughter of Strongbow and Aoife and the new wife of William Marshal, recently appointed Regent to the soon-to-be boy king and trusted adviser to his father before him. Moses had not seen Strongbow since their attendance at the Michaelmas Court, twenty years ago with his wife-to-be, the flaming red-haired Aoife and her father Dairmait. Dairmait was now dead, and for a brief time Strongbow had been the King of Leinster, after his marriage to Aoife. But that was short-lived when the then king, Henry II, invaded Ireland and reasserted his authority. Still, Strongbow had fared well. He was wider around the waist and sported several more battle scars, but he looked content with his lot.

Queen Eleanor's gown was a deep red, made from a combination of luxurious scarlet cloth and silk, trimmed with white miniver fur and that of the darker sable. Moses wished his wife, Douce, could be here to see the women's fashions. Although on reflection, he thought, perhaps not, as she would want to order mounds of cloth to make the same.

The wait was lengthy, but finally when the trumpets blasted the arrival of the Duke of Normandy, soon to be king, Moses turned to see the procession entering the abbey. Beneath their feet was a rich cloth of Tyrian purple. Their arrival was accompanied by triumphal shouting. The procession was led by Godfrey de Lacy, who carried the king's cope. Behind him was John Marshal. John carried in his hands two large and heavy spurs from the king's treasure. Next was his younger brother, William Marshal, the man who had been faithful to King Henry II. He carried the royal sceptre, on the top of which was a golden cross. William, the Earl of Salisbury, held the royal rod with a dove on the top. David, Earl of Huntingdon, who was the younger brother of William I of Scotland; Robert, Earl of Leicester; and Richard's younger brother, Prince John, followed. David, Robert, and John carried three swords with splendid golden sheaths, also from the king's treasure. Sword-bearing before the monarch, at the time of the ceremony, was a mark of honour.

They were followed by six barons, along with six earls bearing a coffer in which the royal vestments were contained, and lastly came William de Mandeville, Count of Aumale. The Earl of Essex, and one time official to Richard's father, carried the great gold crown, encrusted with gemstones.

Richard took up the rear, walking under a canopy of silk, held high by four long lances, each borne by a baron of the realm. The Bishop of Durham, Hugh de Puiset and Reginald fitz Jocelin, the Bishop of Bath, were on his right and left and next to them two novice monks swinging smoking thuribles of pungent incense.

Moses took in the tall figure of Richard; his long legs, his salmon-pink hair, his pale complexion, and his unusually womanly features and the graceful way he held himself. As Richard walked past him, Moses caught his eye. He thought he detected a look of enmity toward him. It was obvious Moses, and his entourage were Jews. They wore the distinctive pointed hat, and their clothes were as sumptuous as the king's. Moses' mood quickly changed, and the familiar downheartedness he hadn't been able to shake since his arrival in London surfaced. He began to wonder if it had been a mistake to come.

When they reached the high altar, Baldwin of Forde, the Archbishop of Canterbury, was waiting for them. Baldwin, a highly spiritual man stood before Richard. He was almost as tall as the new king, but thinner, and where Richard was pale, Baldwin was swarthy. Where Richard had a steely expression, Baldwin's was one of an honest, venerable man.

They were assisted by the Archbishops of Rouen, Trier and Dublin, and the king's half-brother, Geoffrey, the Archbishop Elect of York. Sixteen other bishops and the abbots of twelve great monasteries, including Thomas Carbonel, the Abbot of St Peter's Abbey were present. The Archbishop of Canterbury stood before Richard, who now sat upright on a grand throne on the altar, his expression serious. The nave fell into a hushed silence. Only the faint whoosh of a solitary bat, high in the Romanesque nave, could be heard. The bat swooped down, circling Richard's head, accompanied by a strange-sounding peal of bells. Richard ducked his head, waving his arms to beat away the flapping bat. An audible gasp, from those gathered, rang through the nave. The bat flew away, but the effect of its arrival was obvious. They had witnessed a bad omen, an unsettling start to a king's reign. Richard signalled with a highly agitated wave of his hand to the archbishop to continue with the ceremony. The coronation oath began.

'Will you, all the days of your life, bear peace, honour, and reverence to God and the Holy Church and her ministers all the days of your life?'

'I solemnly promise so to do.'

'Will you exercise right, justice, and law on the people unto you committed?'

'I will.'

Isaac, sitting next to Moses, leant across, and whispered in his ear, 'That won't include us.'

Moses shushed him quiet.

'Will you abrogate wicked laws and perverse customs, if any such should be brought into your kingdom, and will you enact good laws, and the same in good faith keep, without mental reservation?'

'All this I promise to do.'

Having taken the coronation oath, Richard removed his upper garment and his breeches and put upon his feet sandals woven from golden thread. Then the archbishop handed him the sceptre to hold in his right hand with the royal rod in his left. From an ampulla, the archbishop took upon his hands the holy consecrating oil and anointed Richard by pouring it over his head, on his shoulders and on his right arm, with the appointed prayers for each act. The bat, which had been content to zigzag high above their heads, suddenly swooped towards Richard's head once again in an erratic flight. Richard ducked to avoid the collision as the bat flapped its wings in his face before swooping back up to the ceiling. The archbishop followed the bats flight upward, made the sign of the cross, and muttered something under his breath.

Moses was not a suspicious man, but he could not shake the mounting tension gnawing away at his insides. The constricting pain in his chest intensified. The archbishop appeared a little flummoxed by the interruption until Richard scowled at him and told him to get on with it. Baldwin, flustered by the king's impatience, called for the robes to be brought.

A consecrated linen with a cope were placed over Richard's head, and he was dressed in the ceremonial robes, a tunic, and a dalmatic. Afterwards, the archbishop girded him with a sword.

'For constraining those who do wrong to the Church,' said the archbishop.

Then he received the splendid golden spurs and the ceremonial sword. Another promise was made by the king that with God's help everything he had said before would be upheld in good faith. Richard was then dressed in a girdle of gold cloth. The archbishop placed an armill on each of the king's wrists after which the royal stole and robe were placed around his shoulders. In his impatience, Richard rose from his throne, approached the altar, and took hold of the crown himself, handing it to the archbishop. The archbishop looked shocked but continued with an air of dignity. Before placing the crown upon his head, the archbishop once again urged Richard to confirm the oaths he had taken.

'In the name of the living God will you not assume the crown unless you fully resolve to keep the oaths that you have sworn?'

'As God is my witness, I shall faithfully keep the oaths I have sworn. The things which I have here before promised, I will perform and keep. So help me God.'

With that, the heavy crown was lifted above Richard's head, and with great ceremonial show, set upon it, crowning him King of all England and its dominions. The newly crowned king, glorious in his diadem, the ultimate symbol of sovereignty, stood up and led a procession of religious leaders, barons, earls, lords, and others to William Rufus's great hall where a sumptuous banquet was waiting.

CHAPTER

SIX

Brunetta woke early on Sunday morning. She spent her time choosing what clothes to wear before joining her family downstairs for breakfast. When she walked into the room, everyone stared at her. Brunetta immediately regretted her morning's efforts. She had given them cause to suspect her.

'Why are you dressed like that?' Abigail asked.

'Oh, no reason,' Brunetta said with as much nonchalance as she could muster.

Her brother Josce had a mean streak in him. 'You look like one of those Christian whores that ply their trade in Three Cocks Lane.'

Brunetta's mood darkened. She hated her brother. He was mean and saw himself as the great pretender to Moses le Riche. Brunetta knew he would never achieve his ambition. He was not in that family's league.

'Josce, that is a terrible thing to say to your sister. Apologise.'

Glorietta said, 'I think she looks lovely. When I get to her age, I hope I look like her.'

'Is that your only ambition? To be a *zonah* like your sister.'

They were all carping at each other by now in loud voices.

'Enough,' shouted Abigail. 'Sometimes I wish your father were here to deal with you.'

'Well he's not,' said Josce. 'You've got me, and I am the head of the household now. Go upstairs and change your clothes,' he said to Brunetta.

'No, I won't. I'm going out.' Brunetta stood up and ran to the door. 'You can't tell me what to do.'

Her brother ran after her, but she was gone, slamming the door behind her. Brunetta ran all the way to the High Cross. The streets were full of churchgoers and if her brother decided to follow her, she would lose him in the swell of pilgrims. As she walked past Baruch's house, she looked up at the windows to see if she could see him. The house looked empty. She couldn't go back home, not yet, so she carried on to the river. Every now and then she would look behind her to see if he was following her, but he was not. She reached the spot where they had done it and sat down. The hot sun burned the soft flesh of her face. She let out a yawn, her eyelids became leaden, so she stretched out on the soft grass and closed her eyes. The sun burned through her clothes. She loosened the sash tied around her waist and removed her headscarf and drifted off. Then she became aware of a dark shadow above her. Then a deep voice said, 'Waiting for me?'

Her heart skipped several beats. She opened her eyes and sat up. Baruch placed his boot on her shoulder and pushed her back down.

'No please, stay where you were. On your back.'

Brunetta giggled, lying back down on the soft grass. Baruch sat next to her and wasted no time, hitching her shift up above her thighs and climbing on top of her. When it was over this time, Brunetta felt cheated. He had not kissed her, and she longed to feel his lips caress hers.

'Do you want to do it again,' she asked, leaning into him, and smoothing a strand of hair from his cheek.

He snatched her hand away.

'Don't do that.'

'What's the matter? Don't you like being touched?'

Baruch did not answer. He re-smoothed his hair as if wiping away her touch.

'Do you love me?' she said.

Brunetta had not intended to ask such a question. It just seemed to slip from her lips.

'Love you?' Baruch said, smirking.

He stood up and tightened the cord around his breeches. He looked down at her, his expression like a butcher looking at an animal carcass before jointing it.

'Women like you are not for loving, they're for fucking.'

Baruch might as well have slapped her in the face. She felt the full force of his disgust. It made her feel sick to her stomach. As she watched him hurry away from her, the sun disappeared beneath a grey cloud, shrouding him in shadow.

CHAPTER
SEVEN

Moses and his delegation followed at the back of the procession, each delegate clutching a luxurious gift bought with generous contributions from the entire Jewish community. As they entered the William Rufus Hall, the king was already seated at the vast stone table on his marble throne at the far end of the great hall. Moses took in the sight. Lighted candles, thousands of them, some on tall metal stands, others in wall sconces, filled the room with flickering light. Tapestries adorned the walls and decorative hangings draped from the ceiling. The tables lining the hall were covered with pitchers of wine and beer and hundreds of platters were filled with roasted ox, venison, partridges. A roast shoat of pig was the centrepiece. And, of course, the king's grandfather's favourite, lampreys from the River Severn. Richard had spared no expense.

A great murmur passed along the tables as the Jewish procession reached the king's table. Moses could feel the unfriendly stares of the noblemen burning upon his cheeks. He tried to take in a deep breath to settle his nerves, but his chest felt like someone had tightened a band around it. He was having great difficulty breathing. The guests in front of Moses had presented their gifts and been dismissed. At last, he was standing directly in front of the King of England. Jacob of Orléans had been elected their speaker.

'Your Majesty, we bring gifts to honour you and hope that we may live in peace and harmony as we did under your great father.'

The king stared at Jacob. The tension in the hall rose dramatically. Moses could feel it pressing down upon his chest. His heart was beating fast, and a stabbing pain hammered within him. Ignoring Jacob, the king addressed Benedict of York who stood behind him.

'What person are you?'

The new king was a man of few words and known for his terseness. He was known in Occitan as '*Oc e No*' – Yes and No.

'I am Benedict of York, one of your Jews.'

The king turned to Baldwin, Archbishop of Canterbury. 'Did you not tell me that he is a convert?'

'Yes, my lord.'

'Then like a dog he has returned to his own vomit.'

A pain shot down Moses' left arm. His chest felt as if it had the weight of a stone slab bearing down upon it.

'Your Majesty,' said Jacob, his voice calm. 'We mean no offence by coming here, we only wish to–'

The king cut him off and addressed the archbishop. 'What are we to do with him?'

Baldwin replied. 'If he does not choose to be a Christian, let him be a man of the devil. Let him be brought to a Christian trial, as he has become a Christian, and now contradicts that fact.'

'So be it.' The king waved his hand dismissively. His men surged forward and grabbed hold of Benedict.

'Wait,' he shouted. 'Give me that.' The king pointed to the

lavish chest Benedict clutched in his arms. The soldiers wrenched it from his grip and handed it to the king. The king did not accept it but gestured for one of his servants to take it away. 'Take him to the keep.'

The king's men marched him away without struggle.

'And what of these others? Did I not but yesterday banish all Jews from my coronation?'

'Your Majesty, if we had known we would never have...' began Jacob, but stopped mid-sentence when he realised, he was not being listened to.

'I believe you did, Your Majesty.'

'Are my orders as your new king not to be obeyed?'

The king studied the line of Jews in front of him, taking in the lavish gifts of great value they bore in their hands.

'Take the gifts and remove these Jews from the hall.'

William Marshal and several knights, who had been standing by, came forward on the king's orders.

'But, Your Majesty?' pleaded Jacob of Orléans.

'Silence. Get them out of here.'

Moses could not breathe. He clutched his chest, his eyes fluttered shut and he fell to the ground.

CHAPTER
EIGHT

Mirabelle sat opposite her husband, her face as sour as unripe fruit. Elias was in his cellar in the stone fortress they had built opposite the Christian church of St Michael the Archangel, close to the High Cross. He was organising piles of money, gold bezants in one pile, silver short-cross pennies in another whilst Mirabelle entered information onto a sheet of parchment in neat Hebrew lettering.

'*We* should have been at the coronation today, not them,' she said, her lips pursing with bitterness.

Elias said nothing, just concentrated on the task in front of him.

'It's not fair. We work hard, we try our best but still that family continue to do better than us.'

Elias remained silent.

'We even marry our daughter to Isaac of Lincoln to forge an alliance with the greatest dynasty in England, and what happens, the father dies prematurely.'

Elias still did not speak.

'Well, have you nothing to say to me?'

'I have heard all this before. There is nothing I can add.'

Mirabelle's eyes maddened. 'I have to do everything in this household. If it wasn't for me, you'd be nowhere.'

'As you remind me every day.'

Mirabelle dipped the quill she was using into the well of gall nut ink. Next to the Hebrew lettering she entered some figures in Latin. *Quinque marcarum.* Five marks.

'What do you think they're doing right now?' she asked Elias, her tone more conciliatory.

'I have no idea,' said Elias, showing little interest in the conversation.

'I imagine they're in Westminster Abbey this very moment, in all their finery, and soon they will be invited into the hall with their gifts, which we paid for out of synagogue funds, I might add.' Still no reaction from her husband. 'I can see the king graciously accepting their gift and inviting them to sit at the table and fill their bellies with the finest food and drink. Oh, it makes me so mad. That should have been us.'

'I don't know why you make yourself so unhappy by dwelling on such matters. Moses is the leader of our community and he and his eldest son were the obvious choice to send as delegates. There is nothing that can be changed so it's best not to think on things you cannot change. Besides, they won't be filling their bellies. It won't be kosher.'

'Small consolation,' she said, twisting her mouth. 'I see no reason why these things can't be changed.'

Belia, their daughter, came down the stone steps and caught the end of the conversation. 'What can't be changed?'

'Your mother is dreaming again about how things might be.'

'Oh, *Ima*, you're never satisfied. What's the matter now?'

'She thinks we should be at the coronation today.'

'Well, I agree with her there. Why do they always get the best of everything?'

Mirabelle had done a good job poisoning Belia against the le Riche family. In any family disagreement, Belia always sided with her. There was a time when Elias thought Belia might marry Abraham, Moses' son, but Mirabelle had assured her husband in her strident way that that was never going to happen. Mirabelle hadn't spoken to him for two days just for merely suggesting it. Belia was their eldest child, now married to Isaac of Lincoln with a four-year-old daughter, Pucelle. Little Pucelle came tumbling down the steps after her mother.

'*Sabba*,' she cried, holding her arms out and running to her grandfather.

Her voice was shrill, and she spoke with a slight lisp. Elias turned to pick her up and put her on his knee.

'Oh, my favourite granddaughter, Pucelle,' he said, giving her plump little cheek a kiss.

Pucelle clambered onto her grandfather's lap and immediately grabbed for the coins.

'Keep her away from the ink well,' Mirabelle snapped. 'I don't want all my hard work ruined because you can't keep your own granddaughter under control.'

Elias sighed and speaking to the child said, '*Oy lanu*! *Safta* is bad-tempered today.'

Elias entertained the child by letting her pick up the coins and teaching her to say the different names and then helping her to count to ten.

'See how good she is with her counting. She will make a very good moneylender and help her mother in the family business.'

'If we still have one left,' Mirabelle muttered, still in an ill-humour.

Elias sighed. Mirabelle knew why. She had become increasingly obsessed with Moses and his great wealth and, in turn, increasingly preoccupied with finding new ways to make more money, regardless of the means. A thought had been forming in Mirabelle's scheming mind. It first occurred to her when her son-in-law's father, Aaron of Lincoln, died. Aaron had amassed a huge fortune since arriving in England. Rumour was he was richer than the king. This had angered Henry who set about assessing Aaron's wealth. They had set up a separate department in the exchequer and called it after him. *Scaccarium Aaronis*. Men were working full time to establish the extent of Aaron's wealth just so the king could confiscate it. Mirabelle wasn't too happy with this development. It wasn't good news for moneylenders like herself. Up until now she had managed to conceal the full nature of her moneylending activities by not declaring all her transactions. It had been easy to do in the old system of tally sticks and meant the value of her true wealth had been disguised for years. So, in the past, when the king commanded his sheriffs to collect extortionate tallages she had paid less than she ought to have done. Why should she fund his Christian Crusades against the Muslim hordes? How many Crusades would there be? *We are already on the third*, she reflected. When will it all end? The more she considered the unfairness of it, the more the bile of anger rose in her throat.

'Are you all right, *Ima?*'

Mirabelle's hand was grasping the quill so tight she had bent it. Her fingers were stained brown with the gall nut ink. She dropped the quill, smattering the parchment and ruining the entries she had so carefully prepared.

'Never mind the child,' said Elias. 'Look what *you've* done.'

CHAPTER

NINE

braham, intent on the unfolding scene before him, had not noticed his father's increasing distress. Not until Moses fell with a thud onto the stone flags of the hall.

'*Aba*,' he exclaimed, rushing to his father's side.

The hall had, by this time, erupted into hostile chaos. Chants of 'Jews Out' resounded, accompanied by thunderous banging of fists on the wooden trestles. William Marshal pushed Abraham aside, picked up Moses from the floor like he was a stuffed sack, and threw him over his shoulders.

'Where are you taking him?' Abraham shouted, running after him.

'Follow me, boy.'

Behind them the others were being escorted with some force down the middle of the hall and towards the entrance. As Abraham and his father neared the door, they could hear a commotion outside. It seemed news of the king's displeasure had spread to the throng of people gathered outside.

'Here comes a Jew,' said one.

Abraham, standing next to William at the entrance, saw the

man strike a fellow Jew with such force he dropped to the ground, blood pouring from a cut on his forehead. The crowd surged toward the victim, trampling him underfoot. Abraham heard the man's agonised cries and then his cries were no more.

Another yowl went up. 'The king has ordered all unbelievers to be attacked.'

'Kill all Jews.'

'The king demands it,' said another.

Abraham knew from the story his father had told him of the night of his *brit*, when a brutal mob attacked his family, that this could get out of hand very quickly. Abraham had personally never experienced anything such as he was witnessing right now as the relations between the Jewish community and the Christians in Gloucester remained harmonious.

The crowd roared and started attacking those ordinary Jews who had ventured out to watch the king's coronation. The throng of Christians, now a murderous mob, surged forward towards Abraham. William Marshal, a man in his forties, with a lifetime of combat to draw upon, pushed the advancing mob aside and strode past them to a quiet corner on the outside of the abbey. He dropped Moses to the ground, propped him against the stone buttress and turned to leave.

'You're on your own now. My advice is to go home as quick as you can. This lot look like they're out for blood.'

'Thank you for helping us, but I don't understand why?'

'I am a man of war. I like to see a fair fight. This isn't one.'

Abraham thanked William again, then tended to his father whose lifeless body had slumped over to one side. His lips were blue, and his eyes were rolling wildly in their sockets. He didn't seem to be breathing.

'Abraham!'

It was Isaac and his brother. They both had injuries to their faces and head, and their rich garments had been ripped, but they were alive.

'Where are the others?' Abraham asked.

'They ran off into the crowd. We lost them.'

'Help me get *Aba* to his feet. We have to get him out of here.'

The brothers took an arm each and dragged Moses away from the crowd. The walk home was a long one, along the river, cutting through St Paul's Cathedral and along Aldersgate Street. They thought the noise of the baying mob would become subdued the further away they got from the abbey, but it seemed to be following them. They stopped for a while on the steps of the cathedral, just below Paul's Cross, an outdoor preaching pulpit. Moses was gravely ill. Hurrying towards them came the dean of the cathedral, Ralph de Diceto. Abraham recognised him as one of the officiates at the coronation.

'Can you tell us what is happening at the abbey,' Abraham asked him, as he scurried past them.

'They're flogging the Jews in the street, stripping them naked. Women and children. If I were you, I would get to the safety of your homes. They're making their way towards the Jewry.'

Abraham took his father's arm and hauled him up. 'Come on, we don't have time to stop.'

Isaac took the other arm and they set off again, almost running this time with Moses' feet dragging along the ground. At last, they reached the brothers' house in Jewin Street. The house was built of stone, like a fortress, much like Moses' house in Gloucester. Abraham felt sure the worst was over. They carried his father upstairs to the guest bedroom and set him on the mattress. His lips were no longer blue, but his eyes were closed.

'*Aba*, can you hear me, *Aba*? You're safe now.'

Moses moaned, and his eyes opened momentarily.

'He needs a physician. Is there someone nearby I can fetch?'

'It's too dangerous out there. My mother may be able to help.'

Isaac's mother, Joya, was fetched from the kitchen at the rear of the large and rambling house. The house was so big she had no idea that her guests had arrived back. Looking panicked, she asked what had happened. Isaac retold the events whilst Joya examined Moses.

'Has he been feeling ill?' she asked.

'I saw him holding his chest just before he fell,' said Isaac.

'Undress him and get him into bed. I'll fetch something for him.'

'Will he be all right, Joya?' Abraham asked.

'He's very sick. I'll try my best but I'm not a physician.'

'As good as any I know,' Isaac replied.

Joya left, returning with a concoction of willow bark. 'This will help with the pain. It's a waiting game now, I'm afraid.'

CHAPTER
TEN

Arlette sat in the courtyard enjoying the last of the summer sun. At her feet were willow baskets overflowing with autumn fruits and vegetables. Odd-shaped gourds with their vibrant autumn colours. They looked good enough to eat but most of them would be dried and used as receptacles in the kitchen. Lazy wasps buzzed around the basket of apples. Arlette kept an eye on them. They could be unpredictable and sting you for no reason, especially at this time of the year.

In a smaller basket lay bunches of skirrets, their roots looked like fattened up and very long chicken feet. The look of them did not match their taste for they were Arlette's favourite vegetable. A mixture of sweetness with a peppery aftertaste. Douce had introduced her to them. She used them in winter pottage, but Arlette preferred to eat them raw. She had washed them and every now and then she snapped one from the root bulb, popped it into her mouth and crunched on it.

Zev and her son Rubin were busy in the workshop hammering out silver platters and chalices. The business was doing well, and Zev was much happier doing this than he was previously helping his father in the butchery. They had paid back the money that Moses had lent them and were now making a healthy profit. In the evening, she would help with the more dexterous tasks involved in the jewellery side of the business.

She tilted her head to the sky, closed her eyes and luxuriated in the warmth of the sun upon her face. A dark shadow appeared. She opened her eyes. Her son Baruch stood over her, staring at her with his black eyes.

'Hello,' she said, happy to see him.

Baruch had been named after Zev's best friend. Baruch was a man now, tall and muscular with an angular face and nothing like his namesake who had sadly died some years ago. He had the same straggly long hair as his real father. He was looking like and behaving more like him as he grew older. She saw little of her son these days, which saddened her.

'Hello, Mother.'

Baruch rarely called his mother *ima*, the Jewish word for mother. He slumped down beside her, scuffing the ground with his boots as he did so.

'You seem bored,' Arlette said, reaching out her hand to brush the stray hair from his face.

Baruch squirmed and pushed her hand away. 'Don't do that, it annoys me,' he said.

Arlette went back to her work, twisting bunches of herbs and tying them with string so they could be hung in the kitchen to dry.

'Why don't you go and help your father?'

'You know I don't like doing that.'

'What do you like?'

'I don't know.'

'Your father would like it if you helped him out a bit more.'

'I'm sure he would.'

'I wish you two would get on better.'

'Like Rubin does, you mean?'

'You say that like you don't like him. He's your brother. It wouldn't harm you to make more of an effort.'

'What's the point? I only end up arguing with him, then Father gets involved and takes his side.'

Arlette dropped the bunch of herbs she was working on into her lap and sighed. 'If you don't want to work with your father, what are you going to do? You can't just mope around the house doing nothing.'

'I don't know. I don't know what I want to do. I fancied my hand at moneylending like grandfather, but Abraham has that prize.'

'It's only natural that as the eldest he would follow his father, like you should follow yours.'

'I'm content to let Rubin take over. He's much better at it than I am.'

'How would you know? You've never really tried.'

'Oh, Mother, don't go on so. I have enough with Father without you.' Baruch tapped the basket of apples with his boot sending the wasps into a frenzy.

'I know. I'm sorry. I worry about you that's all.'

Baruch leant across and kissed his mother on the cheek, then stood up. 'Don't worry about me, Mother. I'll be all right.'

Arlette gave him a weak smile. She could tell that despite his bravado he was unhappy. She worried about him constantly and wished he would settle down.

'It's time you found a wife.'

Baruch groaned. 'Not that again, Mother.'

'There must be someone you like. What about that girl who comes to synagogue? What's her name again?'

'How would I know; I'm hardly ever there.'

Arlette rolled her eyes in frustration. It would take an

exceptional woman to take on her son. Someone with a thick skin.

'You do know her. She has her hair tied back in braids.'

'You mean the one with teeth like a horse?'

'That's unkind, Baruch.' She laughed.

He did know the girl and it was true. Her teeth did protrude a little.

'Not as unkind as you would be if you made me marry someone like that.'

'I don't think I could make you do anything you didn't want to.'

He bent down and grabbed a stick of skirret.

'Hey,' Arlette said, jokingly. 'Those are mine.'

'Not this one,' he said, crunching it between his teeth and imitating a horse.

'Where are you going?' she called after him.

'Nowhere in particular,' he said and sloped away.

Arlette shook her head. Baruch had always been a problem child. Since birth really, actually since conception, she reminded herself and quickly returned to her work.

CHAPTER

ELEVEN

Rioting had broken out all over the city. The mob was out of control, and it seemed that no Jew was safe in London on this night. All evening Abraham could smell burning and hear the cries of people in the street below where they were being beaten with fists or thrashed with sticks or pelted by stones. Those Jews who had been foolish enough to ignore the warnings or simply didn't know what was going on had found themselves surrounded by an angry mob. Dead bodies lay in the street, their battered and bloodied corpses stepped over by rioting throngs.

Abraham kept watch from the safety of the window, keeping an eye on his father who had not stirred. His mind was in turmoil. One minute he feared for his father, the next for himself. Then he worried about his mother Douce and his brothers and sisters. But most of all he thought of Brunetta, the young woman he had fallen in love with and had set his sights on marrying. Would he ever see her again? His heart ached at this thought. Last night's conversation played on his mind. Isaac's prophetic words, 'Would the new king be good or bad for us Jews?' Well it seemed they had their answer.

A lull in the activity outside on the street had sent Abraham into a nodding sleep where he sat, but loud voices now jolted him from his slumber. It was still dark. A large mob carrying firebrands were making their way down the street, setting fire to wooden doors and throwing brands up to the thatched roofs. The smell of burning thatch leeched through the window opening. The Gotsce house was three storeys high and so might survive a fire attack, but still there was the wooden entrance door at the side of the building. His father stirred in his bed. Abraham wished Moses was well enough to give him sound counsel. He wasn't sure what to do. He was like an animal in a trap. It seemed like history was repeating itself. Abraham called out for the others and soon Isaac and Abner appeared at the door, holding beeswax candles, both still in their day clothes.

'What's the matter? What's going on?' they cried out in unison.

'The mob is back. They're burning the thatch on everyone's roofs and making their way towards us.'

All three went to the window to look out. The whole sky was illuminated by the light of the raging fires and the air was thick with smoke. Grey ash, falling like tainted snow, covered the ledge of the window.

'It's bad. Much worse than we thought,' said Abner.

'What are we going to do? We're trapped here,' said Abraham.

'We can always take refuge in the cellar,' Isaac suggested. 'The stone walls are six feet thick. But let's wait and see what happens first. They might go straight past this house. It's taller than the others in the street. I'm being optimistic, I know, but they just might.'

They watched on, only to see the arrival of a cart piled high with wood and rags, which the mob stacked up against the wooden door of a neighbour, lighting it with sulphurous-smelling Sea Fire, brought from the nearby docks.

'That's Daniel's house. He has a wife and six children living there,' Abner said.

There was a tremendous whoosh as the fire exploded high into the air, its orange flames lighting up the faces of the arsonists. Abraham was shocked to see that they were ordinary men and women, respectable looking, not vagabonds as he would have expected. The fire raged on, crackling and spitting as more wood was thrown on top. It was not long before the door burnt down, and Daniel's possessions were brought out and burned. Screams of young children came from inside the house. Abraham couldn't stand it. He was torn between wanting to do something, and knowing if he did, it would be certain death for him.

He remembered his father telling him when he was about twelve years old that the king, Richard's father, had passed the Assize of Arms Act ordering all weapons in the possession of Jews to be confiscated on the grounds that Jews had the protection of the king, so would have no reason for owning arms. He had gone with his father to the castle and handed over their only weapon to the sheriff. Now, not a single Jew had the means to defend himself when a riotous mob came to call. Isaac was right to be angry. This was a cursed land for Jews.

But what happened next would be branded into Abraham's memory and give him nightmares for the rest of his life. Daniel's thatch had been set alight along with the door. His family had nowhere to go. In a desperate attempt to escape the flames and smoke, Daniel's wife, Judith, with her twins, the two babies, Leah and Rachel, jumped from an upstairs window, hoping to throw themselves upon the mercy of the mob. None was shown. As soon as the mob saw they were going to jump, they held up lances and spears for them to fall upon, piercing the tiny bodies of the babies and slicing into the side of Judith. The children died instantly, but Judith died an agonising death in the blazing inferno. Abraham would never know the fate of Daniel and his sons.

CHAPTER

TWELVE

I n the early hours of the morning, after the coronation
ceremony, the king was still celebrating. Much food had
been eaten and wine consumed. The bones of half
chewed animals were strewn across the floor. Goblets were
turned over, their contents seeping onto the white linen cloths
covering the table. Half-eaten pies, roasted animals and fruit
lay on the table, discarded. Some of the guests lay with their
heads on their folded arms, asleep, others were slumped in
their chairs and still drinking.

Richard had paid no heed to the riots spreading city wide
save for a half-hearted gesture to send a few men to suppress it.
His advisors had counselled that he should not begin his reign
by overtly showing signs of protection for the Jews. As he had
just demanded them to be removed from his celebration feast,
he saw no danger in that. He had been about to call it a night
when the small troupe of men he had despatched returned,
their faces blackened by fire and looking dishevelled.

'Your Majesty, we were too few. The riots are getting
seriously out of hand. We have tried to remonstrate with the

mob, but they are too numerous to control. They are burning, looting and killing the Jews.'

Richard showed no concern. He slumped back in his throne.

'Have a drink for your troubles,' he said, slurring his words and letting out a loud belch. 'What's a few dead Jews? It will be over by the morning, and all will be back to normal.'

'Your Majesty, the city is on fire, and it has got so bad that Christians are killing Christians and burning each other's houses. If it is left any longer the whole city will be ablaze.'

When Richard heard this new development, he sat up, wiped his clammy brow with a cloth and shook his head as if to knock either sense or sobriety into it.

'I sent you out to quell the riots. What use are you?'

'By the blood of Christ, if we had not retreated, Your Majesty, I think they would have killed us.'

'Maybe they should have, you useless piece of *merde*.'

Richard reverted to his French dialect of *langue d'oïl*, but there was no mistaking his meaning. 'Get out of my sight,' he yelled, batting them from his presence.

The men retreated in haste.

'Ranulf de Glanville,' he roared at the top of his voice. 'Where are you? Show yourself.'

Ranulf de Glanville, was the king's justiciar and had been his father's right-hand man.

'Take as many men as you can and use as much force as is necessary. I want this riot snuffing out and I want the ringleaders caught and imprisoned. Now go.'

Ranulf, who had joined in the celebrations, did not immediately move but was seen to sway slightly. For a man nearing his eightieth year he was in remarkable shape, slim and wiry.

'Did you hear me?' the king bawled at him, picking up and throwing the roasted leg of a half-eaten capon at him.

Ranulf ducked the missile.

'Forthwith, Your Majesty.'

As Ranulf gathered his men together, the hall became increasingly empty and still. As the candles began to sputter and burn out, the hall grew darker. A desultory atmosphere descended on the hall.

'I have no stomach for this,' the king said, standing up, and sweeping away the platters and pitchers before him in a rage. 'I am king less than a day and my subjects are already rioting and burning the city to the ground. Damn those bloody Jews.'

THIRTEEN

braham's capacity for watching the riot had dissipated with the sight of the deaths of Daniel's family. Only yesterday, whilst out walking, he had passed the family in the street and exchanged greetings. It was time to take refuge in the cellar. First, they barricaded the door to the house with heavy pieces of furniture to prevent the rioters gaining access, but Abraham knew it was futile. The furniture was wooden and given time would burn through just as it had at Daniel's house.

The atmosphere in the cellar was grim. The few candles they had brought with them were beginning to sputter. Soon they would be in darkness. Isaac's young children clutched at their mother's skirts, whimpering with fear. No amount of reassurance from their mother was helping. Moses remained unconscious, his pallor grey and ghostly in the candlelight. Occasionally, they heard the muffled sounds of the mob. At those times everyone held their breath, Joya putting her finger to her lips, signalling to the children to be extra quiet.

Abraham had spent his time listening intently for any sound that might indicate the mob were inside the house. He prayed for redemption. Not from his sins but those of his persecutors. He had heard nothing for the last few hours.

'Do you think it's safe to go back up now?' he asked the others. 'It's been very quiet. Maybe it's over?'

'It will never be over,' Isaac said bitterly. 'As long as we are Jews, living in a foreign land, it will never be over.'

Abraham was in no mood to discuss the return to Israel and the Promised Land. He wanted to go home to Gloucester where he had always felt safe, to hug his mother and kiss the soft lips of Brunetta and where his father could recover his health.

'I'm going to have a look.'

Abraham crept up the stone steps and listened at the door. All was quiet. He turned the lock and peeped through into the hallway. The barricade of furniture was still in place. No signs or smells of burning. He continued upstairs to the bedroom window to check what was happening outside. Through the dim light of dawn, Abraham could make out the king's men at the far end of the street, rounding up the rioters and putting out the last of the fires. A cart stood in the street piled high with burnt, bloodied and butchered corpses. The riot was over.

FOURTEEN

Abraham had to wait till his father was well enough to travel before returning to Gloucester. Joya had taken good care of him and nursed him back to health. He was now able to walk, although not far, and his speech had improved yet he had become silent and morose. He complained of a weakness in his arm but other than that he seemed to be on the mend.

Abraham was so elated when he saw his father's house, he wanted to jump off the cart and run to it. His mother, Douce, his younger brothers Benjamin and Justelin and his sister, Henne, were all home to greet him, along with Zev and Arlette and their son, Rubin. The only one not there was Baruch, but that was to be expected. Douce had prepared a meal for them, and by the look of the spread on the table, it was fit for a king.

'*Baruch Hashem*,' Douce cried, thanking God for their safe arrival, first giving her husband a hug and then Abraham. 'I've been so worried about you both.'

Douce led Moses to his chair by the fire, which she had lit earlier for him even though it was still a warm September day.

She fussed around him for some time, asking about his health, fetching him a warm cup of apple brandy.

'What can I get you to eat, *cheri*?'

Moses waved his hand and shook his head. The journey had tired him so much he hardly had the strength to talk. It was not long before he was nodding in the chair before a roaring fire.

'We heard about the riot. Everyone is talking about it,' said Henne, excitedly.

Her youthfulness was refreshing, but her lack of understanding could sometimes be irritating.

'It was more of a massacre,' Abraham said, the sight of Judith and her daughters being slain flashed into his mind.

'Henne, go and fetch a drink,' Douce said, sensing all was not well with Abraham.

'What happened? Can you tell me?'

Abraham recounted the entire trip, from his stay at the Gotsce household to the day they left. He left out the most harrowing of details. His mother was a tender soul, and he knew she wouldn't be able to cope. Douce listened attentively, occasionally dabbing the corner of her eye with the hem of her skirt. His siblings listened too, interrupting now and again, with questions he would rather not answer.

'So, your father saw very little of the actual riot?'

'No, he was spared that, *Ima*.'

A hard lump formed in Abraham's throat. He tried to swallow, but this only brought on a fit of coughing. He turned away from his mother's searching gaze. Now that his father was ill, he would have to assume the role of head of the household. He could show no weakness.

'I'm glad he was spared the worst. He never got over that terrible night...'

It was as though his mother had travelled back to that time again. She looked troubled. As a couple they had had their fair share of heartache. Their firstborn, Samuel, had died aged only four years and something else had happened the night of the riot, all those years ago, but he had never been able to get to the bottom of it. Abraham squeezed her hand.

'I heard Benedict of York had converted to Christianity to save his skin. Did he really do that?' asked Henne, more interested in the gorier details.

'He was probably thinking more of his possessions than his life,' said Benjamin.

'Surely not.'

'Have you forgotten the Third Lateran Council edict?'

'I haven't forgotten it. I don't think I ever knew it,' Henne said. 'You know so many odd facts.'

'Not odd. If you want to keep out of trouble as a Jew living in this country, you'd be mindful to know all about the laws these Christians draw up to keep us in our place.'

'Go on then, enlighten us.'

'Ten years ago, the mighty bishops and his majesty the pope held a council to tell us mere mortals about how to live our lives...'

Abraham listened to his younger brother spouting forth bitter criticism of the Christians, noting the similarity to his host Isaac Gotsce. *It must be a trait of the young*, he thought.

'They gracefully told us a Jew who converts to Christianity would not be deprived of any of his possessions because "converts"' – his brother spat out the word 'converts' – 'ought to be financially better off than they were before they accepted the Christian faith.' Benjamin paused. He was looking around to see if he still held their attention. 'See how devious they are?'

Henne said, 'Ooh, yes, they are playing to man's greed.'

'Exactly,' said Benjamin, as if he had also gained himself a convert. Benjamin wasn't finished. 'And then came the *Sicut Judaeis* – the papal bull forbidding Christians – on pain of excommunication...' Benjamin held up his index finger to emphasise this particular point, 'from forcing Jews to convert.'

'But surely that is a contradiction?'

Douce held her finger to her lips. 'Ssh, you'll wake your father.'

'Sorry, *Ima*. I got a bit carried away.'

'So, what happened to Benedict?' Henne said, lowering her voice.

'They took him to the keep. I'm not sure of his fate.' Abraham's answer hung in the silence.

'Do you think he'll convert back?' Henne asked.

'Who knows,' replied Abraham.

Henne continued: 'I'm glad you and Father weren't faced with that choice. I'm not sure what I'd do. What is worse? Lose your life or become a Christian?'

Benjamin snorted. 'Better to be alive than dead.'

Abraham thought of the hundreds of Jews that had died in London that day. Massacred by zealous Christians. He thought of their brutal deaths. What would he have done had they stormed Gotsce's fortress and gained entry? Having seen the fate of others, would he have converted if it saved his life? He thought of Brunetta. He was sure he would have wanted to live just to see her again, but would he be so disloyal to his faith. It was impossible to know.

'How is Brunetta?'

The question brought them all back to the present. Douce said, 'I'm sure Brunetta is well enough.'

Abraham detected a harshness in her tone. 'Why do you say it like that, *Ima*?'

He knew the answer even though he had asked the question. His mother did not approve of Brunetta. She thought her unsuitable as a wife for her eldest son. Eager though she was to see him married, given two of his younger siblings were both married now with small children, she did not want it to be Brunetta. There was something sly about the girl, she had told him. Abraham disagreed. Several young women had been presented to Abraham, as a prospective wife over the years, but he had never taken to any of them until Brunetta caught his attention. Douce didn't answer him. Instead, she fussed over Moses, stroking his hair and adjusting the blanket she had placed over his broken body.

Abraham so wanted to see Brunetta. From the moment he stepped inside his house he had wanted to leave, but he knew his mother would want him to spend time with her. Reassure her that he was well before letting him go. He had told his story, eaten his mother's comforting food, rested, but now he had an unquenchable desire to see Brunetta.

'Do you mind, *Ima*? I would like to see Brunetta...'

'I'm sure she would like to see you.'

Again, a hint of sarcasm marred her spoken intent.

'And how do you know that?' Abraham asked, convinced his mother was keeping something from him.

'Just a guess.'

Brunetta had interest from plenty of boys, including his boyhood friend Mannasser, the son of Josce. When they were at synagogue Abraham would catch his friend staring across at Brunetta. He would dig him in the side and remind him that she was already spoken for, to which Mannasser would reply, 'Not yet!'

'Really, *Ima*?'

'Yes, really. And if you are going to go and see her you will need to take Justelin with you.'

Brunetta was the daughter of Abigail, a widow who had arrived in Gloucester a couple of years ago when Brunetta was a child. She was fifteen now and as far as Abraham was concerned, she was the prettiest girl in Gloucester. Brunetta was not the most conventional of girls, which is why he was attracted to her so much. She brought excitement into his dull life. He ached to hold her. But that would have to be in secret. They were not allowed to be alone together until they were betrothed, but they had found a way. Abraham's brother, Justelin, was just seven and wonderfully naïve. Brunetta had used her considerable charms upon him to persuade him to let them spend time alone together.

'Come on, Justelin,' Abraham said, grabbing his hat and coat and dragging his brother away from a board game he had been playing.

He kissed his mother on the cheek and left. Justelin complained the whole way to Brunetta's house.

'Why do I always have to come with you. It's boring for me.'

'Because Mother cares about what people think and this is the only way I can see Brunetta.'

'What's so great about that?'

Abraham laughed. 'You'll find out one day.'

'You're back,' she squealed, as she opened the door in response to Abraham's knocking.

'Brunetta,' Abigail shouted from inside the house. 'Who's at the door?'

'It's Abraham, *Ima*. He's back.'

'Come in, Abraham,' Abigail said, walking with some difficulty towards them. 'Don't stand at the door.'

'If it's all right with you, I'd like to go for a walk with Brunetta. I need some fresh air and Justelin is here with me.'

'Well... I suppose that would be in order...'

Abigail was not a well woman. She looked older than her years, with greying hair at the temples and lines on her face, a sign she was no stranger to pain. The fight had gone out of her, and Abraham could tell she did not have the strength to argue with her wilful daughter.

'I'll take good care of her, Abigail. I'll have her back before sunset.'

'Mind you do, or I'll have to have words with your father.'

They walked side by side, keeping a respectful distance between them. Abraham watched her from the corner of his eye as the wind blew her chestnut hair, the thick and glossy tendrils swirling around her face underneath the thin veil covering her head. She looked like a wild animal, thought Abraham. Justelin walked behind them, kicking the odd stone and general detritus that lay in the street. As they walked, Abraham told of the terrible events he had witnessed in London. When he talked about the plight of Judith, Brunetta stopped in the street, covered her ears and shrieked.

'Don't tell me anymore. I can't stand to hear it.'

'I'm sorry, Brunetta. I didn't mean to upset you.'

'Can we talk about something else?'

'Of course.'

They walked in silence for a moment or two until they reached the East Gate. At the gate Abraham gave his brother a silver half penny. Justelin looked at the coin.

'Nothing more than a *perutah*,' he scoffed, but pocketed it anyway and walked back into the city whistling.

Abraham knew he would buy a slice of his favourite apple cake from the baker brothers, Janum and Bonel, satisfying his weakness for sweet things.

Beyond the city walls the countryside stretched ahead sweeping up to Robinswood Hill. As a boy, Abraham had often climbed the hill, to look out over the valley towards Wales. Rushing through the long grass they stopped momentarily. Abraham drew Brunetta close to him. Her willowy figure bent in toward him, pressing against his body. He held her close, smelt her hair and breathed in her very essence. He had dreamed of this moment. In the cellar in London, he thought he may never see her again. He cupped her face and kissed her soft, full lips. It was a languorous kiss, full of longing.

'Come,' she whispered.

Taking his hand, she led him to a densely wooded area. He followed her like an obedient dog. Stopping at a sheltered, hidden spot under a pendulous oak tree, she lay down. Abraham lay beside her on his side, looking down at her face. Her eyes were closed, a blissful smile upon her lips. A surge of reckless abandonment took over. Whether it was his near brush with death or something more primal in him, he did not know. He traced his hand gently across her cheek, her lips, her tanned skin, a golden bronze from the long summer's sun. His fingers ran through her glossy hair and down to her neck. Brunetta lay still, only opening her amber eyes to look up at him. They were full of yearning. She grabbed his hand and placed it on her breast. Abraham moaned as he gave it a gentle squeeze and felt the hardening of her nipple. Brunetta moaned in response. Unable to control his passions any longer, he rolled on top of her and kissed her face, her neck. She responded, moving her hips and pressing against his groin. Abraham's passion inflamed. They had kissed and touched before, but this was different. He lost himself in her and she in him. Before he knew it, he was inside her, kissing her and feeling like he was going to explode. Brunetta seemed to want him as much as he wanted her. Maybe it was the thought that he might never have seen her again, he didn't know. He only knew it felt right and he wanted to lose himself in her forever.

When it was over, they held each other tight, Brunetta's long legs wrapped around Abraham's spent body. They lay there for some time, neither speaking. Abraham's consuming passion had subsided, replaced by a sense of immense shame. His moral compass, driven into him by his father and his faith, had somehow gone astray. It was not self-reproach or guilt he was feeling, more a sense of failure that, caught up in the moment, he had succumbed to his primal needs. They had held hands before and once even snatched a kiss, when no one was looking, but it had never gone beyond that. But holding Brunetta in his arms felt so right, so special, it could not be a transgression, a sin.

'Was that your first time?' she asked him, interrupting his thoughts.

'Of course,' he said, somewhat surprised that she would ask such a question. 'And yours?' he asked.

'Abraham, how could you even think...' Brunetta said.

He stroked her soft hair. 'You are my beloved.' Abraham squeezed her tightly. '*Je t'aime*,' he whispered, burying his face into her luxurious curls.

'Do you mean that?'

'Of course.'

'Do you think we should...'

'Get married?'

'Well, now that we've...'

'I'm not asking because of that. I've known since I first met you. When I was in London and the riots were happening around me, I thought I'd never see you again. All I could think of was you. Coming home to you.'

'Really?'

'You have no idea how much I have missed you.' He pulled away from her, his face serious. 'Brunetta, will you be my wife?'

Brunetta's eyes became glassy with tears. A large droplet fell from her lid. Abraham wiped it away.

'What's the matter? Don't you want to be my wife?'

'Of course, I do.'

'Then why are you crying?'

'They are tears of joy, Abraham,' she said, wiping the tears away. 'Don't you know anything about women?'

'Obviously not. But I'm looking forward to finding out.'

It was dark by the time Abraham and Brunetta walked home. Jewry Street was quiet, except for the occasional bark of a hound and the scuttering sound of rats in the alleyways.

'Mother is going to be so mad at me. I've never stayed out this late.'

She quickened her step, but Abraham pulled her back.

'Don't worry, Brunetta. As soon as I tell her we want to get married she'll calm down.'

'Do you think so? You don't know her like I do.'

'I don't, but I do know she'll be happy to make an alliance with my family...'

'I suppose you're right. She's a bit like your mother in that respect. Worried about what people will think.' Brunetta came to a sudden stop in the street. 'Your mother.'

'What about her?'

'I hadn't thought about her. She doesn't like me. She thinks I'm not good enough for you.'

'Brunetta. When does *Ima* act like she doesn't like you?'

'All the time,' she said. 'When she finds out I'm to be your wife, what's she going to say?'

'It won't make any difference to *Ima*. She is not as bad as people think. She likes you; I can tell.'

'How can you tell?'

'I don't know,' Abraham replied, getting frustrated. 'She just does.'

There was silence between them as they carried on towards Brunetta's home. Abraham could not tell Brunetta what his mother really thought of her. That would be cruel. There was always the chance that his mother would come around to the idea of him marrying Brunetta in time.

'Anyway, what about your mother?' Abraham asked.

'What about her?'

'Does she like me?'

'Of course. Who wouldn't?'

'That's not what I asked.'

'Mother likes you.'

There was something in Brunetta's tone that did not convince Abraham of the truth of what she was saying.

'Are you sure?'

'Of course.'

'There's something else, isn't there? What are you not telling me?'

'Well, if you insist. It's my brother, Josce.'

'And what does he have to do with all this?'

'Since we lost our father Josce has taken on the role of head of the household. He might have something to say about us getting married.'

'What sort of thing?'

'I don't know. He can be difficult at times, that's all.'

'I've never had a problem with him before. Look, what if I ask to speak to both your mother and Josce. Would that help?'

'It might do.'

They were standing in front of Brunetta's house. The glow from the fire and the candles inside were a welcome sight. The night air had become chilly. Brunetta put her hand on the metal catch of the door. She turned to Abraham. 'Are you ready?'

'Yes,' he replied, puffing out his chest and straightening his clothing.

At the sound of the catch Brunetta's mother shouted out, 'Is that you, Brunetta?'

'Yes, *Ima.*'

'And about time too. Oh, Abraham is with you,' she said, shuffling into the fore hall.

'Yes, *Ima.* He has something he wants to say to you.'

Abraham greeted Abigail. '*Shalom Alaichem.*'

'*Alaichem Shalom.* Come in, Abraham. Sit by the fire.'

Abraham sat. Brunetta stood by his side. The atmosphere in the room turned awkward. He needed to fill the awkwardness.

'Is Josce at home?'

'He has taken his sister to see her friend.'

Abigail gave Brunetta a look of reproach. Brunetta's sister, Glorietta, was keen on a young man called Ezra and as was custom, Josce was acting as chaperone.

'They're late back,' Brunetta said.

'They are a little, but she is with her brother.'

'And that makes it all right?'

Brunetta's tone was argumentative. She wasn't helping. Abraham placed his hand upon her arm to calm her.

'I'm sorry we were late getting back. I am more to blame than Brunetta. It won't happen again.'

Abigail's mouth relaxed. Brunetta flashed a look of defiance at him.

'She's a very wilful young woman, Abraham. I find as I get older, I'm no match for her. I do what I can.'

'You have done a very good job with all your children; they are a credit to you.'

Abigail gave him a fake smile. *She can see right through me,* Abraham thought.

'Brunetta and I have become very close and being away from her... Well, I've realised. We've realised, we want to spend more time together.'

Abraham was struggling to say the right words. It was an awkward situation to be in. Normally the families would get together and discuss the potential for marriage and then approach the two parties, but it was too late for that. Abraham had to take matters into his own hands. He thought it would be easier approaching Abigail than his parents, but this was proving difficult. He dreaded to think how his mother would take the news.

Abigail's eyes widened. She seemed genuinely surprised. She glanced across at her daughter, then back at Abraham.

'Well, I wasn't expecting that.'

Abraham breathed a sigh of relief. Abigail had understood his meaning and was making it easier for him.

'Yes, we want to get married.'

'Have you spoken to your parents about this?' Abigail asked.

'Not yet. I wanted to speak to you first.'

'Because I am less of a threat?'

'No, nothing like that.'

Abraham had never really spoken to Abigail at length. He had unfairly dismissed her as an old and sick woman. She was much more than that. He could see it now. He hadn't given her the credit he should have. A widow bringing up three children on her own and establishing a respectable, if small-time, moneylending business in the process. There was a noise at the door.

'That must be Josce and Glorietta.'

Josce walked into the room. He stopped when he saw Abraham. Glorietta was behind him, removing her veil and replacing it with her house cap.

'Oh, I didn't realise we had company,' she said.

Abraham could feel the atmosphere change as soon as Josce entered the room. There was tension in the air.

'*Shalom Alaichem*, Josce.'

Abraham walked toward him to shake his hand. Josce strode over to the chair by the fire, ignoring the gesture. The tension built.

'Abraham has come to ask if he can marry Brunetta,' Abigail said.

Glorietta shrieked at this news and ran to her sister,

throwing her arms around her. Josce stood, impassive to the news. Abraham had never seen this side of him. They had only really exchanged pleasantries, either in the street, or at the synagogue. He seemed an ordinary, affable type.

'Why wasn't I told of this?' Josce said.

Abigail opened her mouth to speak but Abraham interrupted her.

'As your mother is widowed, I thought it the best course of action to tell her first, out of courtesy. I meant no disrespect.'

Abraham had learnt tact and diplomacy from his father. It seemed Josce had not learnt any manners from his.

'My mother does not have a say in this household since my father went. I do.'

'I hadn't realised that, Josce. If I'd known, of course, I would have–'

Josce cut him off. 'Brunetta is at fault. She knows.'

Abraham looked across at Brunetta. She wasn't saying much, which was unusual for Brunetta. Whatever was going on in this family? What sort of hold did Josce have over them that he could speak in this way?

'Well, I hope I can make amends. Brunetta and I wish to marry. May we have both your blessings?'

The room fell silent. Abigail chewed her bottom lip, Glorietta stared at her brother, wide-eyed, like a frightened mouse. Brunetta glared at him with the menace of a wild boar. Abraham could not fathom the situation. Brunetta had never talked much about her brother. He wasn't sure how he would stand it if Josce were to deny him the love of his life. Could he do that? The fire crackled, the candles flickered in their sconces, but no one spoke. It felt like the longest moment of his life. Josce seemed to be deliberately taking time to give his answer.

'You may have my blessing.'

There was an audible sigh of relief.

'On one condition...'

This was the deal breaker.

'That I am consulted with all matters concerning the *ketubah*.'

Abraham's mood lifted. He could see no problem with that. His father would be involved in the negotiations of the marriage contract, and he had every confidence in him.

'I see no reason why not,' said Abraham, walking toward Josce with his hand outstretched.

This time Josce took it, and they shook hands.

'*Mazel tov*,' said Josce, rather stiffly.

'Well,' said Brunetta, who had the patience of a gnat. 'What do *you* say, *Ima*?'

'I'm very happy for you.'

FIFTEEN

Telling his parents of his intention to marry Brunetta was easier than he thought. It was late when he finally left Brunetta. His parents had gone to bed, so he decided to break the news to them the next morning. His mother, predictably, objected to the match but his father was more sanguine about the prospect of having Brunetta as his daughter-in-law.

'She is from a good family.'

'How do you know?' Douce said. 'We know nothing about her father. Who was he?'

'We know Abigail and she is a good soul. That's all I need to know. I thought you would be happy that your eldest son is finally getting married.'

'I should be. Why does nothing go as it should in this family?' Douce said, throwing her hands up in the air.

'Well, there is your answer.'

'What do you mean?' Douce said, her voice shrill and high-pitched with frustration.

'When does life ever go as it should? Perhaps if you didn't put such high and impossible expectations upon yourself...'

'What is wrong with wanting the best for your children?'

'We've tried that before and it doesn't always go as we planned.'

Moses was, once again, referring to Arlette. Her betrothal to Deudonne was probably the best match Douce could ever have hoped for. None of her children had ever reached that height since and everyone knew how maddening it had been when Mirabelle announced the engagement of her daughter Belia to Isaac of Lincoln. 'She's been planning this all along just so she can get back at me,' was her response on hearing the news of Belia's betrothal. As usual Douce saw everything that Mirabelle did as a plot against her and her family. Abraham had to admit she was right, up to a point.

When Abraham told his mother that he wanted the ceremony to take place before Rosh Hashanah, which was weeks away, and that he didn't want the usual year long wait between *erusin*, betrothal, and *nissuin*, when the marriage would be consummated, she became suspicious.

'Why in such a rush?'

Abraham avoided his mother's piercing stare. 'This is the way of the modern world, *Ima*. We are not in Rouen now. Times have moved on. Traditions change. Everyone in London is doing it this way now.'

'We don't live in London. I don't see what's wrong with keeping tradition. Tradition is what roots us to our faith.'

'We are still practising our faith, *Ima*. We're just doing it differently.'

'I don't see why we have to do things differently. Your brother and your sister didn't see the need to do things differently. They waited.'

'Yes, but they haven't witnessed what I have. It changes a man.'

'We've all seen terrible things. It doesn't mean the world

has to turn upside down.'

Moses walked over to the wine table and poured three cups of wine, returning with them clasped in both hands.

'Come now. Let us not quarrel over this. As head of this household I shall have the last word.'

Abraham dreaded his father's pronouncement. He was a fair man but did not like to upset his wife, which often meant he sided with her.

'Life is short. What matters is our son is getting married.'

'Exactly, *Aba*. Life is short, and we must make the most of it while we can. We could have died in those riots. I believe *Hashem* saved me for a reason. Maybe it was to marry Brunetta. I have no idea. All I know is she is the one good thing in my life.'

'And your mother is not?' Douce said.

'Tsh, tsh,' Moses interrupted.

'We shall welcome Brunetta into our family with love, but I am with your mother on this. We shall do it the old-fashioned way.' Abraham opened his mouth to protest but Moses raised his hand to silence him. 'We will compromise. We will hold the *erusin* before *Rosh Hashanah* as Abraham wishes, but we will have the *nissuin* in twelve months' time as your mother wishes.'

Abraham could have predicted the outcome. A compromise to satisfy both. He was uneasy with the decision but what could he do. He could only hope his momentary lapse on his return from London had not set in motion a series of events that neither he nor Brunetta would regret, nor give them reason to rush into the marriage.

Moses held out the cup to his wife. 'Take this and let's hear no more of it.'

He gave the other cup to Abraham. '*Mazel tov*, my son. May you have a long and happy marriage just like your parents.'

Douce took a sip of her wine. '*Mazel tov*,' she said, with little enthusiasm.

SIXTEEN

Mirabelle's family sat around the table for their ritual Shabbat supper. The candles had been lit. The *cholent* was simmering away on the range, wafting delicious smells into the great hall, mixing with the smell of freshly baked *challah* loaves. The blessings had been said and it was now time to relax and talk about the week's events.

Bonanfaunt, Mirabelle's only son, sat straight-backed at the other end of the table. He was immaculately dressed in his Shabbat clothes and rather handsome with his jet black, curly hair. His overly large hands were clasped around a silver goblet of wine. In all, he commanded a charismatic presence in the room. His pregnant wife, Genta, sat next to him with their children, the eldest Elias, named after his paternal grandfather and known in the family as le Petit and their second eldest Vives.

'So, Moses and Abraham didn't have such a great time at the coronation,' Mirabelle began, her thin lips pursed into a pleasing smile.

'*Ima*, why do you find such amusement in other people's

misfortune?' Bonanfaunt said, giving his mother a disapproving look.

She did not like to displease her son. 'I don't,' replied Mirabelle, her mouth downturned, as if she were a child being told off.

'Yes, you do,' muttered Elias, helping himself to another cup of wine.

'Don't you think you've had enough, Elias?'

'Oh, leave him alone, *Ima*. He works hard, and he deserves another cup of wine if he wants one. Doesn't he, Pucelle,' Belia said, addressing her daughter.

Pucelle got up from the table and went over to her grandfather.

'*Sabba*,' she cried.

'Ah, Pucelle, *mon petit chou*. You are adorable.'

He lifted her onto his lap. She grabbed for the cup of wine, nearly spilling it and raised it to his lips.

'You indulge her too much,' Mirabelle said.

Elias ignored his wife.

'I heard they nearly died,' said Belia.

'Who died?' said Elias le Petit.

'Moses and Abraham,' his mother explained. 'You don't know them.'

'Yes, I do,' piped up little Elias. 'They are the ones *Safta* doesn't like.'

Everyone around the table laughed, except for Mirabelle.

'You should be more careful what you say around the children, *Ima*,' Bonanfaunt said, in a scolding tone.

Mirabelle crossed her arms and sank back in her chair with a huff.

'Have you heard that Abraham proposed to Brunetta as soon as he arrived back from London?' Belia said.

Mirabelle gave out a derisive snort. 'No good will come of that union.'

Belia turned to her mother. 'Why do you say that?'

'Because Brunetta is an incorrigible flirt,' said Bonanfaunt.

'How do you know?' piped up Genta, giving him an enquiring look.

Bonanfaunt looked flustered for a moment, then composed himself. 'She just is, everyone knows that.'

'I don't,' said Belia, teasing him.

Bonanfaunt scowled at his sister then changed the conversation back to business matters.

'But, seriously,' he continued. 'It was a bad business – the rioting at the coronation – it doesn't bode well for our relations with the new king.'

'But he immediately issued an edict of protection and punished those who were responsible,' said Isaac, finally joining the conversation.

'That means nothing,' said Mirabelle uncrossing her arms and reaching for her goblet of wine. 'We are merely slaves to the king, despite what he says.'

'I don't think we are quite slaves, *Ima*. It's true he has the right to confiscate our wealth when we die, but he only takes one third of it and the family left behind get to carry on the business. Most of the time we are left to run our affairs and our businesses as we like.'

'Except when he goes off on his pointless Crusades, then he takes his pound of flesh again in the form of his legal tallages,' Mirabelle replied.

'There is so much uncertainty now,' Belia said. 'Since my dear father-in-law died and with the king setting up an entire exchequer department in his name.'

Belia was boasting. Mirabelle had married her daughter to Isaac for purely financial reasons to forge an alliance between the two families, but Belia had fallen in love with her husband and now never missed an opportunity to praise him and his family's wealth. It galled Mirabelle as Elias had yet to bring her family great wealth as her own husband.

Mirabelle took a sip of her wine and pointedly placed it back on the table. 'Yes, and while he is calling in Aaron's debts, we are left to find business where we can.'

Recognising her mother's tone Belia countered. 'At least we aren't totally reliant on Aaron's business as Moses is. As Aaron's agent he is having to hand over all his tally sticks and bonds to the sheriff.'

Belia's husband, Isaac, kept very quiet during this discussion. Mirabelle knew why. He was the youngest son of Aaron of Lincoln and by the time he was born, Mirabelle suspected, most of Aaron's lucrative clients were already being dealt with by his older brothers Deudonne and Abraham. Mirabelle hadn't thought about that at the time of Belia's betrothal. If she were honest with herself, the marriage was more about getting back at Moses le Riche. He was one of those men who achieved things in life seemingly effortlessly. Money, wealth. New business found him. He didn't have to go out there looking for it. What galled Mirabelle the most, when she could bear to admit it, was that Moses was a good man. That thought made her almost bring up her meal. She hated him for it. People like that needed to experience hardship in their lives. *Let's see how he copes with that*, she thought, a scheme already hatching in her jealous mind. She looked over at her daughter's husband. Her lip curled. She reached for her wine and drank it down still glaring at him.

Isaac had proved to be an average son-in-law with average abilities. He had none of the aplomb his father possessed, and none of his charisma. Mirabelle was becoming increasingly resentful of him. Because of his father's untimely death, he had brought them no wealth, no business connections. Still, her daughter seemed happy. Maybe it was for the best. The more useless Isaac was the better for her only son Bonanfaunt. She watched as he waved his large hands around, emphasising the point he was making, everyone at the table enthralled. All her hopes now lay with him.

CHAPTER
SEVENTEEN

The penetrating sound coming from the *shofar* as Seth, the *ba'al tokeah*, blew into the ram's horn, slammed into Abraham's soul. The *tekiah*, long and uninterrupted, is the first of the three traditional sounds heard at Rosh Hashanah, the Jewish New Year. It is a time for self-reflection, a reassessment of your life and for repentance. This year Abraham was consumed by self-reproach, so much so, he could not cast off this aching feeling deep inside his heart like it was broken. The *erusin* ceremony, the first of the two ceremonies they would go through to be married had passed without event. The marriage contract had been agreed and drawn up and a toast had been drunk by the two families. Both families had appeared to get on with each other – at least on the surface. Brunetta looked lovely as usual. But despite this, Abraham could not shake his downhearted mood.

Created as a symbolic call to wake up and repent for your sins it seemed to be doing just that. Abraham had agonised over his momentary lapse with Brunetta. Was the *shofar* trying to say something to him, to warn him? Since his return from London, apart from that one time, they had not done it again. But

Abraham so wanted to. The smell of her hair, her skin. He could bury himself inside her forever. Was it as Maimonides said? 'Search your deeds and return in penitence.'

Abraham was certainly feeling penitent this Rosh Hashanah, more so than usual. The thrice mournful sound of the *shevarim* represented tears being shed. He hoped they would not be Brunetta's. He had prayed daily that she would not be pregnant.

It would be the worst thing for Brunetta if she were pregnant before they were properly married. It would bring shame to her and cast a darkness over their whole future life together. Oh, but it had been the most wondrous experience of his life. His morbid thoughts were interrupted by the nine jarring staccato blasts of the horn. Abraham glanced across at Brunetta. Her head was lowered in prayer, the veil shrouding her face. Was she feeling the same? Was she keeping the truth from him? Was she pregnant? It would be a year before they could be fully married. He was overthinking matters as usual, his mind in turmoil, about to explode. Finally, Abraham's mental ordeal was coming to an end. The *tekiah gedolah* sounded, heralding the end of the service. It was another reminder of Judgement Day, when every man would stand before God to give an account of how he's lived his life. Abraham vowed then and there to give a good account of his life when the time came. The feeling of relief, as he left the synagogue to go out into the courtyard, was overwhelming. He never wanted to feel like that again on Rosh Hashanah.

A warm autumnal sun shone into the courtyard lifting Abraham's spirits. He had learnt his lesson. It was time to celebrate. As he stood waiting for Brunetta, he was greeted by Bonanfaunt who reached out his large hands to shake Abraham's.

'*Shanah tova*, Abraham.'

'And to you, Bonanfaunt. Let's hope both our families have a good year.'

Bonanfaunt moved on, greeting people as he went. Abraham bit on his fingernails. He did this until the flesh bled. Sometimes it became very painful, but it seemed to be a habit he could not break, especially when he was nervous. He had an overarching need to see Brunetta and ask her whether she was pregnant or not.

'Ah, there you are. Come with me.'

Brunetta followed him to the corner of the courtyard where a tub of apples stood.

'Is everything all right, Abraham. You look unwell.'

'I'm not sure. I suppose it depends on the answer to my question.'

Brunetta gave him a wary look.

'I need to know, Brunetta...' He leaned into her and whispered, 'Are you with child?'

'I don't think so,' she said.

'What do you mean, you don't think so.'

'Well, it's too early to tell.'

'Oh, I didn't know that.'

She laughed at his ignorance. 'There's a lot you don't know about women, Abraham.'

'When will you be able to tell?'

'A week or so.'

Abraham wasn't sure he could take the torture of not knowing for even a week longer.

'Is there no way of knowing sooner?'

Brunetta smiled back at him. 'If you knew a woman's body, you would understand.'

Abraham scratched his head in frustration.

'What are you two doing?' his brother Benjamin asked.

'I was just catching a quiet moment with my fiancée.'

'There'll be plenty of time for that once you're married, then if you're anything like Father, you'll hide yourself in the cellar,' he quipped.

Benjamin was the joker of the family. Never taking anything seriously, he was a constant source of annoyance to Douce.

'You look like you're scheming something,' Benjamin pressed.

'I leave that to Mirabelle and her clan,' Abraham said, nodding in the direction of Mirabelle and hoping it would distract his brother.

Mirabelle stood by the trestle of food, dressed in her finery. Benjamin and Brunetta turned to look at her. *Good*, thought Abraham, *I have distracted him from any more questioning.*

'What is she up to these days?' asked Benjamin. 'Boiling Christian children in oil?'

'Benjamin,' exclaimed Brunetta. 'That's a terrible thing to say.'

'Don't let Father hear you say that. You know how sensitive he is about such things.'

'Father needs to see the lighter side of life.'

'Well, it's hard when you've experienced such tragedy.'

'We all experience tragedy. Being a Jew is a tragedy.'

Benjamin made a face, feigning tragedy, like in the plays he sometimes watched in the street on market days.

'Don't you ever take anything seriously?' Brunetta asked him.

'I see no point,' said Benjamin, walking away and heading towards the food.

Benjamin could be very annoying, but Abraham was beginning to understand his point of view. He would have to stop worrying about whether Brunetta was pregnant or not. There was nothing he could do about it if she were – except, of course, marry her before next year. He must get on with his life and enjoy every day that God blessed him with.

'Come, let's eat.'

Douce, Arlette, Henne and his mother's friend Bellassez had spent all day in the kitchen preparing the food. It was now displayed on two long trestle tables, looking like a feast fit for a prodigal son. Grilled herring, salmon and carp, still with their heads on, were laid out on platters along with sliced cucumbers, spiced wild mushrooms and white figs. Steaming bowls of *blaunche porre*, a savoury broth made with leeks, stood next to chunks of roasted beef and chickens. For those with a sweet tooth, there were apples cooked in honey. Abraham had little appetite. Despite his best intentions he had given himself a nervous stomach. He picked up a round *challah* loaf and dipped it in some honey. Perhaps the sweetness would take away the bitterness he could taste in his mouth, like the feel of cold pewter between his teeth. Brunetta offered him a cup of *hypocras*, wine mixed with sugar and spices. He took a sip. It perfectly complemented the sweetness of the *challah* loaf, and once he had finished the cup, he began to relax. His lighter mood did not last for long.

'I hear you are getting married, Abraham.'

It was Mirabelle. She was wearing a tunic of fine grey silk. Her hair was entwined with gold and silver threads, visible underneath the diaphanous veil she wore. An opulent *epingle*, a brooch, of yellow gold, studded with emeralds and sapphires sparkled in the sunlight. Abraham could see that as a younger woman she may have been beautiful, but the years of scheming and nastiness had taken its toll on her fine features. The nose was more pinched than aquiline, and her eyes were narrow and cold. Since Abraham was a young boy, he had been afraid of Mirabelle. His father would tell him not to speak to her or play with her children. His stomach began to lurch.

'Yes, that's right,' he said.

'And Brunetta is to be the lucky young girl. Such a pretty thing.'

Brunetta beamed.

'I think so,' Abraham replied, all the while wondering why she was talking to him.

'How is your father? I heard he had a terrible turn in London. Is that why you were delayed there for so long?'

'My father is as well as can be expected. He gets tired quicker than he used to, but he is doing well all the same.'

'I'm glad to hear that. And his business is doing well?'

'I believe so.'

'That's good. I would be saddened to hear otherwise.'

Abraham thanked her for her concern, still wondering why she was talking to him with such a disarming manner. *Perhaps she had been misjudged in the past*, he thought.

'I trust he will be at the Michaelmas Court?'

'He is planning to be, as am I.'

'Let's hope the sheriff is in a good mood. I hear the new king is not best pleased.'

Before he died, King Henry had imposed yet another tallage on his Jewish subjects to fund his Third Crusade. This time he was demanding sixty thousand marks, and the Jewish community were expected to pay the largest share, a huge burden in Abraham's opinion. Since the death of the king, collection of the tallage had been somewhat half-hearted. William fitz Stephen, the city's sheriff, had been appointed assessor of tallages for the whole of the southwest of the country, not just Gloucester. Like his brother, he was a fastidious collector of taxes and a meticulous keeper of records.

'What do you mean?' Abraham asked, feeling a sharp, nervous churn in his stomach.

'King Richard is not pleased at the amounts collected so far.

I hear he is demanding that his sheriffs make an example of those who haven't yet paid.'

'But the sheriff is not responsible for the collection of this tallage. It's the abbot of St Peter who is responsible.'

The venerable Abbot Carbonel was responsible for collecting the tallage, but he had shown a distinct lack of fervour for the task his king had assigned him, despite being a supporter of the Crusades.

'I dare say we shall find out on Michaelmas,' said Mirabelle, giving Abraham the most obsequious smile, before rejoining her family.

Abraham could not shift the feeling in his stomach. The conversation with Mirabelle, although polite, left him with a sense of unease. He must find his father. Giving his apologies and leaving Brunetta, he went in search of Moses. He found him sitting in the great hall, drinking wine with his friend Josce.

'*Aba*, may I speak with you?'

'*Mais certainement*,' said Moses, pointing to a chair for his son to sit down.

His father often lapsed into his native French language, particularly after a few glasses of wine.

'Mirabelle says the sheriff is going to make an example of anyone who hasn't paid the Guildford tallage.'

'Have you been talking to Mirabelle,' Moses said, raising his eyebrows and smiling across at Josce.

'She came to talk to me.'

'That's always a bad sign,' said Josce.

'She will be up to something, no doubt. Don't worry yourself about it, son.'

'That woman unnerves me,' Abraham said.

Abraham left his father and was making his way back to the courtyard when he spotted Baruch. He had not spoken to him since his return from London. Abraham wondered if his cousin was avoiding him, but for what reason he did not know. But then no one knew what was in the mind of Baruch. There was a year between them, Abraham being the eldest, and over the years since childhood, Abraham had tried to get on with Baruch, but had found it hard. They had their childhood squabbles as all children do, but something was not quite right with him, he always took things too far. Baruch now approached with a smirk on his face.

'I see you're going to be married, Abraham,' he said.

Abraham nodded, bracing himself for some slight or insult, for Baruch was incapable of giving a compliment without following it with a slur.

'Sure you want to do that?'

Abraham was going to walk past him. His unexpected question made him stop.

'Why wouldn't I?' he said, giving Baruch an enquiring look.

'Just didn't think she was your type.'

'And what is my type?'

'Oh, you know, someone like your mother.'

Abraham could feel his anger rising at a possible slur on his mother and his future wife.

'And what would that be like?'

Baruch screwed up his face as though he were thinking hard.

'Someone virtuous. Someone Douce would not look down on.' Baruch's screwed up face turned into a broad smile.

'Can't you just be happy for me?' Abraham asked him, not wanting a confrontation.

'I am happy for you, believe me, I am. You've got what you deserve.'

'And what is that exactly?'

'A life of constantly looking over your shoulder, checking on your wife's fidelity.'

Baruch swaggered on by. Abraham was left wondering what the full meaning of his words were. With Baruch there was always a hidden meaning. Did he know something about Brunetta? Had something happened while he was away? With Baruch? The thought made him bilious. Brunetta, his *eschet chayil*, his woman of worth, his everything. Surely not? Abraham decided Baruch was just being mischievous. It was typical of him to want to spoil another person's happiness. He went back into the courtyard where he found Brunetta standing with young Glorietta. Baruch was with them. He could tell from Glorietta's laughter that he was flirting with her. He thought he detected a look of jealousy upon Brunetta's stern expression. Baruch was standing side-on to Brunetta, ignoring her. A nagging doubt formed in Abraham's mind. Damn Baruch, he said, under his breath.

CHAPTER

EIGHTEEN

Abraham and his father set off early to walk to the castle. It was a blustery morning and Abraham was glad of his cap and heavy cloak. He noticed his father's steps were laboured as he walked, bent into the wind, his cloak wrapping around his legs. Over his shoulder was a sack holding the split halves of the wooden tally sticks, which were the only record of outstanding loans. They needed to conclude their business well before the start of Shabbat, and so had set off in good time, hoping to be first in the queue. As they neared the wooden drawbridge, they were joined by others also keen on being seen early. Mirabelle with her husband, Elias, followed by Bonanfaunt and Belia. Bellassez, with her oldest daughter, Muriel and her youngest son, Judah, and lastly Abigail with her son, Josce. Abraham looked for Brunetta, hoping she had accompanied her mother to the castle. The year-long intimate separation imposed upon them was taking its toll on him. It felt like his life had been put on hold.

Ahead of them, within the bailey, stood the imposing square-shaped and turreted stone keep. This was the sheriff's stronghold containing the great hall and the suite of rooms reserved for the royal household. Abraham never felt entirely comfortable crossing the drawbridge. To him it felt like entering enemy territory, but his father would reassure him that in the event of an attack it was the safest place to be. The finely dressed group hurried across the drawbridge, Mirabelle quickening her pace when she saw the others. Abraham took hold of his father's arm and hurried him on. Once inside, they were ushered into the great hall by the sheriff's men.

Sheriff fitz Stephen sat behind a solid wooden desk, his scribes and guards surrounding him. In front of him was a cup of weak ale and several neat piles of the wooden tally sticks, the split halves matching the ones Abraham and the others held in their tally sacks. Abraham studied his face to catch sight of any hostility in his demeanour, Mirabelle's words still clear in his memory. He seemed his usual pernickety self, immaculately turned out in his sheriff's garb. He took a sip from his cup, placed it down carefully, cleared his throat and looked out at the growing number of merchants, lords and other taxpayers who were beginning to fill the hall.

'Let the tallying commence,' he said, looking directly at Moses.

Moses stepped forward, swinging his sack off his shoulder. He laid the sack on the desk and pulled out the halved tally sticks and immediately began to organise them. Fitz Stephen selected a tally stick from his pile and read out the name written in Latin on the notched stick. Moses quickly found the corresponding half. The name on the tally was that of Prince John. He had recently been given land and the title of Count of Mortain by his brother King Richard but before this improvement in his circumstances he had been reckless with money and borrowed heavily. It was time to settle the outstanding debt. A sum of thirteen marks remained.

'I believe this is the matching tally. As you can see there is still an amount of thirteen marks outstanding...'

'I can see that but before we settle this there is the rather pressing matter of the non-payment of the king's tallage.'

Moses stared at the sheriff. Mirabelle's words to his son echoed.

'Have you not received the usual writ from the king to draw upon the *ferm* of the shire to pay this debt?'

'I have not received such a writ.'

Abraham saw his father was visibly shocked at such worrying news.

'King Richard is keen to return to France and continue his father's fervour and establish his kingdom triumphant in the Crusades. The payment of the tallage set at Guildford has been lax, to say the least, and as head of this community, Moses, I must make an example.'

Moses clutched at his chest; his breathing constricted. He took in gasps of air. Sheriff fitz Stephen raised his gloved hand.

'Arrest this man.'

The sheriff's men surged forward, grasped Moses by both arms and marched him towards the exit. Abraham raised his hand to protest but the sheriff dismissed him. There was a stunned silence in the hall.

Sheriff fitz Stephen looked around the room, his grey eyes squinting.

'I suggest those of you who have yet to make payment, make it now.'

Several men and women came forward, pushing past Abraham to reach the front. Mirabelle hung back. As Abraham hurried past her to reach his father, Mirabelle grabbed his arm.

'Pity about your father. He's not looking in the best of health.'

Abraham wrenched his arm from her grip. 'No thanks to you I've no doubt.'

Mirabelle's eyes widened. She was obviously not used to being spoken to like that. Abraham quickened his step and ran after his father. The sheriff's men were dragging him along. Abraham could see his father's feet were trailing lifelessly along the ground.

'Please wait,' he shouted after them.

One of the men spoke. 'Don't interfere with the sheriff's bidding or you'll find yourself in gaol.'

Abraham looked on in panic. His father's face was red, and he could not get his breath.

'I'll fetch *Ima*,' was all Abraham could think to say.

NINETEEN

Brunetta lay on her bed daydreaming. Baruch still dominated her thoughts and the memory of the callous way he had treated her still stung. She had brooded over it countless times. Why did he have to be so mean? Why couldn't he be more like Abraham?

Abraham.

She was now his fiancée and would be married to him next year. She wished it could be Baruch. He was so unlike any other man she knew – not that she knew many. He beguiled her, and she hated him for it. She thought of their intimate time together. Brutal, passionate, exciting. Then she thought of Abraham.

Abraham.

His first and so far, only effort at lovemaking was – she thought for a moment for the right word – disappointing. In fact, if she were truly honest it had been a bit of a disaster, still it had served a purpose. Abraham would not question her virginity. He was so trusting. She had faked it. Try as she may she could not drum up much enthusiasm for his one and only effort. She brought to mind his first short-lived attempt at lovemaking, when afterwards he just lay on top of her and she felt his member go slack inside her until eventually it slipped out, making a squelching sound. The memory of it made her squirm. She compared it to Baruch's rock-hard offering. There was no comparison. She knew what she preferred. Now that she was betrothed to Abraham would she have Baruch again? Her insides throbbed at the thought. She wanted to. She wanted to feel him inside her again. She ached for him.

Baruch.

Her thoughts were in turmoil, flitting from Baruch to Abraham. She knew once Abraham had arrived back from London, she had to do it with him and quickly. She could sense Abraham's eagerness and she had exploited it. Luckily, for her, the timing was right. She knew he was sweet on her, and the thought she could be pregnant with Baruch's child made her do it. She even managed to convince him her tears of relief were actually tears of joy. She had trapped him, but he would never know. Ever since then he had shown remorse for his 'moral lapse' as he called it. He had no cause to worry though. She had started bleeding that morning so was not pregnant by either man.

Unsure how she felt about that, and still in a dreamy mood, she wandered downstairs. Her mother was not in the kitchen but at her desk. Several hazel tally sticks were laid out on the top, along with reams of parchment, all in disarray. Her mother looked worried and didn't look up when Brunetta walked in.

'Is everything all right?' she asked.

'Not exactly,' Abigail said, rummaging through her papers.

'Something's wrong. I can tell.'

'Got your head out of the clouds for once, have you? Back in the real world?'

Her mother infuriated her. 'I was only trying to be nice.'

Her mother looked up from her work with a look that said

Brunetta couldn't be nice. Brunetta's concern turned to resentment.

'Well go be nice somewhere else. I'm busy.'

Her mother went back to her search. Brunetta twisted her mouth and crossed her arms, not sure whether to stay and see if her mother's mood improved or leave her to it, whatever 'it' was.

After a few moments Abigail spoke. 'Moses has been arrested.'

'What?'

'This morning, at the Michaelmas Court.'

'Why?'

'To make an example of us all for not paying the king's extortionate tallage.'

'Have you paid it?'

'Not yet. That's what I'm doing now. Checking my records.'

'Will you be arrested if you don't pay it?'

'Maybe.'

Brunetta thought for a moment. 'Can you pay it?'

'Maybe.'

'Does Josce know? Can he help?'

'Your brother has his own affairs to deal with.' Abigail was still looking for something among her papers, then she stopped. 'Aren't you concerned for your future father-in-law's well-being?'

Brunetta had not given it a thought. Perhaps she should go and speak to Abraham. Console him as a good wife should.

TWENTY

W hen Brunetta arrived at her fiancé's home, it was in a state of chaos. Douce was ranting about how unfair life was; how her wonderful husband was an innocent man and how in all likelihood that harridan Mirabelle was behind his imprisonment. Justelin was crying, Arlette was pacing the room asking where Zev was and Henne was trying to comfort Douce.

'Your father has always had a good relationship with the sheriff. He would not lock him up unless someone had put him up to this.'

'You don't know that for sure, *Ima*. In any case, that's irrelevant now. We need to concentrate on getting Father out of that prison,' Abraham said.

'And how do you propose to do that?'

'I'm not sure. I need to think.'

'Can I do anything to help?' Brunetta asked, her little finger hooked into the corner of her mouth.

Douce replied with obvious sarcasm and unmasked vitriol. 'Not unless you have forty thousand marks to spare.'

'*Ima*, Brunetta is only trying to help.'

'Well, she isn't. No one can.'

'I just thought...' began Brunetta.

'You're not part of this family yet. Don't think for us. We can do our own thinking, thank you.'

'*Ima*!'

Abraham went to Brunetta's side, but she stepped away from him and stood in front of Douce.

'I know you think little of me but, like it or not, I'm about to join this family and your husband is about to become my father-in-law. I think I can help.'

Douce, who was sitting with her head in her hands, shot a look at Brunetta but said nothing. Brunetta continued.

'If you think Mirabelle has a hand in this why not play her at her own game?'

Douce looked puzzled but remained quiet, staring at Brunetta.

'What do you mean?' said Abraham.

'Knowing Mirabelle, she will have bribed the sheriff. That's what she usually does when she wants something. Why don't we bribe the sheriff to get Moses free?'

'This family is honourable. We do not sully our reputation by stooping to *her* level.'

'Then you must be content to let him rot in gaol,' Brunetta said, turning away from Douce, her skirts swirling as she moved.

Brunetta walked past Abraham, who by the look on his face, did not know what to do or what to say. He ran his fingers through his hair, just like his father did when faced with a problem. Brunetta was surprised at her own tenacity. She guessed Douce did not like her and was aware that if she didn't mark her place in the family hierarchy, her life would be miserable in the le Riche household. More so than her own home. Douce was a formidable opponent as a mother-in-law. She had to stand up to her. This was the best moment.

'She might be right, *Ima*. It's worth a try. Father has not been well since his return from London. He won't cope well with the conditions in that filthy gaol.'

Douce let out a frustrated cry. 'You don't need to tell me that. I'm well aware of your father's state of health.'

Undaunted Brunetta pressed on. 'It might help if we knew what Mirabelle wanted.'

Arlette spoke. 'I think she sees an opportunity for her husband to usurp Uncle's position as head of the community. He has not attended the *bet din* because of his ill health. I hear people talking.'

'He has only missed a few attendances at court and none of them were to discuss anything of particular importance,' Douce said in his defence.

Brunetta knew what Arlette was referring to. There was talk about Moses' health and rumours as to how long he had left to live were rife. It was a chink in Moses' armour and Mirabelle would exploit it if she could. Abraham was no community leader. Mirabelle would have heard the rumours, maybe even started them. If that's what she wanted, for her husband or more likely her son, Bonanfaunt, to assume the role of head of the community by undermining Moses' credibility, then they must mete out the same poison.

'What are people saying?' Douce asked Arlette.

'Unkind things. I don't want to repeat them.'

'Moses has served this community all these years and now people are turning on him. Is there no loyalty these days? No gratitude?'

'Don't upset yourself, *Ima*,' Abraham said.

Douce ignored her son's pleas, instead she launched into an anguished tirade. 'Has he not built them a beautiful synagogue with his own money? A school for the children to study their faith. Does he not give wise counsel and help whenever he can? Where would Josce be without his help? What is the matter with these people?'

Brunetta could see that Douce would not be much help in her present mood and Abraham, without his father, was out of his depth. This was her moment. To prove to Douce that she was worthy of joining her family. She might even be grateful to her and that would put her in her debt. An enviable position with which to start her newly married life. She rarely involved herself in the affairs of the community, or her mother's business, but she was not ignorant of its workings. She said little but kept her ears open. Her mind worked overtime to find a way to free Moses and make her life in the le Riche household bearable. Maybe even powerful.

'Abraham.'

Abraham, who was comforting his mother, his arm around her shoulder, jolted at Brunetta's tone.

'Isn't Abbot Carbonel responsible for collecting the tallage and not the sheriff?'

'He is, but it is the sheriff who has imprisoned father.'

Brunetta could see, by the look on his face that he was confused, muddled.

'Is the abbey one of your father's creditors?'

'Yes. They're always wanting money for some repair or grandiose building scheme.'

'Then let's call upon him.'

Abraham looked at Brunetta as if she were mad. In that moment, she could have slapped his face, but that would not achieve her goal and would definitely not ingratiate her in Douce's eyes. She could see that she would have to take the lead once they were married.

'Come on. Let's go now before Shabbat begins. I think this might work.'

Brunetta took hold of Abraham's arm and pulled him away from his mother, despite Douce's protestations. Once out of the hall, Brunetta turned to him.

'Where does your father keep his tally sticks?'

'In the cellar.'

'Good. We need to find those that relate to the abbey. Show me.'

Abraham led the way down the narrow stone steps to his father's cellar. Once inside he pointed at the chest where his father kept the tallies.

'Find one for the abbey.'

Abraham unlocked the chest and rummaged through it. After a while he produced a hazel stick full of notches with writing on it.

'I've found one,' he said, pleased at his efforts.

'How much is owing?'

Abraham studied the tally. 'They owe father ten marks.'

'How much is your father's life worth to you?'

'You can't ask me such a question. I can't put a price on my father's life.'

'You're going to have to if you want him out of that hellhole.'

Abraham knotted his brow. He looked like a court jester playing the fool. He still had not understood Brunetta's plan. She sighed in frustration at his slow-wittedness.

'Give it to me.'

Abraham looked at the stick then back at Brunetta.

'Just give it to me,' she said, snatching the stick out of his hands.

'My father will be angry that we have been in his chest and

taken a tally stick. He is very protective of these sticks. They're worth a lot of money.'

'Your father is no fool. If he's back home tonight and celebrating Shabbat with his family, he'll praise you, not scold you. Come on.'

She marched up the stairs holding on to the tally stick. Abraham hurriedly locked the chest and ran after her. She was out in the street before he caught up with her, striding towards The Cross.

'Brunetta, will you please explain to me what you're doing?'

'Saving your father's life.'

TWENTY-ONE

W hen they reached the abbot's lodgings, a building at the northwest corner of the abbey, she stopped. Abraham was out of breath. On the way there Brunetta had been working out what to say to the abbot. She had decided she couldn't leave this delicate negotiation to Abraham. She would have to do it. She knocked on the door. Moments later, Abbot Carbonel opened it, surprised to see Brunetta standing there. Then he saw Abraham and addressed him.

'Good afternoon, Abraham. How lovely to see you. Your father not with you today?'

'Father has been arrested and thrown in gaol.'

'That is dreadful. I am most saddened to hear this news.'

Brunetta, annoyed at being ignored by the abbot but even more annoyed with Abraham who had not yet introduced her, spoke. 'May we come in Abbot Carbonel? We have business to discuss.'

'Why of course, my dear, come in.'

The abbot's lodgings were not as Brunetta had expected. She thought it would be sparsely furnished, lacking in comfort but she could see into the room beyond and was surprised that he possessed such a large, luxurious bed. They were shown into the main room, filled with comfortable chairs and religious objects of gold and silver. She wondered why the abbot needed to borrow money from Moses when he seemed so well placed here. They sat down in front of the fireplace, the hearth prepared, but not yet lit.

Brunetta began. 'The sheriff has arrested–'

'I'm sorry,' said Carbonel. 'But who are you?'

'My fiancé has forgotten his manners, abbot. My name is Brunetta. You may know my mother, Abigail?'

'I can't say I do,' he said, squinting his eyes at Brunetta. He turned to Abraham. 'I take it congratulations are in order.'

'Pardon?' said Abraham, his mouth slightly open making him look like a bumpkin.

'Your fiancée. Charming.'

The abbot nodded over at Brunetta and gave her an appraising look.

'Oh, yes, of course. Thank you, abbot.'

Abbot Carbonel stretched out his hand to Abraham, giving him a slightly creepy smile. He had no intention of congratulating her or shaking her hand, so she continued. It took all her reserve to keep her temper and not say something sarcastic. Men could be infuriating when they were in each other's company.

'The sheriff has arrested Moses as leader of our community to set an example.'

'An example?'

'For not paying the king's crusade tallage.'

'Oh,' said Carbonel.

Brunetta had to be careful. The abbot, as the king's religious servant, was responsible for collecting the tallage set by King Henry to fund his Crusades. The new king Richard was even more fervent than his father and eager to rejoin his soldiers in the Crusades. She also didn't want to insult the abbot by offering him a bribe. It was tricky for such a novice as she.

'As you know, Abbot Carbonel, Moses values you as an honest and reliable customer. He would like to demonstrate that by a small gesture of thanks.'

She took out the tally stick and held it out in front of her. 'There is an amount of ten marks outstanding on this loan, payable in full at the Trinity Court. My future father-in-law is happy to waiver this final payment to show his gratitude for your loyal custom and hopes to do much more business in the future.'

A smile formed on the thin lips of the abbot. Brunetta knew he understood her. As a final and dramatic gesture, she snapped the stick in half and threw it on the floor at the abbot's feet. She stood up to leave. She saw Abraham's mouth open. She had, by that very action removed any proof of the money owing.

'I'm sure you have Moses' best interests at heart and wish for his release immediately, as does his family.'

'I shall speak to the sheriff and see what can be done to straighten out this matter. I'm sure it is a misunderstanding.' He turned to Abraham. 'My regards to your mother, Abraham, and congratulations again on your betrothal to such a fine young lady. Decidedly charming.'

Abraham thanked the abbot as did Brunetta and they left.

'What now?' said Abraham when they were outside.

'Go home and wait for your father.'

'But how do you know–'

'Abraham, were you not listening in there? Abbot Carbonel has influence. He will secure your father's release in return for the favour we just did him. That's how it works. That's how Mirabelle conducts business. I must go home now. It's nearly

95

Shabbat. Mother will be expecting me. She's already in a bad mood and I don't want to make it worse.'

She stopped when they reached her house. Abraham stood looking like a lost child, not moving.

'Go on then.'

Abraham leaned in and kissed her on the cheek.

'If this works my mother will be eternally grateful to you and so will I.'

Brunetta watched him as he made his way to The Cross, his head down, like a broken man.

TWENTY-TWO

Abraham was shocked when he saw his father after his sudden release. His skin was grey, like an old man's, and he had a hacking cough that would not cease. He was frail beyond his years. Douce bundled him upstairs and put him to bed with a hot drink and extra blankets. She sat by the fire with a small glass of apple brandy, her face etched with worry. Brunetta had been right. Abbot Carbonel had repaid the favour and managed to accomplish the swift release of his father.

'I owe a debt of gratitude to Brunetta. I have treated her unkindly, but I shall be forever in her debt. I fear your father would have died in that prison if he'd lain there another night.'

Her whole body visibly shuddered at the thought. She drank the brandy down in one. Abraham stood to refill her glass. Uncharacteristically, she accepted.

'I saw a different side to Brunetta yesterday. She's not the silly little girl she makes out to be. She has guile. If channelled in a good way that could be a great asset to our family.'

Abraham had never really discussed the family business with his mother before. She tended to keep out of such matters, preferring to be in the kitchen cooking or concentrating on her needlework in the evenings. He couldn't help thinking she was broaching the subject for a reason. One he didn't want to acknowledge. The demise of his father. As if she could read his thoughts, Douce turned to him.

'Your father is not a well man.'

'I know, *Ima*.'

'I think it's time you took more responsibility in the business. Your father needs a great deal of rest.'

'You're right, *Ima*. I will do my best.'

Abraham glanced over at his mother sitting in the chair looking diminutive. Her eyes were glassy with tears. They glistened in the glow of the fire.

'I know you will, and now you have Brunetta to help you and support you. That pleases me.'

'He will get better though. Like you said, he just needs his rest.'

Douce did not answer him. She turned her attention to Mirabelle. 'I swear if I find proof that Mirabelle was behind his imprisonment, I'll...' She stopped. Something had stirred a memory. Her knuckles went white against the cup she gripped.

'Father said the sheriff was just making an example of him.'

The door to the great hall flung open and in strode Baruch looking pleased with himself.

'I doubt Sheriff fitz Stephen would have released him,' Baruch said, appearing at Douce's side.

'What do you mean?'

'Haven't you heard? He's been replaced by the king's right-hand man. Fitz Stephen and his men are gone and replaced by none other than the Marshal, William Marshal. It is he who ordered the release of Father. Apparently, Father met him at Westminster on the day of the massacre. He carried him out of Westminster Hall – probably saved his life.'

Abraham remembered the kind knight who had rescued his father. Then Brunetta's efforts were for nought. And his father had lost ten marks. And his mother would be furious with her.

'How do you know all this?'

'I've been talking to the man himself. He wandered into the tavern with his men-at-arms. He came in to acquaint himself with his shrievalty. I offered to buy him a drink. We got talking. When I told him who I was, and that grandfather was in prison, he ordered his immediate release.'

Baruch looked smug. Pleased with his meagre effort. After all, what had he done but have a chance meeting and a few words over an ale? Any fool could do that. Abraham's hackles rose. Trust Baruch to steal Brunetta's thunder. Her efforts, it turns out, had been fruitless. Another sickening thought. His father had lost ten marks into the bargain. His mother would never let him forget that. Abraham felt nauseous listening to his mother praise Baruch. His own efforts never received such high praise. It was just what was expected of him, being the heir to the le Riche fortune.

He should be grateful to him for saving his father, but he wasn't. Resentful was nearer the mark. Since his snide comment questioning Brunetta's fidelity he had shifted his opinion of Baruch. In the past, he had tried to see his point of view when the rest of the family were against him.

Not any longer.

TWENTY-THREE

'They've arrived,' squealed Henne, as she burst into the great hall.

The family were gathered around the roaring fire, warming themselves on this crisp December morning.

'Who's arrived?' Douce asked.

'The Papal Legate for the Legatine Synod with his entourage.'

'Oh, him,' said Baruch.

'Aren't you excited?'

'Not really,' Baruch said, as he stoked the fire.

'Oh, but he's brought lots of exotic animals and troubadours from France with him. Come on, let's go and see him.'

'What kind of animals?' asked Justelin, suddenly taking an interest.

'I don't know. That's why I want to go. People have been talking about it for weeks.'

'Why does the pope's representative travel with a bunch of animals?' Moses asked.

'It's probably a status symbol,' Baruch answered. 'They say

he is from a humble background in Normandy, and he uses these tactics to extol his merits in public places.'

'I've often found that,' said Moses, scratching his greying beard, deep in thought, 'when a man feels he is lower in social stature he often overcompensates. This fellow sounds like a classic example.'

'He wants people to speak of him as though his equal does not exist on earth.'

'Sounds like he's achieved what he set out to do. Make himself look bigger and better than he is.'

'He's not much liked in political circles. Very overbearing, apparently.'

'How do you know all this?' Arlette asked him.

'You forget, William Marshal is a friend of mine. What he doesn't know isn't worth knowing. He also told me he doesn't like the English.'

'We'll be all right then,' said Benjamin in mockery.

'I'm not interested in any of that,' said Henne.

'Let's go see the animals,' said Justelin, jumping up from his seat.

Moses rested his hands on the chair arms and raised himself up slowly. His old bones were stiff first thing in the morning. 'Come on then. Let's go,' he said.

The family wrapped up warm and went outside in search of the much talked of spectacle. They did not have far to go. They could hear the music as soon as they stepped into Jewry Street. It was coming from The Cross and a large crowd had gathered. Baruch pushed his way to the front. The rest of the family followed. Baruch had never seen anything quite like it. William de Longchamp, the papal legate, was standing on a raised dais, flanked by dignitaries, including the abbot of St Peter, Abbot Carbonel. He was dressed in a scarlet mantle, lined at the neck with ermine. Upon his head he wore a mitre, embroidered in gold and set with precious gems. His garb was of immense opulence, even his shoes were scarlet with golden embroidered orphrey attached. Baruch thought he represented the worst of the pope's obscene wealth. Two white horses with white reins were harnessed to the papal sedan which had carried the pope's representative to Gloucester.

Henne gave out a loud gasp of wonder when she saw the animals. A huge brown bear shackled to his keeper was being led around in a circle, followed by a pack of chained Iberian lynxes. A smaller animal covered with spikes was shuffling along amongst the animals. But most fearsome of all was the lion. Its keeper held a wooden cudgel in one hand and a whip in the other. Baruch wondered what everyone would do if the lion got free. He patted the sword he now kept at his side despite the restrictions placed upon Jews carrying weapons, to reassure himself.

A band of troubadours played their instruments and sang in the Occitan language of the English king. The lyrics were mostly bawdy although one or two songs were humorous. Henne was transfixed by it all.

'Perhaps you should become one?' Baruch said to Henne, a broad grin forming.

'What a troubadour?'

'You'd be a trobairitz. On account you're female.'

'I love music, but I could never live like that. They're never in one place long enough.'

'You could take your kinnor and travel the world.'

Henne sighed. 'I think I'd miss my family.'

'I'd definitely consider it, but I can't play an instrument, or sing for that matter.'

Henne laughed and punched him playfully in the side. Baruch spotted William Marshal in the crowd and went over to him.

'What do you think of all this?' he said to the Marshal, casting his arm around in the direction of the spectacle.

'It's all for show. I don't know why Richard trusts him. He paid him three thousand marks to be given the post of chancellor and now he's the papal legate. It's all gone to his head.'

'He's certainly making an impression. I doubt Gloucester will see such a spectacle again.'

'How's your grandfather?'

'He's as well as can be expected. He's over there watching the menagerie.'

'A bad business, imprisoning him. It seems he was a victim of some skulduggery.'

'That would be Mirabelle. My family's archenemy.'

'She's a dangerous woman.'

'I know. My grandmother has quite a lot to say about her.'

The Marshal laughed. 'Women,' he said. 'They can be quite frightening.'

Baruch was pleased the Marshal had asked after Moses. Not many men of his standing would show such concern for an ageing Jew. A camaraderie between the two men was developing. Baruch liked the man. Perhaps they would become great friends. He was a powerful ally to have.

TWENTY-FOUR

A braham could always tell when his birthday was approaching. His parents sunk into a pensive and often morose mood. Something had happened to mark his birth all those years ago. He knew some of it, but not all, and had always suspected they were keeping something back from him. He knew that a young Christian boy called Harold had been brutally murdered, and that his father and others had been accused of his murder but beyond that he knew nothing. It was as though the spectre of that boy returned and hung over the house, the gloom and sadness so tangible.

In the months since his father's arrest, Abraham had become more involved in the business. Moses was still very much in control, but he tired easily, and often left Abraham to finish the paperwork. He had been in the cellar most of the evening and for a change it was Abraham who was feeling weary. After locking up he joined his parents and his younger brother Benjamin in the great hall. A lot had happened in the family. Henne had become engaged to a young man from London called Vives and Benjamin's wife had given birth to their second child, a little girl called Leah. Baruch was unchanged. Still his brooding self and a law unto himself.

Earlier in the day he had snatched a little time away with Brunetta. They had gone to their secret place, but nothing had happened. Abraham wanted to, but he could not face the intense feelings of regret, sin and guilt that would follow, and the fear that she might become pregnant. They'd had a lucky escape the last time. They were to be married later this year and until then he had to be content with touching her.

His father was nodding in his chair, his mother was squinting at the embroidery pattern she was working on.

'Has your father mentioned the gathering at York to you?'

'No, it must have slipped his mind.'

At the mention of York, Moses woke from his nap, and rubbed at his wrinkled face.

'Ah, yes. I forgot.'

'Were you really sleeping, *Aba*?'

'I never sleep in the day,' he said, offended at the suggestion he had been sleeping. 'You know, since the death of my business partner Aaron, the king has set up a special department in the Great Exchequer...'

'Yes, it's named after him – *Scaccorium Aaronis*. What an honour.'

'Hardly,' said Benjamin. 'Do you know what *scaccorium* means?'

Abraham lowered his gaze. 'Not really.'

He wasn't much of a scholar, or learned, like his father or his younger brother. He tried hard, but it was never enough.

'It's Latin for chessboard.'

'The counting board used by the exchequer?'

'Don't you think it ironic that they call the department for collecting Aaron's debts after the game of chess?' Without waiting for an answer Benjamin continued. 'Just like in the game of chess we are treated like pawns. Moved around this way and that.'

Moses smiled. 'When did you get to be such an angry man?'

'Since we became pawns in the king's game of making money out of us.'

'You're forgetting, Benjamin. The pawn is the least valuable piece in a chess game. To the king we are the most valuable.'

Benjamin nodded in agreement, giving in to his father's superior intellect.

Douce glared at Benjamin. She didn't like it when he became angry. Perhaps it reminded her too much of Baruch. Benjamin went quiet. Abraham steered the conversation back to York.

'What about York?'

'There's to be a gathering of Aaron's principal agents in York to discuss the arrangements following Aaron's death. The king has seized all of his assets and is–'

'Raking in the spoils,' Benjamin said, again interrupting his father.

'Be quiet when your father is talking.'

'Sorry, *Ima*.'

'Aaron's business was of such magnitude that the king is now systematically going through all of his outstanding debts. There are clerks working full time to establish the true measure and extent of his wealth.'

'He's already confiscated his movable goods to pay for his Crusades,' Benjamin said, then his head went back, and he laughed. 'And look what happened to them. At the bottom of the English Channel.'

Douce gave him another glare. 'If you keep talking like this, you'll end up in gaol. It's treasonous.'

Benjamin apologised again to his mother. 'It just makes me really angry,' he added.

'As you know, Benedict of York died of his injuries, after the London riots.'

'Not before he converted again,' said Benjamin with bitterness.

Moses held up his hand to quiet Benjamin. Douce shook her head in sorrow.

'His death and the king's decision to appropriate Aaron's wealth is having a profound effect on our money lending activities. I had a great deal to thank Aaron for. He's the main reason we are where we are today.'

'Your father is not well enough to travel.'

'So, you want me to go in your place?'

'He does,' said Douce, before Moses could reply.

'Why don't we both go?' said Benjamin.

'Only one of you can go. Someone has to stay to keep your father's business going.'

'But I'll be away for *Pesach*.'

'It can't be helped. You'll be here for next year's Passover. I'm sure they'll celebrate it just the same in York.'

'But where will I stay?'

'Your father always stays with Josce of York's family. They'll look after you.'

'How long will the journey take?'

'You're younger than your father, you should be able to do it in less than a fortnight.'

Abraham had run out of reasons why he should not go. The real reason he didn't want to go is that he didn't want to be away from Brunetta for any length of time. He made a mental calculation.

'That means I'll be away for almost a month.'

'I told you it can't be helped. Your father is too unwell. We cannot miss such meetings. It's important our voice is heard,' Douce snapped at him.

She was worried about Moses.

Abraham knew he must accept his mother's wishes. He didn't want to upset her more than she already was. His mother was right. If he was to step into his father's shoes, he must take on all that that entailed. He was being churlish.

'I'm sorry, *Ima*. It's just that I'll miss Brunetta.'

'For goodness' sake, you're marrying the girl. You'll be spending the rest of your life with her.'

When the arrangements were finalised Abraham told Brunetta.

'I'll be away for almost a month.'

Brunetta didn't react. No chagrin, no emotion. 'Oh.'

'I'll miss you.'

Still, she said nothing. It was market day, and she was strolling past the stalls.

'Oh, look at this,' she said, showing him a bolt of expensive cloth. 'Wouldn't I look lovely in a gown made of this? Don't you think?'

'Did you hear what I said?'

'Of course, I did,' she said, turning to face him. 'You're going away, and you'll miss me.'

Abraham sighed. 'Will you miss me?'

'Of course,' she said, fingering the sumptuous cloth. 'I'll miss you and I'll look forward to your return.'

She gave him a cheeky smile that hinted at some future tryst. Sometimes she could be impossible, thought Abraham.

CHAPTER

TWENTY-FIVE

A braham arrived at Josce's house in York on the morning of *Shabbat HaGadol*, the Shabbat before Passover, known as the Great Shabbat. He had been travelling on horseback for the last eleven days, stopping over at village inns to sleep and rest his horse. He was weary and looking forward to resting in a bed without fleas. Josce's house was, as his father had described, one to rival a citadel. He had always thought his father a wealthy man, and the home they lived in reflected that, but this was something else. From the outside its thick stone walls rose higher than any other building in the street. It looked like a castle, in fact, it was probably bigger than Gloucester's castle.

Abraham was shown into the house by a servant and greeted by Anna, Josce's wife.

'You are the first to arrive, Abraham. You must be tired. My husband is not at home. He has business in the city, but he'll be back for Shabbat. I expect you'd like to rest up before we eat?'

'That would be most welcome. I've been travelling for days and, I must admit, I am weary.'

Anna showed him to his room. They walked through an

inner courtyard garden, smelling of rosemary, with a Roman style mosaic path running through it, the stone walls towering above them. At last, they came to Abraham's room. It was only a guest room, Anna had explained, but it was more sumptuous than his own at home. The canopied bed was draped with heavy damask, with matching drapes at the window. Tapestries from Spain and France covered the stone walls and a thick Persian rug, brought back, Anna said, from the Crusades by a noble in part payment of a debt he owed her husband, covered the wooden floor. As soon as Anna left, Abraham fell onto the bed. As he lay on the soft damask, he thought of Brunetta. How he would like to make love to her on this bed, the two of them naked, instead of sneaking off to the woods for a fumble. They both knew what they were doing was wrong and that they should have waited till they were married, but that first time had been so wonderful... still, Abraham was not willing to risk the consequences. It had taken all his resolve to resist Brunetta's advances. He couldn't cope with the aftermath of shame and worry in case she should get pregnant.

Refreshed and eager to meet the other guests, Abraham found his way back to the great hall. The smell of wood burning in the huge stone fire, mixed with the smell of the beeswax candles and the flickering of the cresset lamps reminded him of home but that was the only similarity.

The room teemed with opulence, from the wooden rafters to the gold trinkets adorning the hall and, in the centre, the longest oak table he had ever seen. He imagined this was what a royal household looked like. There were tapestries and rugs from the far corners of the world. Abraham was mesmerised by it all. It reminded him of the king's coronation only the welcome this time was warm and friendly. He had overslept and was a little late. Josce's guests were already sitting at the table.

'*Shabbat Shalom*,' Josce greeted him, rising from his seat at the head of the table.

Abraham wished him and his guests a blessed Shabbat before he took his seat next to Moses of Bristol and his son, Yom Tov. Rabbi Elijah of York was there with his much younger, unmarried sister Antera. The most illustrious guest was Rabbi Yom-Tob of Joigny, a noted rabbinical scholar, who had travelled from France on some religious business. Yom-Tob, who Abraham knew of by reputation had written the *Sefer Hatenaim* or Book of Conditions, which as far as Abraham knew was something about Biblical punctuation and accentuation. Abraham hoped the evening would not be consumed by rabbinical discourse. He was far too tired and, if he was honest, just plain uninterested in the minutiae of his faith.

'I hear you were at the king's coronation?' Josce said.

'And survived,' added his wife.

'How did you manage that, Abraham?' Antera asked him.

Abraham told them all but the gory details. With grim realisation, he knew he would be telling this story for the rest of his days. Already, he was weary of its telling.

'You were lucky to escape,' Antera said, flashing him a smile.

'Poor Benedict. He escaped the riot only to die weeks later in Northampton of all places.'

'They say he converted back to Christianity before he died. Is that true?'

'I don't believe it.'

'He would only have done it to save his skin.'

'It would have been forced upon him.'

'And poor Jacob,' said Rabbi Yom-Tob. 'I met him a few times. A wise man. We had many discussions on the relative merits of Maimonides and Rabbenu Tam.' Yom-Tob pulled on his long grey beard. 'Such a waste of a life.'

Jacob of Orléans had been one of the casualties of the riot that day.

'All of them were,' Abraham said. 'Their only crime was being a Jew.'

'I heard they arrested the ringleaders.'

'That's right. One was hung for robbing a Christian and the other two for throwing a lighted torch onto a thatched roof. Turned out it spread so far it burned down Christian homes.'

'There's Christian justice for you. They only take action when it affects their own kind.'

Abraham wondered if the two hanged men were also those responsible for Judith's death. He hoped so. It would go some way to ameliorating the injustice he felt, make him feel better, lessen the pain. He was still plagued by nightmares of that night.

'Why do they hate us so much?' said Antera.

'They're jealous. They would do anything to be in our shoes and have half the wealth we possess,' said Abraham, surprising himself, sounding like his younger brother. 'They need the money from us, but they don't want to pay us back.'

'Yes, that's true, Abraham,' said Josce, nodding his head. 'Only this morning I had a very difficult meeting with one of my debtors. He seemed to think because he owed the money to Aaron of Lincoln that he need not pay me back. He seems to think all his considerable debts have been cancelled with Aaron's death. But he doesn't understand how the system works. As agents of Aaron we are partners in his business. He doesn't think he ought to pay me the money he owes me.'

'Who was that, dear?'

'Richard Malebysse.'

'Oh him,' exclaimed Anna. 'Even the Christians call him the Evil Beast. That's what his name means. In Latin it is *mala bestia* – the evil beast.' She laughed, popping a dried fig into her mouth. 'I always find it so strange how some people take on the qualities of the name they've been given.'

Josce reached over the table to grab a handful of pistachio nuts. He cracked the shell between his teeth revealing the green nut within.

'He was ranting and raving at me in the middle of the market calling me an enemy of Christ. He said it wasn't fair that I had so much money when he had not enough to go on Crusade.'

'Well, he needs to get his facts straight. We pay for those Crusades through the extortionate tallages the king burdens us with.'

'That's right, and if we don't pay them, there are consequences.'

'Yes, my father was recently locked up in gaol for not paying the Guildford tallage.'

'Let's not dwell on this tonight. We can discuss this on Sunday at the meeting when the others are there. Besides, this conversation is becoming as sad as the face on my dog when he's hungry,' said Josce.

As if the dog knew he was being talked about, the skinny greyhound raised its head, cocking its ear as if listening out for more mention of his name. The dog then got up from its place by the roaring fire and sat by Josce, his sad, pleading face appealing to him.

'See what I mean!'

Everyone laughed, the mood lightened and became more convivial.

'Let's talk about something more enjoyable. Tell me, Abraham, what plans do you have for *Pesach*?' Anna asked.

'Well, as usual my mother will be cooking mountains of food.'

'That's what mothers do,' she replied.

'And I hope to spend it with family and friends and, of course, my fiancée...'

'Oh, you're betrothed?' Antera exclaimed, sounding disappointed.

'Antera has been trying to get a husband since the day she could speak,' her brother, Elijah, cut in.

'That is not true,' Antera protested.

'What's her name? Do I know the family?' Anna asked.

'Her name is Brunetta. She's the daughter of Abigail, a widow, recently settled in Gloucester.'

'I don't think I know the family. What was the husband's name and where did they come from?'

'They came from Northampton. Her husband's name was Ysaac, I think, but she doesn't talk much of him.'

Anna knitted her brows in thought. 'No, no. I don't think I know the family. I remember an Ysaac of Northampton, but he divorced his wife. Quite a scandal at the time.'

'Maybe Abigail's divorced and not widowed,' Antera teased.

'Stop your troublemaking, Antera. You're talking about his future mother-in-law,' said Elijah, rolling his eyes in despair.

'Maybe that's why she teases. To stop you becoming the son-in-law,' Josce said jovially, slapping his friend Elijah on the back.

Abraham was enjoying the good-humoured badinage. It was harmless fun. He wished Brunetta was with him, as his wife, so that Antera would cease being interested in him and stop making it quite so obvious. As well as the good company, the food was exceptional, as was the wine and the conversation flowed easily without dwelling too much on religious dogma. When he could no longer keep his eyes open from tiredness, he stood up to excuse himself for the evening. As he did, there was a frantic banging at the door. The laughter stopped, and Anna gave her husband a puzzled look.

'Who could that possibly be at such a late hour?'

The banging continued, becoming louder and more frantic. Josce rose from the table to answer the door. Abraham went with him. As Abraham got closer, he could hear raised voices.

'Let us in.'

Josce drew back the heavy iron bolts and opened the door. His neighbours Aaron, Milo and Leo Episcopus stood before them with their families. They burst through the door, pushing past Abraham, the women and children hysterical, the men looking terrified.

'Close the door, quickly,' implored Aaron.

'Why? What has happened?' Josce said, bolting the door after the last of them were safely in.

'A mob, led by that Jew hater, Malebysse, broke into Benedict's house. They've slain his widow Esther and all the children whilst they slept in their beds.'

Anna let out a scream. 'Those poor creatures. They have suffered enough.'

'Yes, but now they are at blessed peace,' said Rabbi Yom-Tob.

Anna was not comforted by his remark. She jolted out of her seat. 'I must go to my children.'

The neighbours gathered round, each telling the terrible events at once.

'They've looted his house.'

'And taken all his valuables.'

'And set fire to his home.'

'They've gone berserk.'

'Calm down,' said Josce, finding it difficult to hear above their clamouring voices.

'They're setting fire to all our homes. We don't know what to do?'

Abraham could see the terror etched upon their faces. He

had seen that look before. On Judith in London. How could this be happening again? The king had arrested the perpetrators and distributed a royal writ demanding that Jews be left alone. He had held a solemn Mass where Richard swore to exercise true justice and equity to his people committed to his charge and to abrogate bad law and unjust customs.

Before he left England for the Third Crusade, he'd ordered those responsible to be hanged. Abraham thought if the new king had publicly shown his support, an incident like the London massacre would be a thing of the past. He was so wrong and now, by the worst case of bad luck he could think of, it seemed he was caught up in another attack.

Details of the attack on Esther and her children were hard to listen to. Each time Esther's name was mentioned, Abraham saw Judith's face as she clutched her children before jumping to her death. It was almost as much as he could bear. The others had joined them by now. Anna and Antera took the children into the great hall and tried to comfort them whilst the men remained by the door, taking in the enormity of what was happening. They were under attack, by a murderous mob, led by the Christian devil who went by the name of the Evil Beast.

TWENTY-SIX

Preparations were under way for Passover in the le
Riche household with the usual frenetic activity in the
kitchen. Douce was preparing the *cholent* whilst Arlette
prepared the dough for the *challah* loaves. Henne was holding
the large pan over the kitchen fire, steadying it for her mother
so she could stir its contents.

'You're quiet, *Ima*,' said Henne.

'Am I?' Douce said, wiping the hair from her face, her cheeks
pink from the heat of the fire.

'Are you worried about Abraham?'

'I am a bit. He's never gone away without his father.'

'He'll be all right, he's a man now,' Henne said, still holding
on to the pan with both hands. 'Stop treating him like a child.'

Douce smiled. 'You're all still my children.'

Arlette was kneading the sticky dough, her hands covered in
flour. 'You'll understand more when you have children of your
own, Henne. They never stop being your children.'

Douce finished stirring the stew and told Henne to put the
lid on the pan. It was to cook for several hours in the communal
oven until tender and unctuous. Once the food was ready and

the women had laid the table, they went upstairs to wash and change into their Shabbat clothes. One by one, the men of the house returned, changed their clothes and gathered in the great hall to eat.

Moses had spent the morning in his cellar and the afternoon visiting his customers to collect on outstanding loans. Zev and Rubin had spent the day in the workshop hammering out silver platters and shaping chalices which they sold to the local Christians. Benjamin had visited some local landowners to discuss their loan requirements, and Baruch had not been seen all day. The women joined them, and after the blessings were over, served the food. Conversation centred around how their day had gone and about Henne's upcoming wedding. When Baruch entered the great hall dressed in his Shabbat clothes, his hair combed into neat glossy curls everyone turned and the conversation stopped. It was unusual for Baruch to join them for the weekly Shabbat meal, or any family occasion.

'Please, don't stop on my account,' he said, taking a seat next to his mother and planting a kiss on her cheek.

Arlette smiled and beneath the table squeezed his hand.

'You are lucky to have both your sons with you tonight, Arlette,' Douce began. 'This is the first time Abraham has not been here for *Shabbat HaGadol*. It doesn't seem the same without him. I didn't realise I would miss him this much.'

'Don't fret, *ma chérie*,' said Moses. 'Josce and his wife will take good care of him as they always did with me. He'll be having as much fun as we are.'

Baruch scanned those gathered at the table. 'Where is Abraham?' he asked.

'Well, if you showed any interest in this family, you'd know he's gone to York instead of Moses,' Zev said.

'Please don't start,' said Arlette.

Moses, who sat at the top of the table, held up his hand to silence them.

'I was supposed to go to York for a meeting, but Douce wouldn't let me go. She says I'm too old.'

Douce huffed. 'I didn't say you were too old. I said you weren't well enough.'

'She takes good care of you, *Sabba*. You shouldn't complain,' said Baruch.

'I would never complain about my *eshet chayil*,' Moses said, his eyes watery. 'I don't know what I'd do without her.'

'Oh, tush,' said Douce, a coy smile appearing at the corners of her lips.

'I think it's amazing how after all these years you are still speaking to each other,' Baruch joked.

'Marriage is a wonderful institution, Baruch. You should try it one day,' Moses said.

'I don't think anyone would have me.'

'Oh, nonsense,' Arlette said. 'You are a handsome young man and I'm sure you'd make a good husband.'

'You have more faith in me than I do myself.'

'That's because you have no faith in anything,' Zev said.

Baruch put down his silver spoon in a deliberate manner and turned to Zev. 'Why are you always against me? No wonder I seldom eat with the family. You just can't leave me be. Always some cutting remark or rebuff.'

Baruch scraped back his chair.

'Don't go. Stay and finish your meal. Your father means no harm.'

'You sure about that, Mother?'

Arlette looked down at the table. Baruch was right. Her husband rarely had a good thing to say about Baruch. It was a constant source of sadness to her. Perhaps she did overlook his bad behaviour a little too often, refusing to see his bad points, but it was out of love for her son in the face of constant nagging from Zev. Over the years as Baruch got older it seemed to have got much worse. She wished Baruch would make something of himself, instead of wasting his time with the unsavoury company he kept. Arlette thought if she showed him enough love, and excused his transgressions, it would help him, and he would one day make amends. But she could see it wasn't working. She despaired at times. He was her firstborn and she had failed him.

Zev said nothing. He filled his cup of wine and drained it, refilling it again. That was another cause for concern. Zev liked his drink too much. It had started in the early days of their marriage when they had had some difficulties. Even though those difficulties had been resolved years ago the habit had been formed. It grew worse when he was angry or under pressure. Still, she thought, he was a good husband and a good father to their son Rubin.

Moses raised his glass. 'Come, Baruch, it is pleasing to have your company and I'm sure your mother is enjoying having you sit beside her.'

Arlette reached again for Baruch's hand. He took it and pulled his chair up to the table. 'I'll stay for Mother's sake.'

The rest of the evening passed without further incident. Zev numbed his senses with more wine and Moses regaled everyone with tales of his travels. Benjamin made everyone laugh with his jokes and unique take on life.

At the end of the night Arlette whispered into Baruch's ear. 'I'm so glad you stayed. It's been just like old times.'

'Yes,' he said. 'Father carping at me just like old times.'

'He doesn't mean anything by it. Your father loves you. He's just a little disappointed that you didn't want to join him in the silver business.'

'I think you're wrong, Mother. Even if I did work with him, he wouldn't change. I've accepted it now.'

'Accepted what?'

'That my father hates me.'

Tears formed in her eyes and an intense sadness overwhelmed her. She knew the sadness was because she was also incapable of loving Baruch in the same way she loved Rubin. Was it because he was different or had the lack of her love made him different? Whatever the reason, she could not shake the guilt or sadness that came over her whenever the subject came up.

'He doesn't hate you. How can he, he's your father.'

Baruch snorted in disgust. 'Moses is more of a father to me than him.'

He gave Zev a sideways look. Zev was sitting in between Rubin and Justelin animated in conversation.

'Just look at him, Mother. Do you ever see him behave like that with me?'

Arlette did not answer. Baruch was right. It had been a long time since Zev had shown any interest in her son. Was that why he was so wayward? Showing him love was not enough. A boy needed his father. She must speak to Zev about it.

Despite the altercation between Zev and Baruch, Arlette had enjoyed the evening. Had Abraham been present it would have been perfect, having all the family together. Moses rose to say the final blessing and afterwards Baruch kissed his mother on the cheek, said goodnight and slipped away.

WHEN BARUCH LEFT the great hall, he went upstairs to his bedroom and lay awake for hours thinking about his life, his family and surprisingly Brunetta. His grandfather had said he should get married and for the first time in his life he found himself thinking seriously of marriage. What would it be like to be married to someone? Being faithful to one woman. Was he capable of such fealty? Surely, he would stray. Could he trust himself? Would he be bored? Would he be expected to work for his father and support his wife? He knew enough about moneylending to set himself up in business, but did he want to do that? His casual moneylending activities earnt him enough to keep him in ale but would not support a wife. Besides, what he got up to was unofficial. If he expanded and turned legitimate, he would have to pay taxes.

His thoughts turned to Brunetta. He couldn't quite figure her out. She was more Christian than Jew in her approach to sex. All the young Jewish women he knew were chaste and honourable. They would never let him have his way with them, but Brunetta had given in to him so easily. Both times. He smiled as a vision of her underneath him, breathing hard, her eyes closed, surfaced. He remembered her smell and her soft skin. He'd been avoiding her since the news of her betrothal reached him. He wasn't sure why. It wasn't out of respect for his cousin Abraham. The news that Abraham was away in York gave him an idea. He lay on his back, pleasured himself, and then drifted into a deep sleep.

TWENTY-SEVEN

'Where is the mob now?' Abraham asked.

'They were making their way along Petergate,' Leo said.

'If they made their way from Benedict's house in Spen Lane then they're probably making their way to Stonegate – to Moses' house.'

At the sound of his father's name, Abraham's stomach churned. This could happen anywhere, anytime for the slightest of reasons. For all he knew it might be happening in Gloucester right now. And why? Because people were jealous of their wealth? Intolerant of their faith?

'What are we going to do? They're bound to come here...' Milo said.

'This house is like a fortress. We'll be safe here,' said Aaron.

'I wouldn't be too sure of that. They burnt the thatched roofs of the houses and set light to the wooden doors in London. If they're intent on getting in, they'll find a way.'

'We need to make a decision. It won't take them long to make their way here. I'm probably next on the list after the meeting I had with Malebysse this morning.'

'Do you think that's what sparked this?'

'Who knows. They're like mad dogs. They're deranged.'

'Yes, but they're not stupid. Between us, they owe us a lot of money. This is one way of wiping out those debts in one fell swoop,' Josce reminded them.

'We are under the protection of the king. We could ask the sheriff to protect us. He acts as the king's representative.'

'I'm on good terms with John Marshal. If anyone can stop this attack, surely, he can?'

'John Marshal? Is he the brother of William Marshal?' Abraham asked, recognising the name.

'Yes, it's his older brother. A very influential family here in York, his younger brother Henry is the Dean of York.'

'I know William Marshal. I don't know him well, but he saved my father's life at Westminster, and he managed to free him from gaol.'

Abraham's hopes rose. William Marshal showed kindness to his father – a Jew. Perhaps Marshal's brother would also help.

'He might be willing to offer us shelter in the castle until it's all over,' Abraham said. 'My father always told me the castle was the safest place to go if there was trouble.'

'It's true we are under the king's protection but that hasn't stopped mobs attacking us. Look what happened after the riots in London...'

Abraham had heard nothing of any further riots. 'What happened after London?'

'Don't you know?'

'Nothing of any further rioting has reached us in Gloucester.'

'It seems the riots spread along the east coast. Lynn was the first in January, then the city of Norfolk the following month. They were butchered in their own homes.'

A vision of Judith, the slain Jew, came to him again, unbidden. The accompanying fear in the pit of his stomach also came, unbidden. He could feel the beads of sweat on his forehead and top lip. He wiped them away with the sleeve of his tunic, hoping Josce had not noticed.

Anna, having walked from the children's bedroom to check on them, heard this conversation as she passed by the men.

'Leave this house when those evil men are out there on the rampage. I will not place my children in peril. Let us stay here until it's over.'

'We may not have a choice, Anna,' Josce said, taking her arm and leading her back into the great hall.

When Josce came back, he looked very troubled.

'It's a difficult decision to make. Stay here and trust in the fortifications of this house or take our chances with the sheriff? What does everyone think we should do?'

'The sheriff might side with the mob. He's a Christian after all.'

'Even the king couldn't protect us in London...'

'But the king punished those responsible, so there is a chance that this sheriff will help us for fear of the king's displeasure,' Rabbi Elijah pointed out.

'That's a good point. It may be our only hope,' said Josce.

'I have a good view of the city from my room,' said Abraham. 'I'll go and see what's happening out there.'

Abraham left the men debating their predicament. He ran to his room on the top floor and went to the window where he could gain a good view of the street below and across the city. The shutters had been closed for the night, but he flung them open. The view did not fill him with hope. Fires raged across the Jewry, and he could hear people's screams in the distance. Coney Street was, so far, unaffected, but they were close. He rejoined the men.

'There are fires raging all around us and they're getting closer. I think if you trust this man John Marshal, we should throw ourselves on his mercy and take refuge at the castle.'

'Well, you are the only one with experience of such things. I will take your lead. Are we agreed?'

The men nodded.

'I'm not going out there unless I'm armed,' said Moses of Bristol.

'But we are not allowed to carry arms,' Leo said.

'I have sharp knives,' Josce said.

'Let's hope we don't have to use them,' Rabbi Elijah answered.

Josce and his wife gathered up a few precious possessions, woke the children from their sleep and readied for the short journey to the castle where they hoped to find John Marshal, the sheriff. A northerly wind blew down Coney Street as they headed south towards the royal castle keep. The sheriff and his men would be there to stand between them and the marauding mob. They would be safe.

When they walked past the synagogue, next to Benedict's house, they saw that it had been set alight. Sacred scrolls lay in the street, trampled on by muddy boots, torn, defiled.

By the time they reached the castle keep, their numbers had swollen to over a hundred. Abraham looked up at the tall wooden structure, built upon a raised mound of land. It was much like the castle at Gloucester, only taller. At the portcullis, they were stopped by a guard, who seemed surprised at the number of Jews gathered before him. Josce demanded to see the sheriff. After waiting in the rain, which was now lashing down upon them, the sheriff arrived, looking bleary-eyed and annoyed to have been disturbed at such a late hour. Abraham recognised him from the coronation procession. Surely, the king's representative and the brother of one who had shown kindness to his father would protect them? Still, a deep foreboding came over him. He couldn't help but think that everything showing up in his life had a connection to the terrible events of that night. Perhaps a Jewish curse had been placed upon him.

'What do you want from me at this godawful hour,' John demanded, wiping the driving rain from his face.

Josce greeted the sheriff, who looked somewhat dumbfounded to be standing in front of almost the entire Jewish community of York.

'Richard Malebysse and others have gone berserk and are burning Jewish houses. They've already slain Benedict's wife and her children, maybe more. We're here to ask for your protection in the name of the King, Richard of England.'

John looked up at the night sky across the city. A glow from the fires was visible and the smell of thatch burning was blowing in on the northerly wind.

'Malebysse, you say? He's probably with the rest of his clan, the Percys. Troublemakers those Percys.'

'Will you help us, sheriff?' Josce asked in pleading tones, gathering his family towards him in order to emphasise their plight.

'Come inside the keep. You can take refuge there till it dies down.'

The bedraggled throng made their way through the bailey and climbed the steep steps into the safety of the wooden keep. Inside, a fire raged in the far corner of the castle's great hall. Sheriff Marshal gave orders for his men to leave so that room could be made for everyone. Even so, they were crammed in like salted herrings in a barrel. It was not long before the room was filled with steam from the rain-soaked clothing. Abraham settled himself on the floor in a corner of the hall with Josce, Anna and their children. He heard Josce tell Anna that she had no need to worry and that they would be safe in the keep, but Abraham was not convinced. He could not shake off this feeling of dread.

More Jews had arrived, and the hall now held almost a hundred and fifty by Abraham's calculation. The hall soon became stifling and fusty. He needed some air. He pushed his way through the huddled families to the steps, which led outside to the fortifications on top of the keep. The mob had reached the castle and were clamouring on the other side of the moat, demanding that the Jews be released to them.

Abraham looked out over the parapet. As far as the river beyond stretched a sea of people. The crowd was like a living thing, moving in waves like a school of fishes in a pond, lights flickering from the brands they held.

There was no question about it, they were under siege.

TWENTY-EIGHT

'So, you're going to marry my cousin?'

The voice, deep and sarcastic, made Brunetta jump. She knew who it was. She turned and gave Baruch a defiant look.

'And what of it?'

'Only that I wanted to give you my best wishes.'

Baruch was smirking, his eyes shone with devilment. Her stomach flipped and she knew her infatuation with him was not over. He knew it too. He took her arm.

'I thought I might congratulate you in the time-honoured way?'

Brunetta allowed herself to be led by him. They were walking west from the High Cross. She checked to see if there was anyone around who knew her. She was a betrothed woman and could not risk a scandal. Suddenly, he ducked into Foxes Lane, a narrow, dark alley way that ran between West Gate Street and Smith's Street where the ironmongery trades were located. The alley was seldom used.

'What are you doing?' she said, making a half-hearted attempt at protest.

Anticipating what was to come, her body trembled with excitement and the sheer wickedness of what she was about to do sent a thrill deep inside her. He stopped at an alcove and swung her round to face him. His eyes had hunger in them. He wanted her.

'Is this how you usually express your congratulations?'

'Only when absolutely necessary,' he said, fumbling with her skirts.

'What if someone comes?'

'They won't, trust me. We'll have to be quick,' he said, lifting her up and entering her.

She wrapped her legs around him and put her arms around his neck. He squirmed slightly but let them stay. The alley smelt of urine and dog mess, but she was oblivious to that and to the possibility that someone might see them. She lost herself in him and tried not to cry out in the dark, damp alley. She had to admit it was not the most romantic of places to make love, but it was the most erotic. She held on tight, burying her head in the crook of his neck. Sadly, it was over in minutes. Like an addiction, she wanted more. She hung on to his neck. He reached behind him and grabbed her wrists tearing her arms away. She landed indelicately with a thud against the damp stone wall.

'You're obviously missing your fiancé,' Baruch said, smiling like a man who has made yet another conquest.

Brunetta straightened, patting down her skirts. She didn't answer him but gave him a disapproving look.

'I'm curious. Do you fuck him like you do me?'

'That's none of your business.'

'So, you have done it with him, you little minx.'

Brunetta fussed with her hair.

'What's he like?'

'What do you mean?'

She knew exactly what he meant.

'Does he make you wet like I do?'

'Baruch!'

'Come on, don't feign effrontery. You like to talk about it as much as you like you to do it.'

Brunetta thought about playing the offended one, then changed her mind. It was about time she was honest with him, whatever good that would do. It didn't matter anymore. She was to marry Abraham.

'You do have a strange effect on me. I'm not myself when I'm with you.'

Baruch looked intrigued.

'If I'm honest, I've been wanting to do that since the last time.'

'Happy to oblige, anytime,' Baruch said.

He put his arm around her waist and pulled her to him. Brunetta's mouth was dry, her heart fluttered. He kissed her. The kiss was tender, unlike anything before. While it lasted, she felt like she was melting into him. He pulled away.

'You should do that more often,' said Brunetta.

'Then I'd be in a lot of trouble.'

He walked away in the direction of Smith's Street. Brunetta needed time to catch her breath. Her heart was beating hard. She put her hand to her chest and took a few deep breaths. What did he mean, he'd be in a lot of trouble? Was he falling for her?

Brunetta walked into the grey skies of West Gate Street, a satisfied smile upon her lips, and went home.

CHAPTER
TWENTY-NINE

'Who are the ringleaders?' asked Abraham.

Josce picked out Richard Malebysse. He was not hard to spot. Standing at the front of the mob, lantern-jawed, he had the look of a rabid dog. He was dressed in knight's garb and was having an animated discussion with several other knights. Josce named them.

'That's him brandishing his sword, inciting the others to storm the castle.'

'Yes. I knew that was him. He looks like a demonic creature.'

'And with him is William Percy, that's Malebysse's father-in-law. Next to him is Marmeduke Darell, and next to him that dung-hill knave, Philippe de Fauconberg. All heavily indebted to Aaron of Lincoln. Malebysse obviously wasn't happy when I told him he still had to honour his debts to Aaron. But I confess, I never thought it would come to this.'

'They hate us, Josce, and they hate what we have. They're evil to the core,' Abraham said under his breath, for John Marshal was standing close by and Abraham didn't want him to overhear, in case he withdrew his support.

They watched as the mob grew in number. A monk, distinguished by his white habit, appeared.

'That's the abbot from Fountains Abbey. He's also in debt to Aaron.'

'Who isn't,' Abraham said.

The abbot had brought with him a few fellow monks. Together they held an impromptu Christian service. This calmed the mob somewhat until someone from the fortifications, it wasn't clear to Abraham if it were a Jew or a soldier, threw a stone at the abbot, which hit him on the forehead, stunning him temporarily. For the baying mob, it was the ultimate insult. Demands for the Jews to be baptised and convert to Christianity or be killed rang out.

'I fear this will not end well,' he said to Josce. 'We are under siege and the sheriff is doing nothing to avert a tragedy here.'

'I'll speak with him. See what else he can do,' said Josce, looking around him to seek out the sheriff who was no longer nearby.

'I'll come with you.'

They found John Marshal inside the bailey talking and joking with his men.

'He's not taking this situation seriously. Look at him,' Abraham said.

'It won't get us anywhere if we complain. We must appeal to his sense of honour and his duty to the king.'

Abraham could only hope that John Marshal may have similar values to his brother.

'You're right, Josce, he is our only hope of getting out of here alive.'

John greeted them in an offhanded manner. He was a bull of a man without the royal graces of his younger brother William.

'The mob is increasing in numbers, sheriff. They are calling for us to convert or be killed. I fear the situation is getting out of hand. Is there anything more you can do?'

'We are under the special protection of the king, and he has issued a royal writ after what happened in London that we are to be left alone–' Abraham added.

John cut him off. 'Don't tell me my job, boy.'

'That was not my intention, sheriff. It's just, I was at the coronation. I saw first-hand how these things can get out of control.'

'That was a bad business, you're right.'

'I would hate to see this beautiful city burn like London.'

Abraham was hoping to appeal to his civic duties rather than any concern he may have for Jewish lives.

'That's not going to happen,' John said, signalling to his men to rally. 'I'll speak with Malebysse. He seems to be the ringleader. Let's see if I can talk some sense into him.'

'Thank you, sheriff. We are indebted to you,' Josce said, somewhat obsequiously, almost bowing before him.

John called for his armour to be brought to him.

'He's obviously not taking any chances out there,' said Abraham.

Josce pulled Abraham to one side. 'Whatever happens to me, promise me, Abraham, you will save my wife and children?'

Abraham was not comfortable giving such an assurance. One he was unsure he could fulfil. But with the fear and pleading in Josce's eyes, and the firm grip he had on Abraham's arm, he felt he had no choice but to nod his assent. It was a terrible burden to bear.

The drawbridge, being the only way in or out, was heavily guarded. The mob could be heard on the other side baying for Jewish blood. John, heavily armed with a falchion sword, commanded the drawbridge be lowered and the portcullis raised.

With swift movements, he and a few of his men rushed underneath the moving gate. The mob surged forward onto the wooden drawbridge. Abraham tightened his grip on the hilt of the sharp knife he had hidden underneath his tunic. John disappeared from sight, the gate was quickly lowered, and the mob were kept out.

'Let's go back to the keep. We can see better from there,' Abraham said.

The two men headed for the top of the keep. A set of wooden steps led from the bailey to the door of the keep. It was locked. Abraham battered on the door.

Josce shouted, 'It's Josce and Abraham. Let us in.'

The sound of the metal bolt scraping in its holder was a relief to hear. The heavy wooden door opened. Rabbi Yom-Tob and Moses of Bristol stood at the opening, their ritual slaughter knives – the *shechitah* – firmly held in their hands.

'Where have you been? We thought you must be dead,' Rabbi Yom-Tob said, pulling them in.

'We persuaded the sheriff to speak to the mob. Hopefully, he will be able to put a stop to this.'

'Can we trust him?' asked the rabbi.

'He is our only hope. We'll have to trust him.'

Abraham and Josce went straight to the fortifications. The mob was still there in greater numbers. Braziers had been lit and a camp of sorts set up. As soon as the mob spotted them shouts of 'Kill the filthy Jews' and other obscenities were hurled at them. The pious monk was inciting the crowd. When he spoke, his voice boomed above that of the mob and the people listened to him.

'The Jews are the Antichrist,' the monk bawled. 'They must convert or be smited. Crush Christ's enemies.'

Christian religious fervour mixed with the madness of the mob was working.

'You must storm the keep and convert the Jews by force. God is on your side,' the monk continued.

Abraham could not see the sheriff amongst the mob. He wondered whether he had either given up or been persuaded to join them. It was obvious they were not going to leave until their demands had been met. The choice was a stark one. Convert or die.

CHAPTER

THIRTY

Some hours later, John Marshal returned with a militia of armed men. They crossed the bailey to the entrance door of the keep. Josce and Rabbi Yom-Tob had decided to keep the door locked. When they saw Sheriff Marshal approach, there was a discussion amongst the community leaders as to whether they should allow him and his men to enter. Rabbi Yom-Tob was suspicious of his motives. Josce feared he had brought men with him to arrest them. It was not uncommon for Jews to be rounded up and executed. Abraham was not sure if the sheriff could be trusted. He did not seem to possess the same honour and kindness of his brother. The sheriff shouted up to Abraham and the men who were looking down on him from the turret of the keep.

'Open this door and let me in or by Christ's blood I'll have you all arrested.'

From the angry tone of his voice and his thunderous expression it was clear that the sheriff was incensed at not being allowed back into his own castle keep.

'We want assurances from you, before we let you in, that you will swear on the Holy Bible that we will not be harmed.'

Sheriff Marshal shouted back up, 'I have no Bible on me, but you have my word.'

Rabbi Yom-Tob was not persuaded by this. Still the door remained bolted. After a few more heated exchanges the sheriff moved his men back towards the mob who had managed to push nearer and were gathered on the drawbridge.

At daybreak, the sound of something heavy being pulled along towards the keep drew Abraham's attention. When Abraham popped his head over the parapet, he saw militia men trundling an enormous wooden siege engine in their wake. It would not be long before they would breach the wooden keep.

The siege engine in position there was a lull in activity. The monk who had called for the smiting of the Jews came forward and shouted up from the moat below.

'Safe passage will be given to those who convert to Christianity. Come out now and you will not be harmed.'

The mob, and now it seemed the sheriff, had taken the words of the monk to heart. They were carrying out God's work. Rabbi Yom-Tob called the men together in a huddle far enough away from the women and children so they could not hear.

'There is no way out of this. Once they deploy the siege engine it won't be long before they breach the keep.'

'We'll all be slaughtered once that happens.'

'Unless we convert...'

Rabbi Yom-Tob shook his head. 'It would be against all I stand for to convert to Christianity. We are Jews. We Jews have followed the faith for thousands of years. Ours is the one and only true faith.'

'What's worse, converting to Christianity to save our lives or staying true to our faith...'

'And die?' Abraham said.

'We would die with honour.'

'What good is honour when we are dead?' Abraham asked.

'Let us at least ask them to spare the women and children?'

'You can ask but it will do no good,' Abraham said. 'I have seen what they do to women and children.'

There was a loud thud against the outside wall of the keep. The siege engine was in position. The mob would soon be inside.

'Let all those who wish to convert be given the chance now before it's too late,' suggested Rabbi Elijah.

He jumped onto a table and addressed everyone. 'We are in a desperate situation. They will be in the keep any moment now. If you want to save yourself, do so now. This is your one and only chance. They mean to kill us, every single one of us. They say if we convert, they will not harm us. All those who want to take that chance move to the door, and you will be allowed out.'

A frantic murmur passed amongst them. A mother of three small children spoke up.

'I am a mother. It's in a mother's instinct to do all she can to protect her children. I'll take my chances. Who else is with me?'

Several families came forward. They hugged each other and said their goodbyes to the friends they were leaving behind. The door was opened and the families, as many as forty, mostly those with young children, filtered out. Abraham watched from the fortifications. When they reached the pious monk to throw themselves on his mercy and convert as ordered, Richard Malebysse and his cohorts, on horseback, stormed through the crowd, swords held high. With a slashing motion, they cut down the unarmed group of men, women and children. A small child ran back towards the keep. Richard Malebysse followed her on horseback and struck her down with his sword. She screamed and dropped to the floor. She lay motionless, blood pooling from a gash to her head, turning her flaxen hair pink.

It was over in seconds. The slaughtered bodies lay on the

blood-soaked ground. Malebysse ordered them to be thrown together and burnt. Abraham watched from the top of the keep as the limp bodies of women and small children were thrown on the pyre. The smell of burning flesh sickened him to his stomach. The signs of another massacre, such as he had witnessed in London, were all there. He was not ready to die. He would marry Brunetta. They would be blessed with many children. They would live a happy life in Gloucester. He could picture it all in his mind's eye. He could feel it. Feel the joy. That's what he must focus on. Staying alive and reuniting with Brunetta. He would marry her on his return to Gloucester. The next day if he could. Abraham could watch no more. He returned to the great hall.

'We've been talking,' said Rabbi Yom-Tob. 'The men that is.'

'About?' asked Abraham, concerned at the portentous tone of the rabbi's voice.

'What to do if this does not go our way...'

'And?'

The rabbi said nothing, just shrugged and turned to look at the women and children, huddled in the corner of the room. Abraham knew his meaning. There was almost a hundred men, women and children left inside the keep. Abraham turned away and went to sit in a corner of the hall, exhausted from lack of sleep and utterly sickened by the slaughter he had just witnessed.

Rabbi Yom-Tob was calling for martyrdom. The hall was quiet but for the rabbi's voice and the murmurings of prayer.

'Men of Israel. The God of our ancestors is omniscient, and there is no one who can say "Why doest thou this?" This day he commands us to die for his law; for that law which we have cherished from the first hour it was given, which we have preserved pure throughout our captivity in all nations, and which, for the many consolations it has given us, and the eternal hope it communicates, can we do less than die?'

A few of the women let out pitiable cries, realising their ultimate fate.

'I know I would rather sacrifice my life than transgress the Torah. Who is with me?'

The one hundred souls in the hall, men, women and children, roared in agreement with the rabbi. It seemed they would rather die by their own hand than renounce their faith.

'*Kiddush Hashem*,' he cried. 'Death in sanctification of the divine name.'

That meant only one thing.

THIRTY-ONE

'This world is like a lobby before the *Olam Ha-Ba*. Prepare yourself in the lobby so that you may enter the banquet hall.'

Rabbi Yom-Tob's words were designed to reassure everyone in the room, but they were of little comfort to Abraham. He was not ready to die. He remembered the conversation with his mother after the London massacre about whether he would convert if the situation presented itself. He had his doubts then. He felt trapped, not only by the walls he was imprisoned in, but by his faith. The rabbi was now reciting the *kaddish* prayer, normally reserved for mourners.

'Blessed, praised, glorified, exalted, extolled, mighty, upraised, and lauded be the Name of the Holy One.'

'Blessed is He,' they replied.

'Beyond any blessing and song, praise and consolation that are uttered in the world.'

The throng murmured, 'Amein.'

'May there be abundant peace from Heaven and life upon us and upon all Israel.'

Abraham joined in, but his mind was elsewhere. As clear as though he were standing before him, he saw a vision of his unborn son. Brunetta was not with child from their first time thankfully, and they hadn't done it since so there was no way she could be pregnant. But in the vision his child was a two-year-old boy, and they were playing a game together in the courtyard at the back of his father's house. It was as if he were outside his body watching himself playing with his son. It was so real, yet the child had not been born and still he knew him. He could feel his touch, hear his voice. Something shifted inside him. A prophecy. A renewal of hope.

'This is my future,' he said to himself. 'I will get out of here and I will survive to be with my son.'

Abraham thought he had witnessed the worst when he saw Judith throw herself from the upstairs window of her house, but it was not to be. He could not bring himself to watch as, one by one, fathers took their children to a corner of the keep and slit their throats. Death was despatched quickly with a prayer like the ritual slaughter of an animal.

'May the righteous be reunited with their loved ones after death.'

After the children, the husbands held their wives close to them, whispered words of love and despatched them with swift mercy. As their bodies went limp, they lay them on the ground and kissed them.

The atmosphere in the dimly lit keep was indescribable. Rivulets of blood ran down the walls, blood pooled on the floor. Prayers were chanted, the men shokeling, swaying forwards and backwards, communing with Hashem. A sense of unreality pervaded. Then it was Josce's turn. He took his firstborn and, cradling him in his arms, he slit his throat. This he did twice more. Then it was Anna's turn. Josce had asked Abraham to save his sons, but Josce had chosen death at his own hands rather than have them convert to Christianity, or worse, die at the hands of the mob.

'I love you, Josce,' she said as he held her in his arms. 'I would rather die in your arms than be desecrated by the mob. *Hashem* forgive us.'

'I love you with all my heart and forever,' Josce whispered back.

They hugged each other and then, with the swift movement of an executioner, Josce pulled back his wife's head by her hair, and drew the knife across her throat.

'Forgive me, *Hashem*.'

The blood gushed from the gaping wound in rhythmic spurts. Her body went limp in his arms. Josce clung on to her, sobbing uncontrollably.

Rabbi Yom-Tob had agreed to be the last one. He would despatch Josce, then himself. The far side of the keep had been set alight so that the mob could not defile their bodies. This now raged with some ferocity. The room filled with choking smoke. Rabbi Yom-Tob turned to Josce. 'It is time, my good friend. May you join your family in the world to come.'

Josce handed him the bloodied knife. The rabbi took it from him, recited a holy prayer and without hesitation grabbed Josce from behind and slit his throat. Yom-Tob held him a while until Josce's body went limp.

'*Merci*,' he gasped, before falling to the ground.

Abraham could not breathe. The smoke filled the room and the heat from the fire was intense. The mob was outside, breaching the walls. Soon he would be face to face with them.

Rabbi Yom-Tob looked down at his friend, the knife held loosely in his hand, dripping with the blood of Jews.

'Do you want me to...'

Abraham held up his hand and shook his head. The image

of him playing with his two-year-old son would not go away. It was more real than the sight he beheld.

'Are you sure?' Rabbi Yom-Tob asked.

'I'm sure,' Abraham said, his voice flat and determined.

He could not erase the image of Brunetta or his son. He would be with them. Soon.

'As you wish,' the rabbi said. 'May *Hashem* keep you safe.'

Rabbi Yom-Tob jabbed at the side of his neck with the knife, drawing it down and across his Adam's apple. Blood spurted with force, hitting Abraham in the face. Yom-Tob fell to the ground. Abraham knelt by his side. His eyes were open. They looked heavenward, brightened as if he had seen an angelic being, and then the life went out of his eyes, and he was still.

Abraham was left alone in an ocean of death.

CHAPTER

THIRTY-TWO

From the moment Abraham had entered the keep, he had checked for a possible escape route. From his vantage point on the top of it he was able to map out the castle. Escape seemed impossible. Troops surrounded the keep at every point. His only hope was to change out of his clothes that marked him out as a Jew and disguise himself as a Christian. The atmosphere in the hall was eerily quiet, filled with the massacred souls of the dead. Abraham left and went in search of garments. He found them in a chest, quickly changed and then ran up to the fortifications, hoping to find a way out. On the arrival of the siege engine, the troops had been summoned to help. All were mustered by the engine, leaving gaps in the defence. Abraham scanned the motte. If he were to climb down the outside of the keep on its southern side, he might be able to escape unseen. He was not much of a climber and there was a chance he might fall and crush his bones but what was the alternative? he asked himself.

The mob concentrated their attentions at the siege engine, having scaled halfway to the top of the keep, they were now being hampered by the raging fire consuming the wooden walls. If they were not careful, the fire would consume the wooden siege engine. Abraham lost no time. He lowered himself down the turret and dropped onto the roof of a smaller building below. He landed with a thud. His ankle twisted beneath him. A sharp pain shot along his foot. He got to his feet, in severe pain, and limped to the edge of the roof. The drop was precipitous, but he had no option. He threw himself off the edge, hoping to land on his side and save his foot. He landed awkwardly on the hardened ground of the motte. Winded by the fall, and limping, he made his way to the curtain wall. Keeping close to the wall, he edged toward the southern gate. Hoping that all the guards would be by the siege engine, he approached the gate with some trepidation. It was deserted. Unable to believe his luck, and with the image of Brunetta in her wedding outfit in his mind, he limped through the unguarded gate.

He staggered toward the River Ouse. If he could find a moored boat, he would steal it and make his way south beyond the city and to safety. To Brunetta. He stopped for a moment to rest his foot and get his breath back. He looked on as the keep, now fully ablaze, collapsed into itself in a conflagration of biblical proportions, flaring, crackling and spitting. His friends were all dead, their bodies consumed by fire but at least they were not at the mercy of the murderous mob. They would not be buried beside each other, as was the Jewish tradition, but they were at peace. They had chosen to die by their own hand rather than convert. It was an immense sacrifice.

He could still hear the angry voices of the mob as he untied a small boat moored by the side of the river. He was no more of a sailor than he was a climber but today was the day he would learn many new skills.

CHAPTER

THIRTY-THREE

Abraham was convinced the image of his son had kept him from harm. He could not explain it. He could not wait to see Brunetta, hold her in his arms and tell her of his vision. That thought had been driving him on, pushing him to reach home as fast as he could.

He had managed to row the small boat as far as Selby. Once there, he bought a horse with money he had secreted in his money belt and rode home as fast as he could, stopping only to rest the horse. The poor horse was exhausted by the time they reached Gloucester. He left him at the farriers and went straight to Brunetta's house.

Brunetta answered the door. 'Abraham, what's happened to you?'

Abraham realised he must look a sight. Dried blood covered his face, and his clothes were spattered with mud.

'You look an absolute mess.'

Abraham flung his arms around her and buried his head in her neck. She smelled like rose petals. Brunetta pushed him away.

'Abraham, you stink. You'll ruin my gown.'

It was not the greeting he had expected but he could see Brunetta had a point. He did smell.

'There was a massacre at York. I managed to escape. Oh, Brunetta, it was terrible. The one thing that kept me alive was thinking of you and our son.'

Brunetta looked at him as though he had lost his mind.

'I know I'm not making much sense right now, but I've seen things no man should ever see. Right now, all I know is I want us to be married.'

'We are getting married. It's already arranged for later in the year,' Brunetta said.

'That's too long to wait. If you knew what I've just been through, you'd understand.' He took her hands. 'Come with me to our place. I need you.'

Abraham pulled Brunetta by the arm across the threshold.

'I don't have my cloak.'

'Don't worry about that now. Come on, let's go.'

They ran down the street, running like a pair of wild horses, Brunetta's hair flowing behind her like the unruly mane of a feral pony, Abraham running beside her, his spirit soaring with every step.

When they reached their secret place, Abraham lay down and pulled Brunetta to him. He kissed her, first on her mouth then all over her face and neck. A feeling of ecstasy filled him. It was not sexual in nature but almost a spiritual experience. He knew without a single doubt that they were meant to be together.

'I can't explain it,' Abraham said. 'I thought I would want to rip your clothes off when I saw you and bury myself in you, but all I want to do is hold you. Is that crazy?'

'I'm not sure,' she said.

'Let me look at your face,' he said, sweeping a tangle of

chestnut curls from her face. 'You have no idea how much I've longed to look upon that face.'

'You're acting very strangely, Abraham.'

'I'm acting the way I should act every day of my life. Glad to be alive and with the woman I love the most in all the world.'

The horrors of the last few days seemed far away, never to return. From now on, he decided, his life would be filled with laughter and love.

'I don't ever want to leave you again, Brunetta. You are my whole life and life is so precious.'

'What happened in York?' she asked.

Abraham recounted the events. Everything. Brunetta listened. From time to time, she cried out in horror, covering her eyes.

'I don't know what I would have done if something like that had happened to you. I don't think I'd want to go on living,' Abraham said.

'Don't say such things. Nothing is going to happen to me.'

'Well, it's a good thing I've decided to marry you,' he said, laughing and laying his head on her stomach. 'My child needs a father.'

'What child. You're not making any sense. I told you I'm not...'

Abraham placed his finger on her lips. 'I know.'

Brunetta pushed his hand away.

'I have something to tell you. I know you're going to think I'm crazy.'

'I already think you're crazy,' she said, playing with a blade of grass.

'I saw our son.'

Brunetta looked up and her eyes widened. 'What do you mean?'

'I can't explain it, Brunetta, but I saw him as clear as I can see you now.'

'I don't understand.'

'I don't either, but I know it's the reason I was spared. I'm convinced more than ever that we are meant to be. We are meant to have the child I saw in my vision.'

Brunetta threw the blade of grass away. 'Stop talking like this, you're scaring me.'

'I'm sorry, I don't mean to scare you. I'm fine, we're going to be fine. I'm safe and we're going to be married. I'd marry you today if I could.'

'Today? Are you serious?'

'I am absolutely serious. I don't want to spend another night without you by my side if I can help it.'

'Your mother would have something to say about that.'

'Do you care?'

'A little,' she said.

'I love my mother, but I know what she's like. If she tries to thwart me in this, I will oppose her.'

'You would stand up to your mother for me?'

'Yes.'

'I've never heard you talk like this before, Abraham. You're like a different person.'

'I've realised what's important in life. Come on, let's get it over with and tell her.'

THIRTY-FOUR

Douce was in the kitchen baking bread when Abraham and Brunetta arrived.

'Abraham,' his mother shouted, holding her arms out to hug him. 'You're back.' Then she noticed his dishevelled clothes. 'My goodness what happened to you?'

'It's a long story,' Abraham said.

'What do you mean? Did something happen?'

Then she noticed Brunetta. 'Brunetta, we haven't seen you for a while.' Brunetta smiled at her future mother-in-law. 'How long have you been back?' she asked, turning her attention to Abraham and giving Brunetta a disapproving look.

'Not long.'

'Long enough to call on your fiancée before your own mother?' she said.

Her tone was one of chastisement, but her eyes were smiling. Still, Abraham thought, there was a hint of jealousy there. Mothers were strange things. How could they be jealous of their son's wives? But they were and it seemed his mother was no different. Perhaps he should have left Brunetta at home. The old Abraham would have done that but the new Abraham, the one who had survived, was a different being. It was time he stood up to his mother.

'We want to be properly married as soon as we can. Tomorrow isn't soon enough as far as I'm concerned.'

Douce's jaw dropped. She seemed to stumble back a little. She glared at Brunetta.

'Are you all right, *Ima*?'

'Why so sudden?' she asked. 'The wedding was to be at the end of the year. What has happened? Why such a sudden change?'

'Nothing, *Ima*. There's no need to worry. I have so much to tell you.'

Brunetta stared at the flagstones, twisting her hair into ringlets, avoiding Douce's gaze. Their relationship had gone cold since her attempt to save Moses had gone wrong and ended in losing the family a debt of ten marks.

'You're talking like a crazy fool, isn't he, Brunetta?'

Douce was testing Brunetta. Pitting her against Abraham.

'That's not fair, *Ima*. Brunetta had nothing to do with this. The decision is all mine, not hers.'

'I don't understand,' she said, wiping the strands of hair from her forehead with the back of her flour-covered hand. 'What will your father make of this?'

'How is *Aba*?'

'He's not well. Go and see for yourself. He's next door. Maybe he will talk some sense into you.'

Abraham squeezed his mother's tiny waist. She had given birth to five children and was now in her forties, but she still had her slim figure. Abraham grabbed Brunetta's hand and went in search of Moses. He was in the great hall sitting in a chair by the fire, his head slumped forward on his chest.

'*Aba*?'

'Don't disturb him,' Brunetta whispered, 'he's asleep.'

Moses lifted his head. His bleary eyes focused on the two of them.

'*Aba*, you look tired.'

'Ah, Abraham, you're back. Yes, I am a little tired. Brunetta, how lovely you look.'

'Everything go all right in York?'

Moses had aged since their trip to London. The skin around his neck was loose and wrinkled, his cheeks were hollowed out, but he was still as sharp as a button.

'Not exactly, *Aba*. I'll tell you later but first I have some good news.'

'Good news is thin on the ground these days, my son. Tell me.'

'We're getting married.'

'Tell me something I don't know,' he said, shuffling in his chair to sit up straighter.

'I mean we're bringing the wedding forward. Maybe as soon as next week.'

Moses sat upright in his chair as if a flea had bitten him. 'Have you told your mother?'

Douce appeared dusting the flour from her hands with a cloth. 'He has.' Her voice was stern and almost accusatory. 'Just now.'

'What did you say?' Moses asked Douce.

Abraham answered him. 'She said I'm being foolish.'

Moses gave Douce an affectionate smile. He leaned forward in the chair and reached out for Douce's hand. She took it.

'Well, maybe not that soon...'

'You're not going to talk us out of it, *Aba*.'

'Hold on. Listen to my suggestion before you shut it down.'

'Sorry, *Aba*.'

'You will have your reasons, I'm sure of it. You're a man now, my son. Old enough to know what you want. But don't upset your mother over this. You know what she's like. She likes to have things done properly. How about a compromise?'

'That depends on what it is,' said Abraham.

'Can I suggest the Tuesday after *Shavuot*? That will give your mother some time to organise herself.'

'But that's more than a month away.'

'It's closer than arranged.'

'I suppose so,' said Abraham, his excitement dissipating.

Abraham looked into his father's kind eyes. He could wait a couple of weeks.

'How is that with you, Brunetta?'

'I was happy with the original date but May suits me.'

'Tuesday is an auspicious day to get married,' Moses said. 'Your mother and me got married on a Tuesday.' He looked over at Douce with deep love in his eyes. Abraham thought he saw a tear welling. 'It should be held on a Tuesday.'

'I'm not sure what my mother will say about all this, but it's what Abraham wants. And whatever Abraham wants, I want,' Brunetta said.

Douce huffed, not taken in by Brunetta's show of loyalty. A broad smile spread across Moses' face. The laughter lines around his eyes creased into deep furrows. He chuckled.

'You'll make a good wife, Brunetta. Perhaps you can enlighten my wife. In this house it is always what Douce wants.'

CHAPTER
THIRTY-FIVE

A braham woke on the day of his wedding, his insides
as tight as a knot. He couldn't understand why he
was so nervous. His brother Benjamin told him he felt
the same on his wedding day and that it was just the usual
wedding day nerves all grooms experienced. It went some way
to calming him but not enough. Perhaps it was the thought of
the responsibilities he was about to assume. Having a wife to
support and in time a son. He still saw the vision of his son and
was convinced that one day he would meet him in the flesh.

His mother had organised the wedding in her own
inimitable fashion. The kitchen had been out of bounds for
weeks whilst her, Arlette and his mother's friend Bellassez
prepared the usual mountains of food. Abraham squinted his
eyes as he looked from his bedroom window down at the
synagogue courtyard where the blinding sun was already
heating up the enclosed space, and his guests were already in
place waiting for him. The wedding canopy – the *chuppah* – had
been erected and adorned with silken cloth and May blossoms
of bluebells twisted with fronds of hawknut. In an hour's time
he would be walking towards it and marrying his beloved

Brunetta in front of a host of friends and family. His stomach twisted and tightened a notch.

'Come on, it's time,' Benjamin called from the stairs below.

Abraham looked down at his wedding attire. Sumptuously embroidered and tailored by his boyhood friend Azriel, who had not been gifted with the family's singing voice and instead had become a tailor. His other boyhood friend Solomon was now the rabbi, having taken over from his ageing grandfather after his own father Baruch had sadly died when Solomon was a boy. His wayward cousin Baruch had been named after him. Abraham adjusted the stiffened linen cap, straightened his tunic and went downstairs. Benjamin was waiting for him.

'Too late to change your mind now,' Benjamin said, grinning.

'I'm nervous that's all.'

Benjamin put his hand on Abraham's shoulder. 'It'll be over soon, and you can relax.'

Abraham swallowed and followed his brother out into the courtyard where the guests had already gathered. As he approached the *chuppah*, his guests congratulated him. His mother and father were waiting for him. Douce had been crying and was dabbing at the corner of her eyes with a soft cloth whilst his father wore a look of intense pride upon his face. Although he looked weak and grey, a thin smile appeared on his lips as Abraham drew close.

When Brunetta arrived Abraham held his breath, so taken by her beauty. She looked stunning in her wedding dress of samite silk, a translucent veil covering her face and trailing over her wavy chestnut hair. A lump formed in his throat, and he thought a tear might slip down his cheek but before that could happen, he coughed and looked away towards Baruch.

When the ceremony ended, there was a rousing cheer of

mazel tov. It was time for them to retire to the *yichud* room, a place of seclusion where they would break their fast.

As soon as they were alone, Abraham told her how lovely she looked. Brunetta had removed the veil from her face and was tucking into some bread and cheese Douce had prepared for them. She stopped eating for a second, smiled and continued to chew. Abraham's stomach was still feeling delicate, so he nibbled on a piece of bread.

Despite just being married Abraham sensed there was a distance between them. Perhaps that's how most newly married couples felt. They needed time to get to know one another.

In ancient times, the bride and groom would have consummated their marriage and emerged with the stained virginity cloth to prove that the new wife was a virgin. Thankfully, that tradition had long been abandoned and their secret would not be exposed. They had joked that if it was still required of them, they would use chicken blood to fool the guests.

The meal continued in silence. Abraham's thoughts were upon his wedding night. He had saved himself for this moment. He knew little of the art of lovemaking, but he was determined to get lots of practice now he was married. He had a son he needed to meet.

ONCE THE MEAL WAS FINISHED, they rejoined the wedding celebrations. Brunetta sat with her mother whilst Abraham went in search of his friends. Brunetta watched him as he walked by groups of guests, smiling broadly and thanking them for coming. Brunetta used this as an opportunity to escape. She was beginning to feel suffocated. Her new husband was far too attentive. She wandered over to the stone steps that led to the *scola*, in the basement of the synagogue where the lessons took place and sat on a lower step so she couldn't be seen from the courtyard. She thought about her new husband and let out a deep sigh.

'Bored already? Surely not? A bride on her wedding day.'

Brunetta looked up and saw Baruch making his way down the stairs. He sat beside her, close enough for her to feel the warmth of his body and smell him. A waft of cloves drifted by as he bent to sit down.

'I just needed some time alone.'

'I'll go if you want me to?'

He went to stand. She pulled him back down.

'Don't go.'

'You know what they'll say if anyone sees us together.'

'They can't see us from the courtyard.'

Baruch grabbed her arm.

'Come on,' he said, pulling her up from the stair. 'They won't be able to see us at all in the *scola*.'

'I can't.'

'Nonsense. We'll be quick.'

'Someone will see us.'

'Not down there, they won't.'

'No, it's wrong,' she said.

'Don't be silly. Now you're married it makes it easier.'

'Why?' she asked, trying to pull away from him and looking up to the top step in panic checking no one was watching them.

'It just is. Less complicated.'

Brunetta stopped struggling and allowed Baruch to lead her down the rest of the cold stone steps and into the darkened *scola*. She wanted him. Had done so for such a long time. If they were quick...

Inside the cool, vaulted cellar, Baruch swung her round to

face him. He pulled her to him then slammed her against the cold stone wall. He lifted her wedding dress, spreading her legs apart as he did so. She tried to kiss him, but he turned away, more interested in undoing his breeches. He put his hand on her backside and hoisted her up. She felt his hardness and clamped her legs around his waist. It was like a hunger she had never known. She wanted him inside her. She couldn't wait. When he entered her, she groaned. The sensation of his stiff cock thrusting inside her sent her wild. With each hard thrust, she cried out and tore at his hair. All thoughts of being caught were forgotten. Baruch was hungry for her, and she for him. It was over in minutes. Baruch pulled out from her, stuffed his still hard cock back in his breeches and walked away from her.

'Is that it?' she said.

He turned around. 'What more do you want?'

With that, he hurried back up the stone steps, his boots clattering and echoing inside the stone chamber. Once again Brunetta felt cheated. But at the same time, it had been exquisitely wicked. Damn that Baruch. She straightened her wedding dress. At least there would be no blood to hide this time. And Abraham would never know. She waited a few more minutes, then crept up the stairs checking no one was around before she emerged from the *scola* and into the courtyard.

A crescent moon shone brightly in the clear night sky. The air was fresh and cool. Hopefully it would blow the scent of Baruch from her before she joined her husband.

Abraham.

A heaviness came in her heart at the thought of Abraham. She would be with him for the rest of her life. The wanton abandonment that had consumed her moments before swept aside at the thought of her husband. Is this what her life would be like? A husband who didn't satisfy her, but loved her and a lover who thrilled her, but didn't give a damn about her? What had she done? She had just had sex with a man, other than her husband, on her wedding day. Try as she might to scold herself, a lascivious smile kept reappearing on her lips.

She decided to go into the synagogue rather than join her husband. Her thoughts were a muddle and she needed to compose herself before seeing him again. She opened the door and walked into the consoling silence. The eternal light danced above. She walked to the women's side and sat down. Dark shadows in dark corners were everywhere. The sound of the flickering light soothed her troubled soul. Her mind turned to Baruch in the *scola*. Pure wickedness. Surely, she would be punished. After a while she rose and made her way back to the wedding party.

'There you are. I've been looking for you.'

Abraham's smiling face came into view.

'Where have you been?'

'I was just in the synagogue taking a moment to reflect.'

'Reflect?'

'On how fortunate I am to have a husband such as you.'

Brunetta pursed her lips into a smile. It was becoming easier by the day to lie to him. He was so gullible.

THIRTY-SIX

It was with a heavy heart that Moses remembered the death of his son and the harrowing journey to London, all those years ago. The events and emotions were forever seared upon his memory. The rabid, snarling dogs trailing the cart that carried little Samuel's body, the tearing at the bones of his son's barely cold body with their savage teeth. Moses still shuddered at the thought even after all these years. Almost ten years after the death of his son the king had finally allowed Jews to purchase land outside the city walls to use for the burial of their loved ones. On hearing this, Moses had immediately bought a parcel of land outside the city walls where there was a supply of fresh water. He commissioned the local stonemason to make a memorial stone in memory of his son. It was the first tombstone to be erected on the sacred ground.

Douce had told him time and again that there was nothing anyone could have done to prevent his death, and in his mind, he knew it, but his heart still ached with sorrow for his firstborn. Had he lived, Samuel would have been in his twenties and should have been married to a precious wife who would have given Moses precious grandchildren.

'Judaism teaches that death is not a tragedy, even when it occurs early in life or through unfortunate circumstances. Death is a natural process and death has meaning just as lives do. It is all part of God's plan,' Bellassez would say each year at the service.

This was when Moses struggled with his faith. He could not accept that Samuel's death had meaning. It was meaningless, uncalled for, a waste of a precious life. He knew he would never come to terms with it, and he would never be able to square his faith with what happened. He could only hope that Samuel was at peace in the afterlife where he would be rewarded for the worthy young life he had led.

The granting of the land was too late for Moses to bury his firstborn but not for his father. Old Samuel had died some years later. He buried him next to his son's memorial. Although he was sad, this time it was different. His father was an old man, had lived a good and long life and seen his children and grandchildren grow up. What more could a man want from life? But little Samuel was different. At the tender age of four, Samuel, his firstborn had died of a mysterious illness. Moses had watched as his son became progressively ill. He had difficulty walking at first, then he couldn't swallow and then he lost his sight. It was an agonising time for all the family.

Today was the *yahrzeit*, the anniversary of his death, when Moses visited Samuel's memorial. The sad little procession made their way from the house, through the city gate and across the Roman bridge to the walled burial ground. They were joined by Douce's oldest friend Bellassez and her family.

A pendulous willow tree stood in the corner, fronted by a sorrowful line of tombstones and opposite these was the *bet tohorah*, the cleansing house. Moses had been very specific in the design of this small stone building. A constant flow of living water had been installed, along with a laving stone on which the bodies of the dead were washed. Above the entrance were carved the words *mayim zochalim*, meaning 'living waters'. It was a beautiful place, full of peace and dignity.

Samuels's gravestone bore the Hebrew letters *PN*, for 'here lies', within a carving of the Star of David. Below this was his name and that he was the son of Moses, followed by the year of his death. *4928*. At the very bottom was the epitaph, *May his soul be bound in the bond of eternal life.*

Moses hung his head in sacred remembrance then began to recite the *Malei Rachamim* prayer.

'O *Hashem*, full of compassion, Who dwells on high, grant true rest upon the wings of the *Shechinah*, in the exalted spheres of the holy and pure, who shine as the resplendence of the firmament, to the soul of Samuel who has gone to his supernal world...'

'Amein.'

The small gathering of mourners prayed together. Moses' little granddaughter joined them, speaking in her childish tones, slightly out of time. Hearing his granddaughter's voice, he could not help but think about the children Samuel would have had. Every year this day was a difficult time for him, but today seemed doubly troubling. Perhaps it was being caught up in the horror of the London riots, or perhaps he was just getting old. He felt old. His breathing had not been the same since London and he often had a strange tingling in his left arm and an odd pain in his chest which he never told Douce about.

A few weeds had grown around the stone. Douce knelt to pick them out. As Moses watched her, an enormous sadness swept over him. What would happen to her when he died? How would she cope? His own death seemed closer than ever. A cold shiver shot through his body. A feeling of doom descended upon him like a dark, oppressive shadow. Against Douce's advice Moses had followed the tradition of fasting to symbolise the unforgettable despair he felt on this day. He had not eaten since the previous evening and was beginning to feel faint. Abraham stood by his side. He grabbed his son's arm to steady himself.

'Are you feeling unwell, *Aba*?'

'Look at him,' said Douce, raising herself off the ground. 'The colour has drained from his face.'

'Don't fuss,' said Moses, still gripping the arm of his son.

'Come. Let's get home and get you to bed.'

Moses held on to his son's arm as much for comfort as to steady himself, beset by thoughts of his own death.

CHAPTER

THIRTY-SEVEN

Abraham sat in his father's cellar, counting his morning's collection. He followed the method of accounting that his father had taught him. Moses was asleep upstairs as the heat of the summer sun tired him out and he had taken to sleeping in the afternoons of late.

Abraham's thoughts soon turned to his new wife. The elation he had felt on his return from York had long dissipated, along with his happiness at marrying Brunetta. She was cold towards him. It was strange. The moment she became his wife, she lost interest in him. Their lovemaking, which he was keen to commence, was an awkward affair. Always initiated by him, she seemed disinterested, as though her mind were elsewhere. He wondered where his lustful, delightful fiancée had disappeared to. It was as if a candle within her had been snuffed out. Barely married a few months and already the desire had gone out of his marriage. He wanted to ask his mother whether this was what he should expect from his new wife, but he was too embarrassed to ask and besides, he didn't want to give his mother more cause to dislike Brunetta. There was already a palpable tension between them.

Weary from his taxing figure work, he closed his father's chest, locked it with the key and went upstairs and into the courtyard. It was stiflingly hot in the afternoon sun. Douce was taking a rare moment to rest from her domestic duties. She sat with his cousins Arlette and Henne. Henne, newly married to Vives of London, sat watching her young son, Assel, who was playing in a pail of water splashing it about and making everyone scream. The more they screamed the more Assel splashed.

'Abraham, come and join us,' his mother shouted over.

Abraham sat down on the courtyard floor, next to Assel, thankful for the cold splashes of water from his nephew.

'Where is Brunetta?' he asked.

At the mention of Brunetta, the women went quiet and looked at each other as if the answer was with one of them.

'I haven't seen her since this morning,' said Arlette, a bunch of skerrits at her feet.

'Perhaps she's gone to visit her mother?' Douce suggested.

'No, I don't think she has. I saw her walking out of the city. I expect she's gone for a walk. She likes to walk by the river,' added Henne.

'Why don't you see if you can find her?' said Douce.

Abraham stood up. 'I think I will. I'll see you later.'

'Will you be back for supper? I'm making something cold. It's too hot to cook. Cold chicken with mâche.'

'And raw skerrits,' piped up Arlette.

Abraham gave them a weak smile and left. He adored his mother and normally would have stayed, as he liked their company, but today he was not in the mood. Something was on his mind, and he needed to speak to Brunetta. He went in search of her by the river. It seemed the women in the household knew more than he did about his wife. He had no idea she went for walks by the river. He thought she liked to spend time with her mother and her younger sister.

The river was calm today and the sight of it gently moving along going in the direction of the city calmed him. He walked sluggishly, the intense heat, slowing him down to a stroll. He realised it had been a long time since he went out into the countryside. He seemed to be bogged down by the family business now that his father was unwell. Recently, he had been questioning his life and his role. Was he cut out to be a moneylender? Would he be able to take over the business when his father died? He was beset with self-doubt. More so than usual today.

The vision of his son had not appeared to him for some months. The euphoria he had experienced and the sheer certainty of the existence of his son was fading into a despondent distance. He wondered whether Brunetta was pregnant yet. Had they done it enough? He needed to speak to her. He had been walking with his head down when a noise ahead of him made him look up. Brunetta was walking towards him, her face flushed and her skirts in disarray. When she saw him, her cheeks flushed a deep red, like she had been caught out doing something she shouldn't.

'Abraham, what are you doing out here?'

'Looking for you,' he said.

'How did you know you'd find me here?'

'Henne told me.'

'Oh did she?'

Abraham detected a slight cattiness in her voice. 'Is there something the matter?'

'No, I'm fine. Just surprised to see you.' She looked behind her as if expecting to see someone following her.

'Are you here with somebody?'

For some reason Baruch's words to him at Rosh Hashanah

about looking over his shoulder came back to him. He had wondered what he meant but at the time put it down to Baruch's sense of mischievousness.

'No. No one is with me. Why do you ask?'

'You looked like you were expecting someone to come along the path behind you.'

'Don't be silly.'

She was standing by him now, her cheeks still flushed and a few strands of dried grass in her hair. He reached to pick them out.

'What are you doing?' she said, pushing his hand away and scowling with irritation.

He smiled at her. 'You have grass in your hair. You look like you've been rolling around in it?'

'Do I?' She brushed her hair with her fingertips. Abraham made another attempt to pick out the blades of grass. She let him this time.

'I was tired with the heat. I sat by the river for a while. I probably got them in my hair then. Shall we walk back? I'm very tired now. The sun is glorious but tiring, don't you think?'

She took his arm and swung him round to walk back towards the city along the worn path. Abraham let himself be led. He was grateful of the physical contact, such a rare occurrence these days. As they walked along Abraham thought it a good time to ask her what had been on his mind these past few days.

'Brunetta?'

'Yes, my love,' she answered.

'I was wondering...'

'Yes?'

'Might you be pregnant?'

Brunetta laughed. There was a mocking tone to it as if he was a small boy in the *scola* asking silly questions.

'Why do you laugh?'

'I just think sometimes you are so naïve.'

'Am I? There's so much I don't know. About women, I mean.'

'I promise you, Abraham, you'll be the first to know if I'm pregnant.'

She squeezed his arm. He smiled to himself. He must be more patient.

As they turned into Shipsters Lane, Brunetta turned slightly to check the path behind them. Abraham thought nothing of it. He was out walking with his beautiful wife, and he couldn't be happier.

THIRTY-EIGHT

All was ready in the le Riche household for the celebration of Passover, the most important and joyous occasion of the year. Thousands of other Jewish families all over the world would be celebrating the miraculous escape of the Jewish people from slavery in Egypt at the same time as Moses and his family. As his guests arrived there were hugs and greetings and wishes for a happy Passover. Moses was in a pensive mood.

'*Hag Pesach sameach*. Happy Passover,' Moses greeted his old friend Josce.

His wife, Judea, with their son, Mannasser, and his wife, Belin, accompanied them. Mannasser was their firstborn, the child Josce had announced to Moses on the day of little Samuel's *seudat havra'a,* the condolence meal following his sudden death. He had a special place in Moses' heart as he came at a time when Moses was feeling bereft at the death of his own son. It was a reminder to him of the eternal cycle of life. Mannasser was a grown man now with young children of his own. The children ran past their father and into the great hall to join the other children, the manic excitement of Pesach already upon them.

Next to arrive was Abigail and her family. Moses liked Abigail. She had brought up three children on her own, supporting them as well as she could by engaging in small-time moneylending. He had been pleased to welcome her into his extended family. Her son, Josce, was an abrasive young man, overly protective of his mother and his two sisters, but maybe that was because their father was long dead. Glorietta was a delight to behold. If anything, she was more beautiful than her sister. She had a guileless quality. She reminded him of Arlette when she was Glorietta's age.

The last to arrive was Douce's old friend, Bellassez, with her family. She had filled out over the years, her weakness for sweet foods reflecting in her fulsome figure. Moses adored her, thankful that his wife had a good and loyal friend. She would be of comfort to Douce when he was gone. Thoughts of his own immortality were ever present in his mind these days.

As head of the household, Moses sat at the end of the long table. He was wearing his newly purchased tunic of the finest white linen, tied at the shoulder with a decorative gold clasp. His beard, peppered with grey, was long and wispy and his once thick dark hair was now almost totally grey. His face was lined with the burden of loss and ill health, but it was still a kind face. Passover for Moses had become a mixed blessing. It was a time for rejoicing but also one of sad reflection. He would always remember the brutal rape of his niece, Arlette, and the savage beating of Zev, which left him for dead and caused Arlette to attempt her own life. There was always the worry in the back of his mind that there might be a repeat of the violence at Passover, but he kept these thoughts to himself.

He studied his family who, apart from the children, had joined him around the table. His eldest son, Abraham, and his wife, Brunetta. They had been married almost a year and still no children. Benjamin with his wife, Rachel. Justelin, who Moses had always regarded as a gift from God, coming as he did so unexpectedly at a time when Moses thought their family was complete. At nine years old, he was the most spoilt of Moses' children. Everyone adored him and gave in to his demands at the flicker of his long dark eyelashes. His precious daughter, Henne, sat next to her husband, Vives. His niece, Arlette, sat next to Zev. Rubin, not yet married, sat on his father's side. As always, they were inseparable. There were three notable absences. His firstborn Samuel and his dear father. The third person was Baruch. He was, in all likelihood, drinking in a local tavern with a bunch of gentiles who cared not that he was a Jew, happy to drink the ale Baruch would buy them. He was a law unto himself and seemed oblivious to the grief and shame he put his family through. He didn't fit in and when he was around, he was like an unwelcome guest.

Even though tragedy had touched his family, Moses still considered himself to be a lucky man. He had the best wife a man could ever wish for. She had borne him five children and ran a large household with the efficiency of a military officer. He let out a sigh of contentment and settled back into his chair.

Douce had laid the table, as she always did, with precise attention to every detail. The *seder* platter, containing the richly symbolic foods of Passover, had been placed in front of him. On it was arranged the shank bone or *zeroa*, symbolising the special *paschal* sacrifice on the eve of the Exodus from Egypt, the *charoset*, a mixture of nuts, apples, spices and wine, symbolising the mortar the Jews used when forced to build the Pharaoh's tombs and the *maror*, the bitter herbs, a symbol of the bitterness the Israelites felt when they were slaves in Egypt. Douce always used freshly harvested horseradish, which she grew in her courtyard garden. Next to this was the *karpas*, the green vegetable, symbolising the humble origins of the Jewish people. Later this would be dipped in a bowl of saltwater, the saltwater representing the tears shed whilst in slavery. Douce used lamb's lettuce, or mâche, which she also grew in her beloved garden. Lastly, Moses' favourite, the *beitzah*, a hard-boiled egg, which Douce first boils in its shell then roasts upon the kitchen fire. Moses loved the way the roundness of the egg symbolised the cycle of life, the continuous flow of life to death to rebirth.

The night before Douce had marshalled everyone in the family to cleanse the house of *chametz*, a Passover tradition she ruthlessly abided by, thrusting besoms and cloths into the hands of her children and grandchildren, issuing orders to seek out the *chametz*, under beds, behind doors. Anywhere the unleavened wheat might be found. Her commands were like that of a warrior princess on the battlefield.

'Come on, *Hashem* has commanded us to remove all leaven from our home and take only unleavened bread with us,' she had shouted, following the children from room to room.

Far from being afraid of Douce, the children loved it, scurrying around, crawling under beds, each one in a competition of who could find the most *chametz*.

In front of Moses was the precious family *Haggadah*, richly illuminated with biblical scenes in brightly coloured tempera, which hadn't faded with age. An ancient Hebrew text, Moses used the *Haggadah* to narrate the story of the Exodus of the Jewish people from Egypt. It also guided him and the children in the ritual order of the *seder* meal. Douce had placed a cup of wine in front of him as he would be the one to recite the *kiddush*, the special blessings recited over wine. She called all the children who had been running around and playing games to the table. The noise of children's chatter was almost unbearable but at the same time comforting. Douce placed her finger to her lips to silence them. An expectant air fell around the table and all eyes settled on Moses. A fire crackled in the hearth and the candles Douce had lit earlier flickered in the dimly lit hall.

Moses opened the mighty *Haggadah*. In an exaggerated gesture, he picked up the cup of wine in his right hand, transferred it to his left hand, and then lowered it into the palm of his right hand, cupping it to simulate a vessel. Finally, raising it above the table, he recited the traditional blessing. He drank from the cup, then recited the *shehecheyanu* blessing as Douce refilled his cup for another blessing to remind everyone they were the chosen ones and commemorating their Exodus from Egypt.

Douce brought a basin of water so that Moses could perform *urchatz*, the first of the ritual hand washing. Since his collapse in London and his brief imprisonment, he had become short of breath whenever he stood up or walked anywhere, often having to stop to get his breath back. Douce now did most of his fetching and carrying.

It was time for the 'dippings', an amusing word Moses had copied from his father. He loved to involve the children in this ritual.

'And what does the *karpas* signify?' he asked them.

Zipporah, Moses' granddaughter, piped up.

'Tears,' she burbled in her baby-talk fashion.

'*Nu, nu,*' Rachel, her mother said.

Moses held up his hand to silence his daughter-in-law. 'She's only little, there is plenty of time to learn. No, Zipporah, the *karpas* is us, the Jewish people, the saltwater is the tears.'

Zipporah's face scrunched into a scowl, the beginning of a tantrum. Rachel distracted her by waving a bunch of lettuce leaves in her face to avoid a scene.

It was now time to perform *yachatz*, when the middle

matzoh is torn in half. Douce had already placed three *matzohs* on a platter and covered them with a clean cloth. Moses took the middle *matzoh* from the pile and broke it in half. Then he told the children to close their eyes whilst he hid one of the *matzohs* in a napkin and put the other half back under the cloth. The children would have fun later when they searched for the 'missing' *matzoh*.

The *maggid*, or the telling of the story of Passover came next. Over the years, Muriel, Bellassez's daughter, had been the one to ask the questions. From an early age, Muriel had shown a deep understanding of the Jewish faith. She was now the teacher at the *scola*, which Moses had built beneath the synagogue. Muriel's daughter, Miriam, was a smaller version of her mother. At seven years of age, she was as devout as old Rabbi Solomon. Moses called her '*ma petite gaon*' – 'his little sage' – mixing his native French with the Hebrew word for sage.

'Come, Miriam, it's your turn.'

Miriam stood up and went to Moses' side. He patted her head and she beamed at him. Proud to be given this honour, she stood tall and puffed out her small chest.

She began. 'What is different? Why eat *matzoh*? Why eat *maror*? Why dip the *karpas* twice? Why recline at the dining table?'

Moses and all those gathered answered her in time-honoured tradition. When she was finished, she sat down. Moses caught her eye and winked. Moses then passed the *matzoh* along the table. As he did so, he asked little Zipporah why she ate matzah on this day.

'Because we are hungry?' she replied.

Everyone laughed, except Zipporah whose lip began to curl, signifying an impending grizzle.

'*Aba*, don't tease her. You know how churlish she can get. She's going to ruin the *seder* if you keep this up,' said Benjamin.

'Sorry,' replied Moses, chuckling. 'I can't help it.'

'You see,' Douce remonstrated. 'He's already had too much wine. What's he going to be like when he gets to the fourth cup...'

'The *matzoh*, my dearest Zipporah, shows us the hurried Exodus from Egypt when the Israelites left in such a hurry, they didn't have time for the dough to rise.'

With a broad grin across his face Moses delivered the blessing over the *matzah*. Zipporah stuffed a large piece of it into her small mouth.

'Zipporah,' her mother chided. 'Don't put so much in your mouth at one time.'

'But I'm hungry,' she said, making everyone laugh again.

This time she giggled with them. Rachel scowled at her father-in-law, but he took no notice. For the first time in years, he was enjoying the *seder*. Surrounded by his family, his blessed children and grandchildren, he was reminded of his good fortune. He looked at the roasted egg on the platter. It dawned on him that he had been holding back every *seder*, worrying about what might happen rather than embracing the true meaning of hope and the importance of starting afresh, being reborn. He picked up a piece of the horseradish and with renewed faith said the blessing over the *maror*, the bitter herbs. Out of the corner of his eye he watched as Zipporah put the *maror* in her mouth, only to screw up her face and spit out the bitter tasting herb. He was expecting it and grinned at how gullible small children were. Then he wanted to see her reaction when she tasted the sweetness of the *charoset*. A huge smile came upon her face as she tasted the sugary delight.

'Oh, the bitter sweetness of life,' he said, quietly to himself.

'You are behaving like an old man, *mon chéri*, you are talking to yourself.'

'Or is it the wine?' Abraham asked.

'I have no idea, but he's acting a little odd this evening,' Douce said, rising from the table to bring in the main *seder* meal, the *shulchan orech.*

For days, the kitchen had been out of bounds, the chaos at a heightened level. Moses and Abraham had occupied themselves with business matters, keeping well away. When Douce, Arlette and his daughter, Henne, returned with tureens of steaming chicken soup and several enormous roasted chickens, he imagined for a moment his firstborn son Samuel was sitting at the table, calling his name, *Aba.* As it used to be in the old days. He rubbed his eyes, thinking as he did that Douce was probably right. He had drunk too much wine and was getting maudlin as a consequence or was it old age?

As Douce set down the platter she turned to her husband.

'I thank *Hashem* every day for saving my husband,' Douce said. 'Twice he saves my son. Who can be so lucky? We are blessed.' She reached out to touch his hand. 'What would I do without him?'

Moses covered her hand with his and held it there.

THE MEAL WAS ALMOST over when Baruch arrived. For a moment, the mood in the room altered, became frozen. Everyone seemed to be holding their breath, waiting to see what kind of mood he was in. Arlette quickly broke the spell.

'Baruch, come sit here next to me.'

She rose and gave him her chair, crossing over to a spare chair which she brought back with her and placed next to her son. Baruch had been drinking. She could tell. He had that glazed look in his eyes. He was unpredictable when he had drink inside him. Usually, the family were asleep when he came home drunk, but Passover was different. It was a long night of celebration. Arlette's stomach churned with nerves wondering what mischief he was up to.

Reluctantly, she poured her son a glass of wine. It would have been rude of her not to. He drank it down and looked over at Brunetta. Arlette thought she detected a hunger in his look. She knew that look all too well. She had seen it in his real father's eyes. She shuddered.

'Are you cold, Mother?'

'No, I'm fine.'

Arlette looked across at Brunetta. Her face was flushed. Was that because of the wine she had been drinking? Arlette could not warm to her. She was unkind to Abraham, often showing him up in public. Abraham was like a brother to her, and she hated to see him so unhappy. He should be basking in the heady first year of married bliss. Instead, he seemed to walk around like he was carrying a heavy burden on his shoulders.

Arlette wondered if there was anything between her son and Brunetta. He was more than capable of such deceit, she thought with great sadness. She had hoped Baruch would not have turned out so much like his father. He even looked like him. The guilt of a mother was always with her. Had she done enough for him? Had she loved him enough? Had she indulged him too much because of the lack of love from Zev? It seemed as soon as Rubin was born, Zev lost all interest in Baruch, favouring his own son to the almost exclusion of hers.

Baruch seemed to be in a dark, brooding mood, like a growling dog at the table, he was staring at Brunetta and then at Zev. The look he gave Zev was full of hatred.

'What's the matter, Baruch?'

'I don't belong here,' he said, draining his goblet of wine.

'Nonsense,' she said. 'You're family.'

Arlette's stomach knotted even tighter.

'Why did you marry him, Mother?'

Arlette swallowed hard. She could not answer such a question. Secrets would be revealed and the tensions within the family would increase ten-fold. She lied. 'Because I wanted to.'

'Did you love him?'

She lied again. 'Of course.'

Baruch reached for the bottle of wine. Moses glanced over at her; his eyebrow raised in a question. Arlette shook her head. She didn't want Moses involved. Dear sweet Moses, who was like a father to her.

'Why doesn't he like me?'

'He does like you; you're being silly.'

'He doesn't like me. He's spent most of his life ignoring me.'

Arlette knew there was a degree of truth in what Baruch was saying but she couldn't openly go against her husband. She leant into her son and whispered, 'This isn't the time or the place to raise these issues, Baruch. This is the *seder*. You know how much Moses looks forward to this. Please don't spoil it for him.'

Baruch looked across at Moses. 'Moses has been more of a father to me than my own father.'

'Then please stop this, for his sake.'

'All right then. For you and Moses. No one else.' He stood up; drained his drink.

'You don't have to go.'

'I do, Mother, or I can't be held responsible for what I'll do or say next.'

He glared across at Brunetta.

Arlette let him go.

When the meal was over, it was time for the children to hunt for the *afikomen*, the dessert *matzah*. Miriam was on her feet first, followed by the rest of the children. They hunted everywhere, screaming excitedly, running from corner to corner, looking under the table while Moses sat with a mischievous smile on his face, and when they came close to finding it, a scowl. Moses was hiding it beneath his tunic. When the children weren't looking, he slipped it back onto the table. Rachel saw him and quickly alerted Zipporah. When she saw it, she was wild with excitement, running over to the *afikomen* and snatching it off the table.

'*Nu, nu*, Zipporah. Share it with the others.'

'She is going to be a handful,' Moses said to his son Benjamin.

'She already is, *Aba*.'

Douce poured a third cup of wine while Rachel calmed the excited children. Moses then spoke the special blessing, the traditional *Birkat HaMazon*.

'...may You remember us on this day of Passover to bless us with kindness and mercy for a life of peace and happiness...'

'Amein.'

Moses then drank the third cup, reciting the traditional blessing over the wine. Douce immediately poured the fourth cup of wine, setting aside an extra cup for the Prophet Elijah, whilst Moses went to open his front door to welcome the prophet into his home. He secretly dreaded this part of the *seder*, never sure whether there would be a violent mob outside and that he would, unwittingly, be letting them in. When he saw there was no one there and the street was empty, he let out a sigh of relief.

'*Baruch haba*,' he shouted, as he threw open the door. 'Welcome.'

Moses left the door open and returned to the table.

He raised the last cup of wine, reciting the final *kiddush* and drank from it. The *seder* was almost over. All that remained was the *nirtzat*, the conclusion of the *seder*. It had been a long evening and the children had become fractious, not least Zipporah, who was testing her mother's patience. Arlette had her head on Zev's shoulder, half asleep. Rachel cradled her newborn Leah in her arms, her husband's arm around her shoulder.

It was time to end this blissful occasion and his leading role in it.

Moses recited the poem of his countryman, the Rabbi Joseph Bonfils, or Ben Tov, as he was known. He then reminded everyone that they would one day ask Hashem to bring forth the *Mashiach* – the Messiah, when all of them would be gathered to Jerusalem and dwell in peace. In unison, they shouted:

'Next year in Jerusalem.'

'This year,' added Moses, 'may we all dwell in peace.'

THIRTY-NINE

The next morning Moses felt unwell and remained in his bed, drifting in and out of sleep. It was unlike him. Late afternoon came and he still had not risen. By the evening, he brightened, and asked that all his family gather in his bedroom. They assembled as requested, hovering around the bed, wondering why they had been summoned. They were all there, even Baruch. Benjamin cautioned Zipporah to be gentle with her grandfather as she clambered onto the bed and into his arms. He gave her a hug, kissed her and told her to be a good girl, then bid her goodnight. He did the same with his grandson, Assel. Then he asked to hold baby Leah. He cradled her in his arms and kissed her forehead before handing her back to Benjamin. Then he asked everyone to leave except Douce. Once the room was empty, he spoke, his voice weak.

'My time is coming, *cherie*,' he said, his voice wavering with emotion.

'Don't say that. You'll be back on your feet soon.'

'We both know that's not going to happen,' he said, fixing his gaze upon her.

Douce's lip quivered.

'Come now, I want to see my *eschet chayil* with a brave smile on her face.'

He tried to raise himself to sit up but was too weak.

'I still see him,' he said, his eyes widening and a look of madness appearing.

'Who, *mon cheri*?'

'Brito,' he said, his voice a guttural whisper.

'Don't concern yourself with that business now, *mon cheri*. Rest.'

Douce wiped the beads of sweat from Moses' forehead. The vision of Brito's head, his blood dripping on the virginal snow had haunted her too, but as agreed all those years ago, they had never spoken of it. It had remained between her, Moses and Hashem. It was as if by speaking his name, the evil spirit of Brito had been conjured and was now possessing him. Moses began rambling, jerking his head from side to side, his condition worsening.

'You are safe, Moses. Don't upset yourself. All is well.'

She took his hand. It was cold and damp. His brittle fingernails dug into her palms.

'Remember?'

'*Oui, mon cheri*. How could I forget.'

'We said we would take it to our graves.'

'*Oui, cheri.*'

'I have kept my promise. Promise me when I'm gone, you'll do the same.'

'I promise, husband. You don't need to ask.'

'We did the right thing.'

'Of course we did.'

'Arlette is happy now with Zev. They have made a life together.'

'Yes, they are very happy and have Rubin to be thankful for.'

Baruch had not complied with Moses' request to leave the

room. Suspecting some deathbed confession was about to be heard, he had sneaked back into the room and hidden behind the damask curtain which covered the door and helped to keep out the winter draughts. He was listening intently but when he heard Rubin's name and not his own when expressing his parents' happiness an anger so violent raged within him. He gritted his teeth and curled his hands into fists. Staying perfectly still he listened on.

'Baruch is a disappointment to me.'

'Sssh,' she soothed, stroking his forehead. 'Don't say that, *cheri*.'

'I can only say this now. Now it's my time. I've tried to love him as my own son, but it's been hard. He won't let anyone love him. Not even his mother.'

The words seared through Baruch's cold heart. The steely armour he wore pierced by a truth he knew to be true. He pushed people away. *Even his own mother.*

'Arlette loves him. She has never treated him differently,' Douce said.

She no longer attempted to silence her husband. This was a conversation long overdue. It was best such things were said now. Moses should meet his maker with a clear conscience.

'Zev has always found it difficult. I believe he loves Abraham more than Baruch.'

Baruch had always sensed a chasm between him and his father. Now he thought about it, that was probably the reason for the tension between him and Abraham – the fact that his own father had always shown him more attention. And of course there was Rubin, the golden boy. Zev had always treated him differently. Now he knew it wasn't his imagination, it was the truth, and everyone in the family knew. But why did his father not love him? What had he done to deserve his contempt?

'It's hard for a man to love a child who's not his own.'

The blood drained from Baruch's beating heart, replaced with the bitterness of hatred.

Zev was not his father.

Was this the family secret he had so long suspected? That the man he thought was his father was – as he long suspected – not his father. It all fell into place. The constant feeling he had, even as a boy, that he was the black sheep of the family. He didn't belong. His father always favoured Rubin. Always defended him in an argument. He even favoured Abraham above him. In the pecking order Baruch was at the very bottom. The rage inside was unbearable. How could his mother keep such a thing from him? He remained still, clenching his fists, until he could no longer feel the pain.

Who was his real father? Was it this fellow Brito? What business was it they shouldn't talk about? He listened on. Moses fell into a muttered rambling he could not make sense of. Quietly, he slipped away from his hiding place and out of the room.

CHAPTER

FORTY

Next year in Jerusalem.

The prophetic words echoed in Abraham's mind. They would be the last words he would hear his father utter. There would be no next year for Moses. Abraham looked on as his father's motionless body lay there, his sunken eyes occasionally flickering open and looking heavenward, glazed and vacant. Not a word had he spoken. Abraham and Douce had kept vigil at Moses' bedside throughout the night and into the next morning. There was no change.

Douce held his hand and whenever he opened his eyes, she spoke to him in soft tones, stroking his hair and reassuring him that he was not alone. Abraham could hear bird chatter outside and sensed it must be nearing dawn. He lifted the latch on the wooden shutters and let the icy fresh air in. The courtyard below was in dark shadow and eerily quiet. He closed the shutters and returned to his father. Moses' breathing had settled into a rhythmic pattern of shallow rapid breaths, followed by long periods where he did not take a breath. With each exhalation, Abraham thought he had taken his last, but then he would begin again without effort as if he had just forgotten how to breathe for a while. Abraham watched as his chest rose and fell, then became still and then rose again. As time went on Moses appeared to get smaller. His breathing had moved from his chest to his lower abdomen, more rapid this time. Douce let go of her husband's hand and stood up.

'I'm going to make some peppermint tea. Would you like some?' she asked.

'I think it might help us to stay awake,' Abraham replied, giving his mother a weak smile.

Douce smiled back at her son and with her head bowed slightly with tiredness and despair, she left the room. Abraham took hold of his father's hand. In the dim light, he could see his fingernails were turning purple and had become gnarled like a knot in an ancient tree. His breathing continued, rapid and rhythmic and then it stopped. Abraham waited, as before, for it to start again but it didn't. He had taken his last breath. Finally, he was at peace.

Some moments later his mother walked back into the room. She instantly knew he had gone. The contents of the walnut cups she held in her hand spilled across the wooden floorboards. She hurried to the side table and placed them there where the tea slopped onto the oak surface.

'*Mon chér,*' she cried.

Burying her head in his chest she let out a wail of inhuman proportions, followed by deep, wracking sobs. Abraham had seen his mother upset before but never had he witnessed such grief. Unsure how to comfort her he went back to the shutters and flung them open, allowing his father's soul, which was already loosening its ties, to be free. Next, he picked up the bowl of standing water and emptied its contents out of the window.

Eventually his mother stopped sobbing, wiped her eyes, then kissed Moses on the forehead and said goodbye.

'Help me place him on the floor,' she said, her voice lacking emotion and yet her face unable to hide her sadness. 'We need to light the candles.'

'*Ima*, do you need to do that now?'

'Your father would want it this way. I must do this last thing for him.'

Abraham saw that his mother was grey with grief. Her youthful face was lined with the pain of sorrow. Her pale blue eyes were misted over, but there were no tears. It seemed to intensify his own grief and he crossed over to her and hugged her, letting his tears fall.

'Come,' she said, pulling away from him and turning back to the task she was now so eager to perform.

Abraham supposed it was her way of coping with losing the man she had spent almost all her life with, the father of her children. It was a way of honouring the love they had shared, his dedication and his respect for her. Abraham realised in that moment he had to be strong for his mother. With great difficulty, they lifted Moses from his bed and placed him upon the white linen shroud that Douce had laid out upon the straw covered floor. The candles were close by, in readiness. Douce placed one at his head and lit it.

As was the Jewish custom, Moses' body could not be left alone.

'Stay here, I'll go and get Bella.'

Bella, apart from being Douce's oldest friend, was also a member of the *chevra kaddisha* or holy society, a group of women who cared for the community's dead. Abraham now took on the role of the *shomerim*, the person, or group of people who stayed with the body until burial. It was an honour.

Abraham sat on the wooden floorboards next to his father's body. A pale morning light filtered into the room, casting dappled shadows on the walls. He wondered where Brunetta had got to. She was probably still asleep. He needed her. The bird chatter was rousing, full of life, hailing a new dawn and yet the death of his father felt to Abraham like the end of everything.

The end of an era.

Moses had been the lynchpin of the family. It would now fall to Abraham, as the eldest son, to take the lead. He seriously doubted he could replace the enormous void his father had left with his passing.

Even so, sitting by his father's side, he silently vowed to honour his memory by doing all that he could to protect the family and defend the empire his father had built up.

To the end of time.

CHAPTER
FORTY-ONE

B aruch sought the company of men. Moses' words were still echoing in his head and he needed to drown them out. He needed to drown his sorrows. He had worked up quite a thirst.

At the bar, in the Lich Inn, stood a group of knights. It was obvious from their conversation they had not long returned from the Crusades. The chapel on the London Road had been founded in part to take care of the fighters who returned from the Crusades. They arrived home with unknown diseases, blindness, skin lesions, and most feared of all, leprosy. Those affected were quickly despatched to the chapel of St Mary Magdalen to be cared for. Many never left alive.

Baruch ordered an ale and stood close by to listen to their tales. They spoke of violent battles, death, brutality; of exotic, dark brown whores they had bedded. In his present mood, it all sounded preferable to the life he was living. After all, what had he to return to? A mother who lied to him, a father who wasn't his, his grandparents unable to love him. In comparison, a life as a warring knight sounded adventurous, appealing. After a few ales, he approached the men. Their conversation was raucous, lewd and loud.

'How do I sign up?' Baruch asked.

The men looked at him. He was dressed in clothes that marked him out as a Jew. One of the men spat at his feet. Baruch's temper spilled over. He took the man by the neck and with the other hand punched his jaw. Baruch was no weakling and the bile running through his veins probably contributed to his strength. He had knocked the knight clean out. The man fell from Baruch's grip and thudded to the floor. Out cold. The knights looked impressed rather than angry.

'Never seen a Jew do that before,' one of them said, shoving his hair back over his scalp.

'I'm not a Jew,' Baruch said.

'Could have fooled me,' said another.

'Who do I need to ask to join you on the Crusade?'

The man he hit was still out cold. One of the men looked down at him then back to face Baruch.

'Well I suppose you've proved yourself as a worthy opponent. If you're serious then seek out the sheriff. He'll be at the castle with that lovely young wife of his.'

He made a lewd gesture and Baruch grinned. The man on the floor groaned. The sheriff was none other than William Marshal with whom he had struck up an acquaintance.

'He'll be all right. We'll look after him.'

He couldn't see the sheriff looking like he did. Like a Jew. The guards at the castle would not let him pass. He would have to change out of his Jewish clothes. Baruch had no money on him either. Even though he had vowed never to return to that house he would have to. He swigged the last of his ale and left the inn.

As he entered the house, he could hear wailing coming from

Moses' bedroom. He crept up the stairs and peeped in. Moses was laid out on the floor, lighted candles surrounding him.

The great Moses le Riche was dead.

For a second, Baruch felt an emotion close to grief, but then he remembered his grandfather's words.

'Baruch is a disappointment to me.'

'I've tried to love him as my own son, but it's been hard.'

His anger spiked. He knew just who to take it out on. Maybe for the last time.

Instead of gathering his things and leaving he went upstairs to Brunetta and Abraham's bedroom. Brunetta often lay down in the day for a rest. He opened the door. She was lying curled up on her side her backside facing out towards him. Was she asleep? No matter. She loves it, can't get enough of it. If he felt any guilt about seducing his cousin's wife, it was gone. He loosened his breeches as he tiptoed to the edge of the bed. She stirred. He lay down beside her curving his body next to hers, his cock as hard as his anger. He lifted her skirts, she turned her head, he pressed it down into the mattress, spread her naked buttocks and entered her. Brunetta struggled and cried out. He covered her mouth with his hand.

Having no respect for her, he rammed his cock into her as hard as he could. With each thrust he thought of the injustice his whole family had meted out to him his whole life. The betrayal. His mother. How could she do that to him? The only consolation he could think of was that his mother had been unfaithful to her husband. Zev. The man he thought was his father. He must be as spineless as Abraham if he married a woman who he knew was carrying someone else's child. He had tried to make his father love him, but it was obvious that was never going to happen and now he knew why.

Oblivious to Brunetta's protests, he lost himself in his

wrath. If Abraham was to walk in on them now, what of it? He would thrash the spineless buffoon to within an inch of his life.

When he had finished, Brunetta was sobbing.

He left her, changed into his Christian clothes, then went in search of his mother's money box.

ARLETTE WAS DEVASTATED by the death of her uncle Moses. He had been like a father to her. Kind, protective, wise and loving. She was going to miss him terribly. The house felt cold and empty even though everyone was home observing the *shemira*, the guarding of Moses' body until the time of his burial. Even in death, his absence could be felt.

Arlette had crept out to go downstairs for something to eat. She was just helping herself to some bread and cheese when Baruch stormed in. The emptiness and solitude in the kitchen was immediately filled with menace. She did not have to look at him to know he was in one of his tempers. She had neither the energy nor the inclination to argue with him. She turned her attentions to the block of cheese in front of her gradually aware that he was staring at her. She could feel the threatening nature of his eyes boring into the back of her neck.

'What's the matter?' she asked.

'Don't you know?'

Arlette jumped when she heard the tone of his voice. He practically growled his answer. She was used to him returning to the house drunk and belligerent. She was the only one in the family who could calm him down. Zev usually managed to make things worse. She was grateful he was still upstairs. This time she sensed something more ominous.

'Surely you must know?'

Arlette spun round. 'What is it this time? Lost more than your money at dice?'

Baruch threw his head back and laughed at her. Arlette's throat went dry. She had never seen him like this. He reminded her of his real father. The memory made her feel sick to her stomach, her hunger gone.

'Losing money I can recover from, but this...'

He waved his arms in the air. Arlette was at a loss. She had no idea what he was so upset about. Was it Moses' death?

'What? Why are you acting like this?'

The sickness was turning to fear. She thought it best to leave, let him stew on whatever was troubling him and talk in the morning. She moved to walk past him.

'I'll speak to you in the morning when you're in a better mood.'

'I won't be here. And I won't be in a better mood.'

Arlette stopped. 'Where are you planning on going?'

'As far away from *you* as I can get.'

She covered her cheeks with her palms as if he had slapped her across the face. There was undiluted hatred in his voice.

'Please don't talk to me like that.'

'How should I talk to you? With respect? You're no better than the whores I lay with.'

Arlette raised her hand to slap him. He caught her wrist and twisted it, drawing her close to him.

'Why don't you tell my father about my bad behaviour?'

'I will when I go back upstairs.'

He let go of her wrists and pushed her away, laughing at her. 'But he isn't upstairs, is he?'

Arlette caught her breath.

'I know, Mother. I know he isn't my father.'

Arlette's chest tightened; her throat constricted. 'You've been drinking, you don't know what you're saying.'

'Actually, Mother, I'm quite sober for a change and I know exactly what I'm saying. I heard them.'

'Who?'

'Douce and Moses.'

'Moses is dead.'

'He might be now, but he was quite talkative when I last set eyes on him, telling Douce about how hard it must be for a man to love a child who isn't his.'

Baruch almost spat the last few words at her. She staggered back at the force of his anger. Had her son discovered the secret she had hidden from him these long years?

'That's just the ramblings of a dying man.'

'Oh, come on, Mother. Don't lie to me. You've done enough of that.'

He crossed over to the food and picked up a piece of cheese. He seemed to be enjoying speaking to his mother with slant regard for her feelings. Baruch picked up the knife from the table and pointed it at her.

'You know I've never felt part of this family. I know why he favours Rubin... because Rubin is his.'

'You're both his.'

Baruch stabbed the sharp point of the blade into the wooden tabletop. Arlette flinched.

'You can stop all that now. No point in denying it. Your secret is out.'

Tears ran down Arlette's cheeks. He might as well have stabbed her in the heart.

'I would have loved to experience that. The love of a father.'

The pain she felt for the son she loved was unbearable. Although he was angry with her, she could tell he was hurting. Knowing that he had always felt out of place made her feel immensely sad. She thought she had done enough to make him feel loved, to make him feel wanted.

'Who was he anyway? Who was it tempted you away from that paragon of virtue you call your husband? What was it Moses called him?'

Baruch ripped the knife out of the wood, ran his fingers along the blade in contemplation. Arlette could hardly breathe. If he said his name, it was proof that he really did know.

'Brito?'

Arlette took a sharp intake of breath, and her fist went to her mouth. A cruel smile stretched across Baruch's features.

'I can tell I'm right, Mother. You can't hide it. Your face says it all. So Brito is the name of my real father, not Zev.'

He knew. After all this time. He knew.

'I've always loved you. I still do.'

She reached out her hands to him. He batted them away.

'I don't need your love anymore, Mother. I'm leaving.'

He picked up the remaining cheese and bread and stuffed it into a small hessian sack.

'Where are you going?'

'As far away from this place as I can possibly manage and I'm not coming back. If I never see you again...'

He faltered. Arlette was hanging on to his arm, pleading with him to stay. He shrugged her off, like she was a filthy beggar.

'Get off me, you whore,' he said, pushing her to the floor.

Without checking to see if his mother was hurt, he left, slamming the door behind him.

After that the house fell empty again.

Empty and cold.

FORTY-TWO

W hen Baruch left, he slammed the door behind him without a shred of regret. Such was his anger he forgot to look for his mother's money box. With a swagger he strode to the castle. His Christian clothes were perfect. As soon as he put them on this time he felt like a different man. More Christian than Jew. At the drawbridge the guard barred his way with his pike. Baruch demanded to see the sheriff.

'The sheriff's busy.'

Baruch had never been in the castle. Abraham always accompanied Moses there to conduct business. He had to think of a reason why the sheriff would want to see him. Christians generally despised Jews. Dressed as a Christian, the guard would have no way of knowing he was a Jew. He lied.

'I have important information about the Jew, Moses le Riche. It is to the sheriff's advantage he speaks with me.'

The guard relented and let Baruch pass through. He entered the keep and was shown into the great hall where William Marshal stood with his back to him.

'You have news of Moses le Riche?' he said, turning around.

'I have come to report his death, sire.'

William looked genuinely touched at this news. 'Baruch. Your grandfather is dead. I am sorry to hear that.'

There was an awkward silence. Baruch could sense he was about to be dismissed.

'May I speak with you in private?'

'Is it to do with Moses?'

'On another more private matter.'

William looked intrigued. He studied Baruch, his fingers pulling at his beard.

'Very well.'

He dismissed his men and walked over to the grand fireplace. He was a tall man of handsome proportions. Square-jawed and muscular. He stood by the unlit fire. A table stood nearby upon which was a bottle of wine.

'Can I offer you a cup of wine?'

Baruch accepted and took the cup from William.

'What is it you wish to say?'

Baruch suddenly felt foolish. Why would this great knight be interested in his personal tragedy – for that was what it was. A tragedy of birth. He swigged the cup of wine down in one. What did he have to lose? His life was a mess. This might be his one last chance to make something of it.

'I have just learned from Moses that the man I thought was my father isn't my father.'

'Then Moses is not your grandfather?' Marshal, said, his interest piqued.

'No.'

'But I thought you said Moses was dead.'

'He is. Before he died, I overheard him talking about a man called Brito.'

William's eyebrows rose in recognition.

'Do you know of him?'

Baruch had wondered where his father was and whether he was alive still. He wanted to get to know him. Find him.

'It's an unusual name. I know of only one man named Brito.'

'Is he here?'

William scratched at his head. 'If it is the Brito I knew, then I'm sorry to say he's dead.'

Baruch's hope of meeting his father was short-lived. He was dead and he would never know him. Never feel his love. In that moment he hated his mother more. Why hadn't she told him his father was dead. William seemed to sense Baruch's disappointment.

'If it is the same man, he served our king well.'

It was as though William had pricked him with his sword. He was intrigued. A royal connection.

'My father served the king. Are you sure?'

'I have served three kings so far in my lifetime including the present king. I've known many of the men who served them. If I'm right, your father served King Henry loyally. He was a formidable knight.'

'What happened to him?'

'It is said he was murdered by some brigands whilst in Gloucester.'

'What was he doing in Gloucester?'

Baruch was trying to make sense of how his mother, a Jew, had come to be with child by a Christian man who served in the royal household. There was much he did not know about his mother.

'No one knows exactly. At the time King Henry was concerned about losing his lands in Ireland. An Irish king had taken advantage of the king's favour and amassed an army to fight over there.'

'What has that got to do with Gloucester?'

'A Jew from Gloucester called Josce was funding him. He

and some unknown others made it possible. As a result the king almost lost control of Ireland.'

Baruch wondered if the Josce he referred to was his grandfather's best friend, Josce. There was so much he didn't know.

'So you think his death was something to do with this Irish king?'

'I believe at the time no one was punished for the crime and as is the way it was forgotten about.'

'How did he die?'

William hesitated, took a swig of his wine and fixed his grey-green eyes on Baruch.

'They cut off his head.'

Baruch showed no emotion at this news. All he could think of was whether his family had somehow been involved in his murder. There had to be some link. After all, his mother had at one time lain with him. He was living proof.

'You haven't come here for a history lesson,' William said, placing his cup on the table and straightening up.

'I've come to ask if I can join you fighting the infidels.'

'But you are Jewish. Why would you want to get involved in our battles?'

'I am Jewish only because my mother is Jewish, but my father was a Christian and a brave and loyal knight. I want to honour my father and someday avenge his murder.'

'Do you have experience of soldiery?'

'No, but I have good sword skills, and I can ride a horse as good as any man.'

The Marshal studied him for some time. Baruch could feel the weight of his stare. It made him shuffle on his feet. He became impatient.

'Well then?' he said.

'We could always use men like you.'

Baruch put his cup down.

'I won't disappoint.'

'Make sure you don't.'

The sheriff was a busy man and Baruch sensed he had taken up too much of his time and the Marshal wanted him to leave. He stood looking down at his feet, not knowing what to do, not wanting to leave. What now? How did this work? He had no idea. He lingered.

'Must have been a shock to find out who your real father was,' William said.

Baruch nodded.

William shouted for his men to return.

'Go with this man. He'll sort you out with a uniform and some food. We leave for France tomorrow to join the king.'

'What's your name, young man?' the soldier asked as they walked into the bailey.

He was just about to say Baruch then changed his mind. Baruch was such an obvious Jewish name it would give him away.

'Brito,' he said with pride. 'My name is Brito.'

Baruch followed the soldier to a storehouse bustling with activity. Horses were being shoed. Weapons were being cleaned and inspected, repaired by the blacksmith. Baruch's spirits rose. It was as though he had been born to this life.

FORTY-THREE

Brunetta held her stomach. Something felt like it had shifted inside her. With difficulty she managed to move to the edge of the bed. When she looked at the covers they were stained with blood-coloured semen. She ripped off the cover and hid it under the mattress, then soaked a cloth in the bowl of water that stood on the side and lodged it between her legs. It was cool and soothing. Then she climbed back on the bed. The pain inside grew stronger.

How foolish she had been. Baruch was nothing but a savage brute and she wanted nothing more to do with him. If he had damaged the baby growing inside her she would kill him. Her protectiveness towards the child surprised her. She hadn't given much thought to the life growing within. She hadn't even told Abraham. She had been putting it off, not wanting to witness the cloying sentimentality he would display about the son he was so convinced he had already conjured in a vision. Would it be a son or a daughter? Abraham would be bitterly disappointed if it were not a son. Would it be his?

Had Baruch damaged the child? It was hardly a child. She

was probably only two months pregnant. Her stomach not even swollen. She pulled the covers over her and lay still, praying that no damage had been done. She must have drifted off to sleep because she woke with a jolt. Someone had climbed into bed with her. For a moment she thought it was Baruch again. About to launch an attack, she was surprised to see Abraham. His face was stained with tears.

'How is Moses?'

'He's dead,' he said, his voice breaking.

Brunetta had not given a thought to Moses. She had not kept vigil with Abraham. Not supported him or her mother-in-law in their hour of need, preferring to go back to bed and sleep. Abraham nodded and buried his face into her neck. Brunetta put her hand around his neck to comfort him. She was relieved it was not Baruch. The pain in her stomach had gone and she hoped there was no lasting damage. Now was probably not the best time to tell Abraham of the child. He had just lost his father. But then again maybe her news would cheer him up, help with his loss.

'I have some news, Abraham.'

'Is it good news? I couldn't cope with bad news, not right now.'

She gave him a look. Like she had a secret to tell him. He stared back at her.

'What is it?' he said, curious to know.

'I'm with child.'

'You're certain,' he said.

'Positive.'

'How long have you known?'

'Not long. A day or so.'

'I wish you had told me sooner, rather than on the day of my father's death.'

Brunetta hadn't expected this reaction from Abraham. She expected him to gush over her pregnancy, suffocate her with his affection, proclaim the news to all his family.

She was relieved to have been spared all of that.

FORTY-FOUR

When Mirabelle heard of Moses' death, a thin smile appeared upon her lips.

'*Ima*,' said Bonanfaunt. 'You shouldn't rejoice at someone's passing. Just think how you would feel if father died.'

Mirabelle contemplated that scenario and tried hard to imagine how she would feel if Elias died. She could not summon up an emotion. For years she had resented Moses le Riche and his family. His prominence in her community and that of the Christian community. Whenever there was a problem, it was Moses le Riche that members of the *bet din* consulted with. Not her husband. It was Moses who the wealthy Christians went to when they needed to borrow large sums. But now there was a chink in the le Riche armour and his name was Abraham. Abraham was weak. She could see that, and she would exploit it.

'At last,' she said. 'We have a chance to take our rightful place in this community.'

'You're obsessed, *Ima*. It's not healthy.'

'What's wrong with wanting the best for my family?'

'Nothing. But there are limits.'

Elias, who had been sitting quietly in the corner, raised his eyebrows.

'You should know your mother by now. She has no limits.'

'I don't see you complaining when I bring in lucrative deals,' she barked.

Elias jumped in his seat at her aggressive tone towards him, then shrugged his shoulders in defeat.

'I feel sorry for Douce,' said Genta, who was pregnant again and holding the latest addition to her growing brood, her son Jacob. 'They were so much in love. She was distraught at the funeral.'

Genta, living under the shadow of her mother-in-law Mirabelle, rarely spoke her mind and never got involved with family conversations.

'Don't be such a dreamy-eyed fool. That woman has bled her husband dry over the years.'

Mirabelle gave her such a sour look that Genta turned away from her with tears in her eyes. Bonanfaunt scolded his mother.

'*Ima*, sometimes you don't realise what you're saying.'

'I think she does,' said Elias under his breath to Genta.

'What was that?' Mirabelle snapped.

'I didn't say anything,' said Elias, winking at Genta when Mirabelle wasn't looking.

'I've been thinking about how we can make the best of this situation. Elias, you must approach Moses' old customers and offer them a better rate of interest than Abraham is offering.'

'I can't do that.'

'Why not?'

Elias stammered when Mirabelle asked him to do tasks he wasn't comfortable with. The stammer returned.

'It's, it's...'

Mirabelle ignored her husband.

'Start with the abbot from St Peters. Thomas Carbonel. If we get him, others may follow.'

'But...'

'Never mind that. I'll speak with some others. Find out what they think of Abraham. Put some doubts in their minds as to his suitability to carry on Moses' business. That should do it.'

'It's not exactly ethical, *Ima*.'

'When was business ever ethical? You have a lot to learn, Bonanfaunt. Sometimes you have to do unpalatable things to survive.'

'You wouldn't have done this when Moses was alive. Why now?'

'Moses had support in high places. Abraham is weak. He's not up to the task.'

'Aren't you worried this will backfire on you?'

'Not really. I'm going to make my own powerful allies.'

'Like who?'

'Like John, the Count of Mortain.'

'The king's brother. You're treading on dangerous ground there. John is unpredictable and vindictive.'

'That may be so but he's going to be our next king.'

'Richard isn't dead yet.'

'No, and I may not live to see him die, but you will be alive. I'm doing this for you and your children's children.'

Mirabelle reached out to Bonanfaunt and touched his arm. It was the closest she ever came to showing affection to him. Genta looked resentful and squeezed his other arm in a territorial gesture.

'John is in Wales,' Mirabelle continued. 'I'm going to travel there and ask him for an audience.'

'What's he doing there?'

'Carrying on an illicit liaison with Queen Clemence – of course she's not a real queen but has a high opinion of herself and insists everyone addresses her by that title. There's talk of a child. I believe her name is Joan.'

'How do you know all this, *Ima*?' Bonanfaunt asked his mother, somewhat incredulous at her depth of knowledge about the royals.

'I keep my ear to the ground,' she replied. 'A little knowledge can be a powerful thing.'

Elias joined the conversation. 'You might not like her methods, son, but she knows what she's doing and usually gets what she wants.'

Mirabelle gave a snort of agreement. 'John hates his brother and is constantly plotting against him while he's away fighting in the Crusades. He has designs on the crown.'

'So?'

'My son, you have a lot to learn.'

'What do you mean? You're being deliberately vague.'

'John needs money to plot against his brother. I'm going to make sure he gets it. A generous source of credit, not questioned, not recorded, not taxed – to call upon whenever needed. John would be indebted to us, and when he becomes king, he will not forget us.'

'It's a risky strategy, *Ima*.'

'There's little risk. Moses is dead. Aaron of Lincoln is dead. Virtually the entire York community perished in that massacre along with the major moneylenders and sources of ready cash. There are fewer major players in the market – leaving a very convenient void.' She paused a moment, puffed out her chest and a hint of a triumphant smile could be seen lingering between her thin lips. She took in a deep breath. 'And I intend to fill it.'

She reached for a date from the fruit bowl and popped it into her mouth. The smile still there as she ate.

'This is our time.'

CHAPTER
FORTY-FIVE

Baruch travelled across the English Channel, through Europe and arrived at the city of Acre in the Levant. The siege had ended a few months ago and the king's army were now making their way towards Jaffa along the magnificent coastline of glistening turquoise sea and sandy beaches. A flotilla of supply ships followed them, keeping them fed and most importantly watered. Baruch had never known such thirst or such heat.

William Marshal, or the Marshal as the men called him, was an impressive character. He was never far away from the king's side offering advice and sound counsel. Baruch had great respect for him. Life in the king's army was hard, harder than he realised. Back in England he was lazy, dissolute. Now he had a purpose. To fight. The cause was unimportant to him. He was neither Catholic, Muslim or, for that matter, Jewish. It had been easy to convince the men he was a Christian having spent more time in whorehouses and taverns than many of the men he now camped with. Baruch was now known to everyone, including the Marshal, as Brito. He had used his father's name and reputation to ingratiate himself with the Marshal and the king and having fought side by side with them over the last few months, he had proved himself in battle.

One evening, after a long day of marching, he sat by the fire drinking wine, reflecting on matters back home. Baruch enjoyed the life of a soldier, far more than his life in England. He thought he might miss his mother, but he was still angry with her and had no urgency or desire to see her again. He wondered how the family were faring now that his grandfather was dead. Would that pathetic excuse for a son be able to run the business in the same way Moses had? Doubtful. Then his mind wandered to Brunetta. He wondered how she was. Whether she was happy married to Abraham. The only person he felt anything for was Henne. They had always been close.

An old soldier approached and lowered his weary body down next to the fire. Baruch nodded at him. The soldier spoke.

'Are you Brito's son?'

Baruch jumped at the mention of his father's name.

'Yes, did you know him?'

'I knew him well.'

'What was he like?'

A wide grin appeared on the soldier's weather-beaten face. 'He was a fine soldier.'

'And?'

Baruch could tell the man was holding something back. The soldier rubbed his chin as though he were trying to recall something.

'You never knew what he was up to.'

'What do you mean?'

'He was secretive.'

'I was told he worked for the king.'

'That's right, he did.'

The soldier's taciturn manner was beginning to annoy Baruch.

'But we never knew what he was up to half the time.'

'Were you with him at Gloucester?'

The soldier raised an eyebrow. 'Aye.'

Baruch's lips were dry. He took a gulp of wine.

'Was he doing work for the king?'

'I believe so.'

'Can you tell me anything about it? Did you know my mother?'

The soldier stared at Baruch, a puzzled frown creasing his forehead.

'My mother. Her name was Arlette. She would have been very young then.'

'Did she work at the whorehouse? He was fond of a young woman there.'

Baruch could feel the anger building inside him and the instinct to defend his mother's honour was strong.

'My mother was not a whore.'

A light of recognition or an understanding shone in the old soldier's eyes.

'You did know her?'

The soldier gathered his things and stood up to leave, avoiding Baruch's stare. 'I'm tired. I need my bed,' he said, keeping his gaze to the ground.

Baruch grasped his arm and held on tight. 'You know something about my mother and Brito.'

The soldier shook his head. 'A bad business,' he muttered.

Baruch shook the man. 'Tell me or so help me I'll...'

The soldier cowered. 'I had no idea,' he said. 'I wouldn't have spoken if I'd known.'

'Known what?' Baruch shouted, drawing the old soldier closer to him.

'You have his eyes and his temper,' the soldier said.

As if the old soldier were on fire, Baruch let go of him. The soldier staggered backwards, then composed himself. He walked away then stopped and turned.

'Your father was a fine soldier but when it came to women, he was a brute. He raped your mother.'

The words hit Baruch like the swipe from a hammer. Baruch slumped back down by the fire. His mother had been raped and he was the product of it. No wonder she had kept it from him. Did Zev know? Did he marry her to protect her honour? There was no doubting Zev's love for Arlette. Baruch had to admit, grudgingly, that if that were the case, Zev had done an honourable thing marrying his mother. His thoughts turned to the last time he saw her. He had said some awful things. Things he should never have said. He sunk his forehead into his hands and made a promise. If he survived this Crusade, he would return and make it up to her.

THE NEXT MORNING Baruch woke with a thick head. Dawn had barely broken and already the sun was hot. He was relieved when they were afforded a brief respite from the relentless sun as they passed through a dense cool wood. But this was soon over when they emerged into the bright sunshine. The stone fortress of Arsuf loomed before them, high on a promontory, at the edge of the coastline. Dazzling turquoise sea stretched out beyond it and above a clear azure sky. The main gate was flanked at both sides by semi-circular towers at each corner. A towering octagonal keep dominated the entire fortifications. It was as good as – even better than – many English castles Baruch had seen. Then the terrifying din of the enemy started up again. Beating of drums and the discord of cymbals were nothing to the screeching and screaming of Saladin's men. It made the hairs on the back of Baruch's neck prickle. He gripped his sword, ready for battle.

The enemy were closing in.

CHAPTER

FORTY-SIX

Since the death of Moses, Brunetta noticed Abraham had gone into a dark place. He was morose, hardly spoke to her and was no longer interested in having sex, which suited her fine. She was near her time, and it would not be long before she gave birth. She still thought of that last time with Baruch. He had been brutal with her. She worried he had damaged the baby. And then he was gone. No one knew where he was, where he had gone, what he was doing. At the time of the assault she didn't much care for him but then, when she heard he had left the family home, she began to wonder why. Was he upset? He was a complicated man. Brutal and vulnerable at the same time.

For the first time in her life, she found she cared for someone other than herself. Her baby. This unknown thing inside her had changed her. She couldn't explain it. She wondered whether Abraham's vision would come true. Was she carrying the child he so vividly saw in his vision? If so, was she part of some wider plan?

She had been feeling tired that morning so had gone back to

bed. Her swollen stomach made it hard for her to get comfortable and sleep. Mid-morning, she was woken by a sharp pain and the feeling of wetness underneath her on the sheets. Moments later a severe pain tore through her lower back. She held her breath until the pain subsided. The baby was coming. She screamed out to alert someone in the house. She could not get out of bed. She screamed again. This time with the pain.

Why wasn't anyone coming to her aid? Where were they all? Anger turned to panic when she realised she might lie there and no one would hear her screams. She would die along with the baby. Did she deserve that? She did. The tears came then. She had been wicked. She had been adulterous without a care for anyone's feelings but her own base sexual needs.

The pain intensified until she could bear it no more and screamed again for help. Would anyone hear her at the top of the house? A wave of white-knuckle pain gripped her. When she thought she could bear it no longer she thought she heard footsteps on the stairs. She shouted Abraham's name. The door opened. It was Douce. She hadn't always liked her, but Brunetta was never so pleased to see her.

'How long have you been like this?'

Brunetta had lost track of time. 'I'm not sure.'

Douce felt her stomach. 'What sort of pain is it?'

'Like a sharp pain, only it comes in waves.'

Douce stood up. 'I think you're about to have your baby, Brunetta.'

'Is it going to be all right? The baby, I mean?'

'Why wouldn't it?'

Brunetta thought of the savage attack on her unborn child by that beast.

'I don't know.'

Douce's eyes softened. She laid her hand on Brunetta's and patted it.

'It's your first child. It's always a little...' She stopped, searching for the right word.

'Scary,' said Brunetta.

'You'll be fine. I'll go and tell Abraham,' she said, going to the door.

'Douce.'

Douce turned around. Douce was helping her, even though she hated her. She realised she was selfish to the core and didn't deserve her help.

'I'm so sorry, Douce.'

Douce said nothing and left the room. Hours later, with her help, Brunetta gave birth to a healthy boy.

ABRAHAM JOINED Brunetta after she gave birth. Douce had assured him that the birth was no place to be and Brunetta was in good hands. Abraham was grateful to his mother. She always knew best. Perhaps the birth would bring the two women closer. He hoped so. It would ease the tensions in the household. It might even bring him closer to Brunetta.

Abraham would have loved his father to be here for the birth of his first son. It was not to be. And yet it was strange. He could almost feel his presence in the room.

Brunetta looked exhausted, her brow wet with sweat and her hair plastered to the sides. He kissed her on the cheek and asked her how she was, but in truth he was more excited to see his son. He couldn't wait to meet him in the flesh. The son of his vision. He walked over to the basket and looked inside. Large indigo blue eyes stared back at him. Here finally was the son of his vision. He held his tiny fingers. The baby's touch convinced him that this was the child. The one who had saved his life. Although his son would not be officially named until his *brit*,

Abraham had already decided on a name, Tzuri. It meant 'my rock'. It was odd but Abraham felt the need to thank his son even though it was ridiculous to expect a newborn to comprehend anything he was about to say. He held the child close to his chest and whispered, 'I'm so glad to meet you at last. Thank you, son.'

An indescribable joy filled his heart. The prophecy had come to pass. He kissed his son, allowing tears of gratitude to fall. As the tears fell, they turned into tears of sorrow at the aching loss of his father, the fact he would never know his grandson. He was overwhelmed by a great sadness. He placed the baby back in his basket and left the room unnoticed.

The enormity of the loss he felt hit him with such ferocity it shocked him. He sought refuge in his father's cellar, unable to face anyone. The tears pooled down his face and in the quiet solitude of the cellar, he sobbed. He was no longer the son of Moses. He was head of the le Riche household with all the responsibilities that went with that. He still owed the king 300 marks in death duties.

The burden of his new role lay heavily upon him. It frightened him. Was he up to it? How would he cope without his father there to guide him? His mother and all his siblings now relied on him to keep the business going successfully, to keep a roof over their heads, food on the table and more. He looked at the parchment *shetarots* and tally sticks. They were still laid out on the desk where he had been working the night before. He looked through them. Was there anything that needed attending to today, anything pressing? His hands became clammy. He rubbed the back of his neck. Nothing helped. Overwhelmed by the onerous task before him, he made his way back up the stone steps, each step an effort. He wanted to hide somewhere so he didn't have to face any of it. He reached the top of the stairs and realised with chilling certainty, there would be no refuge.

He had a son. It terrified him.

CHAPTER
FORTY-SEVEN

Since Moses' death Douce had become morose, Abraham seemed lost, and Arlette missed her uncle. The black thoughts and mood that had plagued Arlette for much of her life had descended once more, with such suddenness and with no warning. Her argument with Baruch played on her mind. That was a year ago. She had not seen him since and had no idea where he was. She prayed each day that he would return and they could be close again. Zev seemed unconcerned that Baruch was missing. For him, nothing had changed. If anything, he seemed a little happier. Their arguments over Baruch had ceased and Zev, probably sensing her mood, had been more affectionate towards her. Try as she may, she could not discard her dark thoughts or the feeling that there was a gaping void in her life.

It was her time of the month, and she was visiting the *mikveh* to carry out her regular ritual washing to make her pure. It would soon be time for her monthly visits to stop altogether. She was feeling old and tired. She would wake at night drenched in sweat and unable to sleep. She often snapped at people for no reason. Douce told her she was probably coming to the end of her childbearing years, and her monthlies would stop. Arlette couldn't wait. Each time she visited the *mikveh* the memories of that night visited her with such freshness. The sound of the water in her ears, her breath leaving her body. Her long recovery. Physically she was healed, but emotionally, she doubted she would ever be truly free of the trauma.

Baruch knew Zev wasn't his father. How did he know that? Who would have told him? He mentioned Moses. Did Moses know Baruch was not Zev's son? Did Douce know? She always thought they knew but the subject was off limits in the le Riche household. She hadn't mentioned any of her conversation with Baruch to Zev. His relationship with Baruch was bad enough. The news that Baruch knew he wasn't his father would only make matters worse.

Baruch even knew the name of his real father. How was that possible? For a year she had wracked her mind to understand it all. It exhausted her. She dressed and walked back to the house.

Douce was in the kitchen, as usual, preparing a meal with Henne. To her surprise, she found Abraham sitting by the fire in the great hall, his head in his hands.

'Is something wrong?' she asked him.

Abraham started when he heard her voice. 'No, I'm fine.'

'You don't seem it.'

Abraham sighed and slumped back in the chair.

'Is it your father? Do you still grieve for him?'

'I do.' There was a pause then he continued. 'It's not that.'

'Then what it is?'

Arlette went to sit next to him.

'Can I help?'

'I wish you could,' he said, chewing nervously on the knuckles of his right hand.

Arlette had been so caught up in her own troubles she had not realised that Abraham was suffering too.

'Talk to me. Maybe I can help.'

Abraham rubbed at his eyes with the flat of his hand, took a deep breath and began. 'When father died, I had to take over the business.'

'And you're doing well.'

'That's it. I'm not. I don't have the skills father had. I'm just not in his league.'

'You do yourself an injustice.'

'Mirabelle has been stealing father's oldest clients and I don't know how to stop her. There is much less money coming in than when father was in charge. And the king wants three hundred marks from me in death duties by Michaelmas. Everything is in a mess, and I don't know where I am with anything. Mother and Brunetta expect me to support them. I'm really scared. I think we may lose the business. I promised my father I would defend his interests from the four parts of the world and until the end of time. I've failed him.'

Arlette had never seen Abraham so distressed. He looked haunted.

'I didn't know. I'm sorry.'

'You see, there's nothing you can do. There's nothing anyone can do for me. It's hopeless.'

'Have you spoken to Brunetta?'

'No. I haven't mentioned any of this to mother or anyone else.'

'I won't say a word to anyone. I just think Brunetta is your wife. Surely you can share your troubles with her.'

'She's not that kind of wife.'

Arlette did not know what to say to him. They had a young child and should be happy, but it seemed Brunetta was of no comfort to him. Since their marriage Brunetta had lived in the house. Two years had passed but still Arlette hardly knew her.

She knew nothing of the world of finance, but she could see Abraham was burdened by it. She had nothing to offer him.

'Perhaps you should have a word with Zev?'

Zev was like a father to Abraham. When he was a boy Abraham would play with him for hours, ignoring Baruch until Rubin came along. The bond between man and boy had been established and they were still close.

'I don't think Zev can help me. I'll have to work it out for myself.'

'I'm sure you will, Abraham.'

Abraham stood up. 'Thanks for listening, Arlette. I appreciate it. I better go back to the cellar. I have work to do.'

'Don't spend all day down there. It's not good to be alone. Go for a walk later. Take Brunetta with you. The fresh air will do you both good.'

Abraham nodded, and with his head bowed, and looking like he had the weight of the world on his shoulders, he left the room. Arlette knew she was speaking platitudes to him but didn't know what else to say. She had a good idea how Abraham was feeling. She knew only too well how dark thoughts crept insidiously into your head, making you think there was no point in living. No hope left.

CHAPTER

FORTY-EIGHT

The ship carrying King Richard back to England pitched violently in the black waters. The unforgiving wind tore through the ship's square-rigged sail, the rain lashed against Baruch's face like icy needles and the entire ship creaked and groaned under the attack of the elements. He had fought bravely at the Battle of Arsuf, killing many of Saladin's men but had never felt fear as he did now. Being in the middle of the ocean in what was effectively a wooden box was something he knew he would never get used to. He wished the journey was over and he was back on terra firma.

When the storm started Baruch lashed himself to the side of the ship as he had seen others do to stop him being tossed overboard. To calm his nerves, he held on tight to a flask of dark liquor he had bought from a wizened street trader the name of which he could not pronounce. It was warming and soporific. The storm raged on. Baruch looked to the sky. It was black. No moon, no stars to guide them. Was this what the Christian hell looked like? At some point he must have slept from sheer exhaustion for when he woke, he was immersed in vomit and sea water, but he was alive. The first light of dawn was a mere crack on the eastern horizon. Voices barking orders had woken him. Baruch was untying the ropes around his waist when he realised the ship was not moving. He stood up and saw that they had been forced off course and the ship had run aground on the rocks. How could he have slept through such a perilous event? He would never make a sailor and he had no wish to. The damage to the ship was significant. The sail was in tatters and the mast had split in two. Many of the king's men had perished in the sea. They were shipwrecked.

Preparations for disembarking were already underway. Baruch gathered his things and made his way down the gangplank. He could not be more relieved to set foot on dry land. Since joining the Crusade, Baruch had built upon his father's position in the king's service and with the help of the Marshal he was occasionally allowed into the king's inner circle. The king was in a terrible mood, shouting at his men and cussing in his language of Occitan. Baruch had kept well out of his way for most of the morning. He could be unpredictable when he was in that kind of mood and Baruch wanted to stay in his good books. Because of the shipwreck they had landed in unfriendly territory and were hundreds of miles away from any ally. The nearest was the king's brother-in-law Henry, the Duke of Saxony, who was married to the king's sister, Matilda, and he was in Braunschweig in Germany. It was going to be a perilous journey fraught with danger and with a king who still looked very much like a king they were left open to attack. Against his better judgement Baruch approached him.

'My lord, may I make a suggestion?'

The king turned to him, his face red with rage. 'What is it?'

'We are few in number and if anyone should mount an attack against us in these unfriendly lands, we will be sorely outnumbered I fear.'

'Go on.'

'You might want to change into a disguise so that no one recognises you...'

The king stared at Baruch for some time before answering. He seemed to be gathering his thoughts.

'You're right,' he said. Then turning on his aides he shouted, 'Why didn't any of you warn me of the dangers? Isn't that what I have you around me for? Useless idiots.'

The king then spoke to Baruch. 'What sort of disguise do you suggest?'

'I would dress in the guise of a servant, my lord. That way no one will take any notice of you, and we may pass through these lands unhindered.'

The king pondered upon this. Baruch could tell from his expression that he was not convinced his suggestion was the right one. One of his trusted aides piped up.

'How dare you suggest that the king dress as a servant. Why, it's an outrageous suggestion.'

'What would you have me do?' the king asked him.

The aide had not expected this and from his prolonged stammering it was obvious he hadn't thought through a solution.

'Well, it's unbecoming for a king of the realm to dress as a servant.'

Another aide stepped in to help. 'Why not dress as a Knight Templar? That would be more fitting, my lord.'

The king considered his suggestion. 'I think that's an excellent suggestion.'

Baruch bowed to the king and walked away. His attempt at gaining permanent inclusion into the inner circle had failed. He hadn't accounted for the king's arrogance and vanity.

By mid-morning, the heat of the sun had dried out Baruch's clothing and they were on their way northwards riding towards Gorizia, a city at the foot of the alps in the hands of Count

Meinhard – an ally of Duke Leopold of Austria. The duke had been humiliated by King Richard at the battle of Acre. After the capture of the city from Saladin's forces, Richard and King Philippe of France cast down Leopold's banner from the battlements of the city. It was a deliberate act and a sign that he and Philippe were unwilling to concede Leopold any share in the spoils. At the time Baruch thought nothing of the gesture, revelling in the triumph of victory. But now they were in enemy territory the king may have cause to regret his actions.

They reached the outskirts of Gorz late that next evening. Earlier Baruch had noticed the snow covering the alps even though the sun was shining. But it was dark now and the weather had turned increasingly bitter. A light drizzle began, and it was decided to make camp for the night. Baruch kept a close watch on the king. The group was small, and he worried that if an attack were to happen, they would be sorely undermanned. The night passed without incident. However, as they left the city of Gorizia behind them and rode along the road northwards in the direction of Vienna Baruch thought he spotted a figure on the far hillside. Moments later as they rode through a narrow valley a barrage of arrows hailed down upon them. One of the king's aides was killed; a few others were injured. Baruch dug his stirrups into his horse's nether regions and pulled up alongside the king.

'There's nothing else we can do but try to outrun them, Your Majesty.'

And with that Baruch took his crop to the king's horse and gave it such a swipe that the horse reared up and galloped off ahead. Baruch and the rest of their retinue followed. The tactic worked and within a few minutes they had outrun the ambushers.

Later that evening when they had made camp Baruch was called to the king's tent.

'Sit down, Baruch, and take some wine with me.'

The only other person in the tent with them was the king's servant. He came forward and poured the wine. Baruch studied the king's face. His pale skin was covered in freckles and his sand-coloured hair was messy and tattered. His long legs stretched out in front of him as he leaned back on the sumptuous cushions. Despite his appearance he still looked every inch a king filling the space with his regal presence.

'You saved my life today. I am in your debt.'

'It is an honour to serve, Your Majesty.'

'I understand your father served my father well before his untimely demise.'

'He did indeed, Your Majesty, but I have very little knowledge of him. My father died when I was but a baby.'

'It is a shame for a son not to know his father.'

Baruch did not reply. He did not want the king to know he had been born of a Jewess and brought up in the faith. He had kept his real identity a secret from everyone except the Marshal who was not about to reveal his secret and nor was he. Ever. He had concocted a tale of how after his father had died his mother, grief-stricken, had died of a broken heart and he was left to fend for himself. Anything was better than admitting he was a Jew.

'I've been thinking about what happened today.'

'The ambush?'

'Yes.'

'I think your enemies know you are here, and they are watching the roads. We will have to be more vigilant.'

'I've also been thinking of your suggestion the other day.' Richard paused and took a swig of his wine. 'That I should dress as a servant.'

'I didn't mean to be disrespectful, Your Majesty.'

Richard held up his hand to silence Baruch. 'I know. It was

my own folly that I did not adopt the guise of a servant. You were right.'

'I was only thinking of your safety, sire.'

'I realise that now and so from tomorrow I will dress as a servant and God willing, we will not be attacked again.'

'May I make another suggestion, Your Majesty?'

'Go on.'

'We need to keep away from the main roads as much as possible. It will delay our journey but if the roads are being watched...'

'Right again,' the king said, finishing his wine and putting his cup down.

Baruch took it as a signal, and he stood to leave. 'I bid you goodnight, Your Majesty. It's been a long and tiring day.'

'Just one more thing...'

Baruch hesitated. The king was unpredictable. He waited to be admonished.

'Tomorrow, I want you by my side.'

'It will be an honour, Your Majesty.'

As he left the tent Baruch's face split into a broad smile. His father would be proud of him.

FORTY-NINE

With the king in disguise and by keeping off the main roads they reached Erdberg, a suburb of Vienna near to the Danube River. Over the last few days the weather had worsened. Thick snow fell, and the temperature at night reached freezing point. They had decided to stop over at a local inn to rest the horses and eat something warming and substantial. It was risky but essential. They were exhausted. Baruch calculated it was a risk they could afford to take as there had not been one incident since Gorizia. True to his word the king had remained in disguise and on their travels had not drawn suspicion. Baruch worried that although he remained in disguise he still acted like a king and still expected to be treated like one. This regal behaviour would definitely give him away in the company of strangers. He had to say something to him.

'Your Majesty, I am concerned that your disguise may be uncovered this night.'

'Why so?'

'If I may be so bold. When in your disguise you look like a

servant, but your manner is not that of a servant. I fear your true identity may be revealed.'

'What would you have me do?'

Baruch had to keep the king on his side. He was keenly aware that he could fly off the handle at the slightest thing. He would have to summon all his diplomatic skills. Baruch swallowed hard.

'Perhaps if you did not give orders to the rest of us and behaved more like a servant...'

'Go on.'

'For example, at this evening's meal. Rather than wait to be served perhaps you could help and then when the food is ready serve yourself. No one would know you were a king.'

The king tilted his head backwards and roared. Baruch, relieved that he had not taken offence, relaxed a little.

'Very well, my friend, I will do as you ask.'

Baruch could not settle for although the king was acting as he had suggested, he was still drawing inquisitive looks from the other travellers and the locals. Baruch kept watch from a seat in the corner by the fire, constantly aware of everyone's movements. When Richard got up to stir the stew or turn the spit of the roasting chicken, a few of his aides rose with him. Baruch stared them down and remembering his instructions they sat again. When the meal was ready Richard stood up to help himself. He went to grab the handle of the ladle when a surly man who had been drinking alone in the opposite corner leapt up and grabbed the handle at the same time. The man planted his hand on top of the king's, then whipped it away but kept his gaze firmly on the king's hand. Baruch wondered why, then following the stranger's gaze his heart skipped a beat. The king had not removed the gold ring of St Valerie. It was rectangular in shape, oversized and solid gold. The man continued to stare at Richard's hand, then back at his face with a questioning look. Baruch approached. It was obvious that the serf had noticed the ring and was wondering why such a poor-looking servant would be wearing such an expensive-looking piece of jewellery. The serf muttered an apology and sat back down at his seat. Shortly after, he left without eating. Baruch made enquiries as to who he was, but it seemed he was a stranger to the inn, and no one knew him. Baruch hoped he was a nobody, and they would not see him again.

Baruch went outside to relieve himself and left the king sitting at the long oak table tearing apart a leg of chicken. The night was exceptionally cold, and he was glad they had made the decision to stay at the inn. Baruch watched the steam rise as he pissed in the white snow staining it yellow. He had just finished when he heard the thunder of horse's hooves. He crept to the window to look inside. The king was still at the table oblivious to the scene unfolding outside. Before he could warn the king, Austrian soldiers armed with swords burst through the door and into the inn. The man from earlier stood with them. He pointed at the king and shouted, 'That's him over there.'

The soldiers rushed at Richard. His trusted men surrounded their king and tried to protect him. They were no match for the soldiers. Outnumbered they fell one by one until there was only the king left. Richard did not attempt to fight back. The soldiers seized him and held him in an iron grip as the captain approached. The captain addressed the king in broken English.

'You are Richard the King of England?'

The king said nothing. The stranger spoke again.

'Look at his ring.'

The soldiers grabbed hold of the king's hand and held it out in front of him. The opulent gold ring looked incongruous on the hand of a shabbily dressed servant. The captain nodded his head in confirmation.

'I am arresting you on the orders of Leopold, the Duke of Austria. You are to come with me.'

'How dare you lay your hands on the King of England.'

The captain ignored him, motioned to his men who then dragged the king out of the inn and into the cold night. Baruch watched as he was bundled onto a wooden cart and driven away. Baruch could still hear his protests as he disappeared into the darkness of the night but could only look on helpless. He knew it was hopeless. The soldiers were well armed and there were many of them. To protest was futile. The stranger in the inn must have recognised the king and betrayed him. It occurred to Baruch that he might have been a spy working for the Duke of Austria. He slammed his flat palm against the stone wall of the inn, cussing as he did so, partly out of frustration when it dawned on him that he should have known and partly out of guilt for doing nothing to help the king.

Baruch remained outside the inn for some time. He stared into the blackness of the night, the heavy snow falling all around him and landing on his lashes. He thought if he stared long enough along the empty track the abductors would realise their mistake and the king would emerge atop his horse. But that moment never came. Not able to feel his feet and the snow freezing his face, he took one last look into the inn. The scene was one of carnage. Men he had fought with, marched with, broke bread with lay on the floor soaked in blood. The fire no longer seemed welcoming. There was nothing else for him to do but try to find out where they had taken the king.

CHAPTER
FIFTY

Almost two years had passed since Abraham lost his father and still, he was not coping. His father's debts were taking a long time to settle, and without his father's wise guidance to bolster him, Abraham was floating around in nothingness. Untethered. The solid ground his father had forged for him had vanished. It was like walking on a cloud of thick fog. His head was full of dust, empty of rational, focused thought. He did his best to hide it, and so far, it was working. But for how long?

Brunetta continued to make demands upon him. Not sexually. She seemed to be totally uninterested in that side of their marriage. Abraham could not remember the last time he had done it with her. They were as far apart as they could ever be. Strangers sleeping side by side. Her demands were monetary. Whenever he refused her money, it ended in an argument. He would accuse her of being unreasonable, she would tell him he was mean and end it with the usual slur.

'I wish I'd never married you.'

At times Abraham thought the same. He could barely remember the love he once felt for her. His only concern was the

234

child. As long as she looked after him, and Tzuri was happy, Abraham could tolerate her. His son was one year old now and beginning to take on his own personality. He was Abraham's only source of joy. If it wasn't for the child, he didn't know what he would do.

Abraham had taken to hiding in the cellar, rarely venturing out. It was quiet down there and no one disturbed him. No one could ask him awkward questions about the business, so he was surprised when he heard hurried footsteps coming down into the cellar. His brother Benjamin was out of breath when he came bounding in.

'Have you heard?'

'Heard what?'

Abraham loved his brother but his cheeriness, jocularity and zest for life made him feel more depressed than ever.

'The king has been kidnapped.'

Abraham took some time to digest this news.

'Kidnapped,' he asked. 'How can that be? By whom?'

'They say he was returning home from the Crusades when he was shipwrecked.'

'Who says?'

'Everyone is talking about it.'

'Who's everyone?'

Benjamin snorted in frustration. 'It doesn't really matter who. The point is the king has been kidnapped. Come upstairs. I want to tell the others.'

Abraham followed his brother up the cellar steps and into the great hall. Benjamin gathered them round and told them what had happened.

'He landed on the coast of Italy and made his way as far as Vienna. He dressed as a lowly servant to try and evade capture but was betrayed by someone at the inn. Duke Leopold's men arrived and took him prisoner.'

'Who's he?' asked Justelin.

'The Duke of Austria.'

'So, he's not a king.'

'It's like a king. Anyway, he forged an alliance with Henry the Sixth, the Holy Roman Emperor, and they've been holding him in various prisons around Germany.'

'Can they do that to an English king?'

'Apparently.'

'Now they're demanding a ransom before they'll hand him back.'

'How much?' asked Abraham.

'One hundred and fifty thousand marks.'

There was an audible intake of breath as everyone heard Benjamin announce the enormous sum that was being demanded. Abraham had expected as much. The ransom would be paid, and as ever, the Jews would be expected to pay more than their fair share.

'The king's chancellor, Richard Longchamp and his justiciar Walter of Coutances, have been despatched to Germany to negotiate his release.'

'Can't they rescue him?' said Justelin. 'Then we don't have to pay the ransom...'

'Or better still, not pay the ransom, and leave him there,' said Abraham.

'He might as well spend his days in captivity for all the difference it would make to us. He's never here,' said Henne.

'I don't think he's been in England for more than a few days since his coronation,' Arlette added.

Douce said, 'And we all know what happened then. Moses never really recovered from that experience. I swear it's what put him in his early grave.'

Henne put an arm around her mother's shoulder to comfort her.

'I'm sure they'll try to rescue him rather than just pay the ransom. Whatever you think of him, it's outrageous that someone from another country can just kidnap the King of England,' said Zev.

'I'm sure someone's thought of that already. He must be somewhere well defended for them to even consider paying the ransom.'

'They say he's been moved several times to a secret location, so we can't find him,' said Benjamin.

'I bet he's not in the best of moods,' said Justelin, giggling.

'Heads will roll,' said Benjamin, grinning.

'It's not a laughing matter,' snapped Abraham.

The room fell silent, and all eyes were on Abraham.

'Don't you realise we'll have to find the money to pay for this? They will bleed us dry. We'll be ruined.'

Abraham stood rigid, his hands were balled into fists, and he was visibly shaking. His family stared back at him, a sea of shocked faces. He stormed out of the hall and went back down to his cellar.

'What's wrong with him?' Benjamin said.

'He's not well,' said Douce, her face etched with concern. 'He misses his father.'

'Don't we all,' Benjamin said, giving his mother a reproving look.

FIFTY-ONE

Despite his best efforts, Baruch had been unable to locate the king. He could hardly believe that the Duke of Austria had the audacity to kidnap the King of England. It was an outrage. Dispirited and hungry, Baruch finally returned to England six months later.

Whilst away, he had plenty of time to think about his family, particularly his mother. He desperately wanted to see her and apologise for his behaviour. She must have suffered at the hands of Brito. His guts twisted at the thought of how alike he was to his real father, especially when it came to women. Perhaps he owed Brunetta an apology.

When he found himself walking through the South Gate towards The Cross, his stomach was fluttering with nerves. He couldn't quite understand it. He had fought in the fiercest of battles, killed dozens of men and yet he was trembling at the thought of seeing his mother again.

When at last he reached Moses' house, his tabard was sticking to his back with sweat. Tentatively, he opened the door. The smell hit him first. It was of home cooking. The smell of home. As he walked toward the kitchen, he could hear women's voices. He could picture the scene. Douce would be organising everyone. His mother would be making a batch of bread and Henne would be stirring a large pot of something.

As he entered the kitchen, he saw his mother first. She looked exactly as she had done when he left two years ago. He stood and watched them for a few moments. Douce was there, looking old and grey. Henne sat shelling peas in the corner. Brunetta was cradling a child on her hip. The child was about two years old. His hair was jet black and curly. *Could he be mine?* thought Baruch momentarily. Then his mother spotted him.

'Baruch,' she screamed.

Everyone turned to look at him. His mother dropped the spoon she was holding and ran towards him. She threw her arms around him and hugged him for a few long moments before standing back to look at him.

'You look different. Your skin is so brown.'

She touched his cheek and ran her hand over the light-coloured scar he had on his chin, an injury from a Saladin fighter.

'Hello, Mother,' he said, wiping his brow with the back of his hand.

The kitchen was warm and making him hotter than he already was. Douce was next to hug him, then Henne. Brunetta held on to the child and glared at him in sullen silence.

'Where have you been?' Henne asked.

'I've been abroad, fighting with the king.'

'But the king has been kidnapped.'

'I know. I was there.'

There was an audible gasp from the women.

'Tell us all about it, Baruch. How exciting,' said Henne.

Baruch was bombarded with questions about where he'd been, what the king was like, how did he get his scar. So many, in the end, he raised his hands to quieten them.

'Go through to the hall,' Arlette said. 'I'll bring you a drink and some food. You must be hungry.'

Baruch's trepidations at his homecoming were unfounded. His mother could not be happier. He spent the next few hours regaling them with tales of hot sun, turquoise seas and exotic lands. He left out the gorier details of the battles he had fought. Then he told them how the king had been kidnapped, that he'd tried to find him but gave up after months on the road.

'I thought you were looking thinner than when you left,' Arlette said. 'Here, have some more.'

Arlette had prepared a platter of meat, cheese and bread. Baruch had eaten three quarters of it.

'I've had enough. There's more food there than I've seen in months.'

Baruch sat back in his chair, holding on to his stomach, a smile stretched across his face. He had not expected such a warm welcome given the circumstances he left in. The only person not in attendance was Brunetta. She was still angry at him. It was inevitable. He couldn't blame her. He had acted like the vilest of beasts.

'Where are the others?' he asked.

'Abraham is down in the cellar and Zev and Rubin are at the workshop.'

Not much had changed. Rubin and Zev were still working together. Abraham had obviously stepped into the shoes of his father. It seemed odd, though, that Abraham had not ventured out of the cellar when he heard his sister's shrieks. There would be plenty of time to catch up with the others. For now, he was content to sit amongst the women in the family.

He had missed them.

FIFTY-TWO

Baruch was exhausted by all the questions and his long journey from Portchester. He asked his mother if his room was still available, unsure of his status in the family now he was back.

'It is as you left it, Baruch. Don't you want to wait till your father gets home?'

Baruch winced when he heard his mother refer to Zev as his father. Now was not the time to talk to her about it. He was too tired.

'I can see him later. I really need to sleep.'

Arlette hugged him and let him go.

'I'm so happy you're back, Baruch. I've missed you so much,' she said when they reached the bottom of the staircase.

'I've missed you too, *Ima*.'

Baruch kissed his mother on the cheek and climbed the stairs to his room. He had called her '*Ima*', not 'Mother'. He wondered if Arlette had noticed. He hoped so because it was a sign of his deep love for her. It was time he changed and this was a small but not insignificant gesture. There was a comforting familiarity about the house, his room. It was, as she said, just as he had left it, apart from the untidiness. Arlette had cleaned and made his bed. He sunk down into the mattress and shut his eyes. His mind was racing, and he found it hard to sleep. He thought about Brunetta. He had treated her badly. He would apologise when he had a quiet moment with her alone. He wondered if the child was his. How ironic that would be. History repeating itself. He wondered if Brunetta was happy with Abraham. She hadn't looked happy but that was probably more to do with her seeing him than anything else.

It wasn't until his mother flung her arms around him that he realised just how much he had missed her. He was even more ashamed of his behaviour towards her. He wondered about Zev. How would he react to his return? Be openly hostile or welcome him back. Rubin would not be a problem nor, he thought, would Abraham. Not much seemed to have changed since his absence.

Eventually Baruch drifted into a heavy sleep. When he woke up it was early morning. He went downstairs to the kitchen. He had a terrible thirst. When he walked in, he was surprised to see Brunetta sitting there with her son. Alone.

'You're up early,' he said, trying to keep his tone jocular.

Brunetta ignored him and carried on feeding her son some frumenty mixed with eggs.

'Are you not talking to me?' he said, sitting opposite her at the table.

'Why should I?' she snapped back, raising her gaze to glower at him.

Baruch had had a lot of time to think about his behaviour. He swallowed hard.

'I'm sorry,' he said in a quiet voice.

'Pardon?'

'I said I'm sorry.'

'So you should be.'

'I treated you badly, Brunetta. I was angry at everybody even my mother. I took it out on you the last time I saw you.'

Brunetta wiped the dribble from her son's chin.

'What's his name?'

'Tzuri.'

'That's a nice name. It means "your rock".'

'Yes, I know. Abraham chose it.'

Baruch had not seen any of the men of the household yet as he had slept most of the evening. He wondered how their marriage was.

'How is Abraham?'

There was a pause, then Brunetta said, 'He's all right.'

Baruch detected a slight curtness in her reply. It told him she was no happier now than she had been when he left. He studied her. Her figure had filled out a little, but she was still an attractive woman. He noticed the early morning light sifting through the window cast a shimmer through her hair, highlighting the chestnut tones. A surge of desire for her flooded his loins. Like the old times. But he was not the same man. He forced himself to control the burgeoning swelling developing underneath his breeches. He decided that to talk about the child would dampen his ardour.

'How old is he?'

'Almost two.'

Baruch made a quick calculation in his head. The timing was right. He could be his.

'He's not yours if that's what you're thinking.'

'How do you know?'

Brunetta picked up Tzuri and placed him on her lap. She didn't answer him.

'He could be mine...'

'He has too calm a nature to be yours.'

Tzuri gurgled contentedly. He had been fed and seemed

happy to sit on his mother's lap. The child gave Baruch an inquisitive stare. *Does he know who I am?* thought Baruch. *Perhaps he senses I'm his father.*

'There seems to be a pattern developing in this family,' he said, standing up.

'What do you mean?'

'Oh nothing.'

He walked out of the back door to fetch fresh water. When he returned his brother Rubin and Zev were helping themselves to some bread and cheese. Brunetta had left.

The three men stood looking at each other for an uncomfortable few moments. Neither knowing how they should react. Now that Baruch knew Zev had married his mother to protect her honour, he saw him differently. He decided he should be the one to break the ice. He put down the pail and walked towards Zev, put his arms around him and hugged him, patting his back in a manly fashion. Zev hugged him back.

'Son, it is so good to have you home.'

His mother must have told Zev that he knew he wasn't his father, yet Zev addressed him as son. It was time to bury the hatchet.

'*Aba*, it's good to see you.'

Rubin, sensing there would be no tension or argument threw his arms around Baruch.

'It's great to see you, Baruch. I want to hear all about your travels.'

Baruch then spent the next hour retelling his tales from yesterday. The atmosphere was convivial. Something he wasn't used to. When Arlette arrived and saw the three of them talking and jesting amiably, she put her arm around Baruch's neck and kissed him on the cheek. When he was almost finished, Abraham arrived. Baruch could tell immediately he was different. He appeared surly and uncommunicative. When Baruch tried to hug him, Abraham shrugged him off.

'I have business to get on with,' he said, his face scrunched into a scowl. 'I don't have time to waste.'

Abraham grabbed a piece of cheese and bread and left the kitchen by the stone steps that led to the cellar. The room remained silent until they heard him close the door.

'What's up with him?' Baruch asked.

Arlette was putting a pan on to boil. She turned to Baruch.

'He hasn't been the same since Moses died.'

CHAPTER
FIFTY-THREE

Baruch learned later that after his kidnapping at the inn in Erdberg, the king had been passed from stronghold to stronghold in the German-speaking lands controlled by Henry and Leopold. Initially, he had been taken to Durnstein Castle, a stronghold of the Duke's on the banks of the Danube fifty miles to the west of Vienna, then on to Ochsenfurt Castle around March of the following year. This was where two English emissaries – the abbots of Boxley and Robertsbridge – were despatched to begin the long negotiations for his ransom and eventual release. He spent some weeks at Trifels Castle and then back to Ochsenfurt. His mother, Queen Eleanor of Aquitaine, worked tirelessly to raise the ransom, and it had taken almost a year to broker his release. Eventually, the huge ransom of 150,000 marks had been raised and paid, and the king was finally released in early February 1194. He returned to England a month later whereupon a triumphant procession to St Paul's Cathedral was conducted. Baruch had made no attempt to attend. He had been home almost a year and had decided to stay in Gloucester. His fighting days were over but his fighting skills, however, were useful to the sheriff who was his old mentor William Marshal. Baruch became a *skermiseur*, a fencing master. He became known as Baruch le Skermiseur. Others knew him by the less complimentary name of "the personal Jew of Sheriff Marshal". Baruch knew it was meant as a slur, but it mattered not. For the first time in his life, he had discovered his place in life and where he fitted in, and had finally crossed the divide that existed between his community and those of the Christians. Knowing that his father was Christian, his mother a Jew made sense to him now. He knew himself better and the interminable battle in his head, those negative thoughts, the anger, had evaporated and a sense of peace had entered his heart.

Ten days after the procession through London, King Richard convened a meeting to be held in Northampton to put pressure on each Jewish community to pay the 5,000 marks he had imposed upon them as part of the 150,000 marks ransom paid for his release. Every Jew over the age of ten and those who paid taxes had to attend. There would be no exceptions. Baruch was in the great hall when Benjamin arrived to tell them the news. Abraham had been fetched from the cellar for the announcement. Baruch studied his face as he listened to his brother. His expression went from sullen to diabolic as he heard that he was to be taxed and that he had to attend the *donum* at Northampton.

'This is outrageous,' Abraham shouted.

'No need to upset yourself,' Douce said, trying to calm her son.

'It's not enough that the king wants to mulct us to the hilt. He expects us to travel all the way to Northampton for the privilege. It'll take at least a week to travel there. Add on accommodation costs and the journey back.'

Abraham ran his fingers through his hair, now grey at the temples. He looked like he was already adding up in his mind the cost of the journey and the amount of tax he would have to pay.

'We'll have to start making preparations now if we're going to get there by the thirtieth. Isn't it enough that we pay our fair share, but no, he wants more and more. It's never going to stop.'

Baruch had noticed since his return home that the family behaved differently when Abraham was around. Like they were fearful of him.

'What does he want the money for?' Justelin asked.

There was a hint of frustration in Abraham's voice. He looked haunted by some demonic force.

'It's our share of the ransom.'

'And an unfair share at that.'

'He's not pleased we haven't paid it all.'

'It does seem odd that the sheriff can't collect the tax like he has in the past,' Douce said, giving Abraham a concerned look.

Abraham raised his voice. 'We just paid a ransom of 150,000 marks. He expects us each to pay 5,000 more. If that's not unfair, what is?'

'That's why he needs the money. His royal coffers are empty.'

'Huh,' Abraham scoffed. 'And he expects us Jews to bail him out – again. What kind of a king is he? Bleeding his subjects dry? You can't get blood from a corpse.'

Abraham shot a menacing glare at his brother as if Benjamin were personally responsible for the king's excesses.

'Don't blame me,' Benjamin said, his shoulders raised in a shrug, adding, 'he probably needs it for his fight against the French king, Philippe the Second.'

'But he's only just been released from captivity and already he's planning on going to war – again.'

'Wars cost money. They say he needs 300 ships to sail to Normandy.'

Abraham did not answer him. He stormed out of the hall and disappeared back into his cellar. The room fell silent. Baruch looked at his grandmother. She was staring after her son, a worried look upon her face and fidgeting nervously with her wedding ring. Baruch turned to look at Brunetta. She had Tzuri on her lap and was humming a song to him and rocking him back and forth.

LATER THAT DAY Baruch set off to the castle. On his way there he spotted Brunetta at The Cross. She had been avoiding him since he arrived home and they had hardly had a moment alone. She was walking on her own without her son. Baruch watched her as she walked ahead of him remembering her willowy figure and the familiar sway of her hips. He hurried to catch up to her.

'Where are you off to?' he asked her.

Brunetta jumped and stopped abruptly.

'Sorry, I didn't mean to startle you.'

'I'm not used to being accosted in the street.'

'Where is Tzuri?'

'He's at home with Douce. She's looking after him.'

'So where are you going on your own?'

Brunetta hesitated for a second. 'Not that it's any of your business but I'm going to visit my mother.'

'Ah, and how is the lovely Abigail?'

'She's not lovely and she's not well.'

'I'm sorry to hear that.'

'No, you're not.'

Brunetta carried on walking. Baruch pulled at her arm to halt her. They had stopped by Maverdine Lane. He guided her into the narrow alleyway.

'You have a very poor opinion of me.'

'Justified, don't you think?'

'Look, I've already apologised. What else do you want me to do?'

Something flashed in her eyes. Baruch was pleasantly shocked when he detected a hint of longing there. Could she still want him after all that had happened between them?

'Are you happy with Abraham, Brunetta?'

She glared at him. 'I don't wish to discuss my marriage with you.'

'What have you done to him? He's a nervous wreck. He does nothing but sit in the cellar all day and chew his nails. He visibly shakes when you try to talk to him.'

'I'm not the cause of that.'

'Are you happy with him?'

Brunetta turned her face away.

'Are you happy, Brunetta?'

'What would you know about happiness?'

Her tone was bitter. Her eyes welled with tears. Baruch had never seen her show any emotion toward him except hatred or lust. Something inside him softened toward her. He reached out and wiped away the single tear that had spilled from her eyelid. She flinched.

'Is Abraham good to you?'

'He is indifferent to me.'

'You're not the kind of woman who should be treated like that. You need comfort. You need love.'

Brunetta gave him a confused look.

'I know you think me incapable of love, but I have changed, Brunetta. I've grown up since I've been away, found out things about myself.'

'You aren't the same person that left us. I have noticed that.'

'You've been avoiding me.'

'I have a little.'

'Are you afraid of me?'

'A bit.'

'I'm the same Baruch I always was, just nicer.'

Brunetta gave a weak smile. He was bringing her round to him.

'You know the funny thing is I still have feelings for you.'

'I'm not interested in those kinds of feelings. I've also grown up, Baruch.'

'Can we agree to be friends?'

She smiled. This time it was an engaging smile. Then she nodded. Baruch leant towards her and kissed her cheek, then the other and once more. He had seen French men and women make this gesture of friendship. She smelled divine. Of rose petals and jasmine. He gave her a hug. She let him. The stirring of desire rose up within him. Since his return he had not frequented the whorehouse in Three Cocks Lane, and he had no desire to. He pulled himself away, worried that he would take things too far and the ground he had gained with her would be lost.

'I'll see you later at supper?' he said, walking away from her and crossing to the other side of the street, ducking into Foxes Lane, taking the shortcut towards the castle.

CHAPTER

FIFTY-FOUR

Since the summons to attend the *donum* at Northampton the whole of the Jewish community was plunged into a frenzy of activity to prepare for the long journey. A *bet din* had been called to discuss the *donum* and to make the necessary arrangements. It was decided that they would travel together, for safety reasons. They set off a few days later like a band of troubadours in a travelling show. When Abraham arrived at Northampton, he was exhausted and in one of his worst moods. The journey had been arduous and the lack of privacy and the constant requirement to be sociable had taken its toll on him. He would have preferred to stay at home in his cellar. Still, he was thankful there had been no vagabonds on the road to rob them.

As he approached the West Gate leading into the town he took in the imposing motte and bailey castle on the banks of the River Nen where the *donum* would be held. It was much bigger than the castle at Gloucester. He had arranged to stay in the Jewry in the communal buildings set aside for such visits. With him were his brothers, Benjamin and Justelin, and his brother-in-law, Vives. Justelin had just turned twelve and yet, because he was considered a taxpayer from the age of eleven, he had been required to attend.

They made their way along Drapery Street turning into Sheep Street where the Jewry could be found. They were stared at by the Christian community of Northampton as if they had never seen a Jewish person before. They had probably never seen so many at one time, thought Abraham as he walked along, his head bowed to avoid their gaze. A small gathering of Jews were standing outside the synagogue. He recognised one or two from his visits to London with his father. Several Jewish magnates were in attendance, the major ones being Jacob le Vieil of Canterbury and Deulesault Episcopus of London.

There was a notable and tragic absence from anyone representing the York community. This brought back horrendous memories for Abraham. Scenes from that massacre came flooding back and the uncontrollable sweating and trembling and the jangling of every nerve in his body returned. He made his excuses and left the group, wandering down to the river for some peace and quiet, telling Justelin and Benjamin he would return soon.

On his return Abraham noticed Mirabelle and Elias talking to the brothers Abraham and Judas Gabbai of Bristol.

Abraham despised Mirabelle. He wondered what scheme she was cooking up now. Abraham Gabbai was the treasurer of Bristol's Jewish community and as such was an important and powerful man.

Mirabelle had been quiet since King Richard's return. Abraham had heard she had supported Prince John whilst the king was incarcerated in Germany then withdrew her support when the king's ransom was paid. Mirabelle, mercurial as ever, simply switched her allegiance back to Richard and with luck on her side Richard forgave his brother. Mirabelle, once again, came out of the situation smelling of roses or as his mother's good friend Bellassez used to say, 'That Mirabelle. If she fell into a cesspit, she'd come out smelling of rosemary.'

They were huddled in a closely formed group. *No doubt plotting something*, thought Abraham, *knowing Elias*. He liked to appear as the more trustworthy partner to Mirabelle, but Abraham had never trusted or liked him. He was like a silent snake hiding behind his formidable wife. He wondered what they could be talking about. He decided to walk past them. As he did so Elias looked up, noticed him and coughed loudly to silence the group.

'*Shalom alaichem*, Abraham,' Elias said. 'You know the Gabbai brothers Abraham and Judas?'

'*Alaichem shalom*,' Abraham greeted them. 'We've never met but I recognise you from my travels with my father.'

Mirabelle stood, tight-lipped, barely acknowledging Abraham's presence.

'Ah yes, we were sorry to hear of your father's passing. He was a great man.'

A hard lump lodged in Abraham's throat as he thought of his father. He missed him as keenly now as he did the day he died. He swallowed hard, desperately trying to hide his emotions. 'Thank you,' was all he could manage. He nodded a communal goodbye, and like a small child lost and bewildered amongst a sea of people he hurried on to the synagogue where he hoped to find solace and gather his thoughts. To his dismay, rather than find the synagogue empty, it was full of jostling Jews from all around the country. He nodded politely as he passed by people he recognised. Finally, he found a bench to sit on in a quiet corner. When he sat down, he realised his heart was racing and his palms were clammy.

~

THAT EVENING ABRAHAM joined his brothers at a communal reception that Jacob, the leader of the Northampton Jewry, had arranged. A conversation struck up with Isaac of Stamford and it turned out he knew Abigail, Brunetta's mother.

'You're married to Brunetta. She was a pretty little thing. Shame what happened to her parents.'

Isaac was getting on in years and liked a drink. Abraham poured him another goblet of wine. He was keen to learn more about his wife's family. He remembered the comments in York about a scandalous divorce.

'What happened?'

'Messy business. Ysaac found Abigail in bed with another man. There was no denying it. Such a scandal.'

Abraham could not imagine the woman he knew as Abigail being found in a compromising situation.

'Are you sure we're talking about the same Abigail?'

'I believe so. She had a son called Josce.'

It must be the same family. Glorietta was much younger than Brunetta. Was she a half-sister to Brunetta? Born out of wedlock? No wonder Abigail never spoke about her husband, telling everyone she was a widow when, in fact, she was an adulteress. Abraham thought of Brunetta with bitterness. Was she a liar and an adulteress like her mother? Is that what Baruch meant about not looking over his shoulder? A noxious bile filled his throat, he hawked and spat on the ground.

The conversation turned to the king's soon-to-be-introduced system called the *Scaccarium Judaeorum* – or Exchequer of the Jews.

'It's a natural development from the *Scaccorium Aaronis* set up after our good brother Aaron of Lincoln died. The king has nearly exhausted the spoils from that venture, now he needs to find another source of income,' argued Abraham Gabbai.

'Since the massacres across the country and the burning of the deeds of debts due to us Jews, the king has suffered a considerable loss,' said Jacob.

'At our expense,' said Abraham, giving Jacob an accusatory stare.

Abraham did not appreciate Jacob's tone. It seemed he was defending the king's actions. They were traitorous words.

'I didn't say I agreed with the king,' Jacob replied defensively.

'I hope not,' muttered Abraham.

He flashed a dark look at the faces around the table. They all seemed to be staring at him. There was a slight lull in the conversation. Abraham dropped his gaze, aware they were staring at him, and uncomfortable at his outburst.

'I've heard there's going to be a whole new way of recording every loan we transact, doing away with the tally sticks and using parchment chirographs that are to be stored in a locked chest and involving Christian key keepers,' Jacob said.

'Can we trust them?' Abraham asked, his head thrust up sharply on hearing the word 'Christian'.

'I doubt we'll be given a choice,' said Benjamin.

'What's a chirograph?' asked Justelin.

'It's a written contract to prove to all parties the amount of the loan,' replied Abraham, his brother.

'Does that mean people like Richard Malebyisse won't be able to burn down synagogues like he did in York looking for tally sticks to destroy?' said Isaac of Stamford, pouring himself another cup of wine.

'It's designed to stop forgery. Whether it will or not is to be seen,' said Abraham Gabbai, ignoring Isaac's reference to the burning of Jewish debts.

~

THE NEXT MORNING, he walked to the castle with his brothers. He had spent a sleepless night despite feeling weary. All he wanted now was to attend the *donum*, pay his dues and go home. Back to his quiet, cold cellar.

They entered the castle by the imposing barbican entrance at the North Gate. It was heavily guarded, and Abraham was again reminded of the tower in York and the scenes therein. Inside the inner ward ahead of him stood the tall square keep and to his left the great hall. The castle was a hive of activity. Separate huts existed for stonemasons, blacksmiths and carpenters. A stable block with horses and kennels for hunting dogs stood against the high stone wall of the bailey. The sounds of horses nickering, dogs barking mixed with the sound of blacksmith's hammers and the chiselling of stone and the sawing of wood. The scent of roasted meats wafted across the inner ward. The scene was so far removed from his own insular world of cellar and synagogue. A trail of Jewish moneylenders led from the barbican to the great hall, all clutching chests and money bags, their distinctive garb contrasting with that of the soldiers and workmen.

Once inside the great hall Abraham was corralled into a corner with the rest of his community representing Gloucester. The other communities were similarly grouped. Those from Northampton were called forth first. Jacob and his daughter, Pucelle, were first to be called. Jacob stood before a long table at which sat Willem de Buking. He was a man of solid proportions with a hard stare, brought in by the king to manage his taxes with an iron hand. His large hands gripped the quill and as each taxpayer stood in front of him, he would look up and give them a look that said he was not to be trifled with. In front of him was a long roll of parchment and a well of ink. Jacob emptied the contents of his chest onto the table. Willem directed his clerks to count the amount. Once counted and rechecked he noted the amount onto the roll of parchment, beckoning the next. A long queue had formed. Abraham let out a deep sigh. It was going to be a long day.

CHAPTER

FIFTY-FIVE

Baruch had spent the last few days with Douce, Arlette and Henne whilst Zev and Rubin spent most of the day out of the house. Baruch was enjoying the company of women. He loved being pampered, waited upon, listened to. It was a far cry from the battlefield. His every want was tended to from sweetmeats to glasses of fine Gascony wine. The only downside was his widening waist. Perhaps it was just his age. He was now in his late twenties and expected to be married with children of his own. His mother had given up on him and never mentioned it. Since their truce, Brunetta had still been avoiding him and spent most days at her mother's.

What he needed right now was some energetic exercise to keep him in shape and it wasn't fencing. The one thing he had his mind upon most days was lying with Brunetta. He thought he had got her out of his system but as soon as he returned and particularly when she looked at him a certain way, those lustful feelings for her came back. They weren't the destructive, base feelings he used to have for her, or most women for that matter. It was a different kind of lust. He hadn't experienced feeling like this ever. Had he misinterpreted her looks? He was eager to find out.

The family were out at a community event that evening. Everyone would be there. Would Brunetta attend? She rarely involved herself in family occasions. Perhaps this evening would give him a chance to talk to her again. Alone.

Baruch stayed in his room until he heard the last of his family leave the house. Brunetta was not with them. He gave it a few more moments before he raised himself off his bed and made his way to Abraham's bedroom. He listened at the door. It was quiet. He knocked. There was silence. He took hold of the latch and opened the door. Brunetta lay asleep on her bed, a thin blanket covering her. Tzuri was in his cot on the other side of the room. He tiptoed towards him to get a closer look. The child had thick, black curly hair. He was asleep but something in his expression reminded him of himself. He could not shake the nagging feeling that the boy was his. Brunetta stirred in her sleep. The noise was breathy and sensual. He crept towards her and looked down at her reclined and vulnerable body. Her skin was an olive colour and she reminded him a little of the exotic women who followed the soldier's camp, selling their bodies to any taker. He leant over to sweep back a tendril of hair from her cheek. As soon as he touched her skin Brunetta opened her eyes wide. She looked a little startled at first, then closed her eyes and gave out a soft purr. Baruch had an overwhelming desire to kiss her. On the lips. He bent down and placed his lips on hers. They were soft. He kissed her gently. Just the one tender kiss. As he pulled away from her, he felt her hand on the back of his neck gently pulling him back towards her. He kissed her again and this time she responded. The kiss lasted a long time. He was lost inside her embrace. He threw back the blanket revealing her curvaceous body and began kissing her in places he had never kissed a woman before. Her neck, her clavicle, her breasts, between her thighs. Her moans grew louder. At one point Tzuri stirred in his cot. She ignored the child and he fell back to sleep. Her back arched to his touch, his kisses. He waited until she drew him to her. They kissed again until he could not restrain himself a moment longer. Their lovemaking lasted an eternity. Unlike the other times, it was loving, tender, full of passion, not lust.

When it was over, he kissed her again. Her eyes were closed. Not a word had been exchanged. He lay by her side and put his arm across her stomach. They lay like that, relaxed and breathless. Baruch was overcome with a warm, contented sensation. He did not want to move.

'I've wanted to do that since I came home.'

'I've thought about it,' she said, shuffling into a more comfortable position.

She was on her side, her back arched into his groin. He kissed the back of her neck. She reached her hand back and ran her fingers through his hair.

'You've changed,' she said.

'Why do you say that?'

'You never would have lain with me like this before you went away. I tried to kiss you so many times, but you always turned your face away.'

Baruch let out a snort of laughter. 'I wasn't a very nice person, was I?'

'You weren't very nice to me.'

'But now I'm making up for it,' he said, feeling his hardness press against Brunetta's soft flesh.

'What are we going to do?'

'Can't you tell,' he said, pressing against her.

'Not that,' she said, responding to his move by pushing her backside toward him.

Baruch turned her onto her back and brushed the hair from

her face.

'Do you mean Abraham?'

'Yes,' she sighed. 'Abraham.'

CHAPTER

FIFTY-SIX

W hen it was Abraham's turn he strode up to the table and held Willem de Buking's hard stare. He wasn't sure where this sudden surge of bravado had come from. He had been stewing in the corner on the unfairness of it all. The whole of the English community of Jews were virtually being held to ransom in this great hall at the king's whim. If the king hadn't been stupid enough to get himself captured, if he bothered to spend more time in the country he was king of, maybe Abraham wouldn't be standing there like a raging but compliant bull waiting to hand over money he didn't want to hand over. If it were up to him the king could have stayed in Germany. They could have him. He wondered if Willem could read his thoughts. If he could, he would be strung on the highest turrets of Northampton castle and made an example of.

'And you are?' Willem asked.

'I am Abraham, son and heir of Moses le Riche. These are my brothers, Benjamin and Justelin.' As he said this, his brothers stepped forward.

'Ah, the great Moses le Riche of Gloucester.'

Abraham detected a note of sarcasm in his voice. He took affront.

'My father built up a successful business and provided for his family. Many of your associates would be nowhere without his ready source of hard cash. In the same way the king would be now without our resources, which I might add are not limitless.'

Willem stared hard at Abraham. The corner of his lip curled.

'You dare speak harshly of the king?' Willem roared.

Abraham was rendered momentarily speechless by the man's gruff voice. He realised that inadvertently the words he was thinking had come out of his mouth. He hadn't intended them to. Benjamin stepped nearer.

'Sire, my brother meant no disrespect. He has had a tiring journey and has not been well of late.'

'That's no excuse,' Willem replied tersely. 'What is your promise today?' he said to Abraham.

Abraham replied, 'One hundred and five marks.'

Willem did not reply. Abraham opened his father's chest and tipped the coins onto the table. He counted them and then they were rechecked by de Buking's clerks. While they were counting de Buking studied Abraham, his eyes narrowing. Abraham watched as he entered the words *De Heredibus Mosse de Gloucester*. Writing the numbers in Roman numerals he ended the entry with the words *pro eodem*, in Latin, meaning 'the same'.

Abraham gave out a sigh of relief. It was over.

'Arrest him,' Willem shouted to his guards.

There was a metallic jangle as his men drew their swords and a thudding of boots as they swooped towards Abraham, accompanied by an audible gasp from those gathered in the hall. Benjamin shielded his brother. Abraham was wild-eyed with fear.

'What for?' Benjamin shouted, incredulity rising in his voice.

'For speaking against the king,' Willem answered, motioning to his men to take Abraham away.

Abraham was flanked either side by the guards, each holding on to his arms.

'Wait, you can't do that. He didn't say anything.'

'He said enough.'

CHAPTER

FIFTY-SEVEN

Brunetta lay in bed after Baruch's visit somewhat baffled about what had happened but also not entirely unhappy about it. She hadn't lain with Abraham since the birth of Tzuri. He seemed to have gone off it since the death of his father. Brunetta had been relieved. There was something else about Abraham that concerned her. He had become more morose and lately had not been interested in his son. That was unusual as Tzuri, in Abraham's eyes, had been a gift from Hashem. She had thought him a little crazed when he returned from York and told her about the vision of his son and wanting to get married so soon. She had her own reasons for wanting to marry earlier than planned, so she went along with it.

If only Baruch had been like he was now, back then. Maybe she would have married him. Maybe he would have wanted to marry her. Why was everything in life upside down or the wrong way around? Life was so unfair. Why was she lumbered with a morose and complaining, verging on boring, husband? She should have married Baruch. He was handsome, beguiling, sexy. She turned onto her side. Her legs were still trembling from the pleasure. He had been so tender, so attentive. She wondered what could have happened to make him change so towards her. Now she thought about it he was nicer to everyone, including his father Zev.

If it wasn't for Abraham's sullen moods, life in the le Riche household would be bearable. More than bearable.

Her thoughts turned to how she would react when she saw Baruch again. She had been avoiding him as much as she could since his return. Now she wanted to see him. To lie with him in bed naked and kiss his lips and other parts of him. She would need to be careful. Douce was a wily old fox and would sniff out any hint of infidelity, particularly when it concerned her precious son Abraham.

Like a biblical revelation, Brunetta realised how unhappy she had become. How utterly miserable she was. It was time to change. She needed loving and that is exactly what she got from Baruch. For the first time ever an intense feeling of happiness mixed with excitement enveloped her. She felt the need to pleasure herself, something she hadn't done in a long time.

THE NEXT MORNING Brunetta rose early. Tzuri had woken her up and for once she was happy to greet his chubby, smiling face. She lifted him from the cot. He was getting heavier by the day. She studied him. There was a look of Baruch in him. Could he be his and not Abraham's? Rather than the thought giving rise to disgust, this time she entertained the possibility.

She crept downstairs hoping to see Baruch in the kitchen. There he was. Had he been waiting for her?

'How are you feeling this morning?' he asked.

She blushed. 'I feel very well, and you?'

'A little confused.'

'Why?'

'Last night. I hadn't meant that to happen. I wasn't...'

'I know you weren't looking to do what you usually do.'

She sat Tzuri down at the table on his chair and began to prepare some warm frumenty. Tzuri looked from her to Baruch with a child's inquisitiveness, his large eyes wide and unknowing. He looked like he was trying to understand their conversation.

'It's a good job he can't understand what we're saying,' she said, stirring the pot of frumenty.

'It won't be long and then we'll be in trouble.'

Brunetta laughed. 'I think we're already in trouble.'

Baruch stood up and went to her. He put his arms around her waist and kissed the back of her neck. The feel of his lips on her neck was delightful and sent tingles down her spine. She turned to look at Tzuri. He had a quizzical look upon his face.

'He's wondering what's going on. I don't think he's ever seen me being loving with his father.'

'Is he his father?'

Brunetta turned around to look at Baruch. His look was a searching one, a needy look almost.

'I don't know.'

Baruch let go of her and went over to Tzuri. A wooden toy lay on the table. Baruch picked it up and gave it to him. Within minutes Tzuri had dropped it. Baruch picked it up again. This happened several times.

'You don't know much about children, do you?' she said, pouring Tzuri's breakfast into a bowl and setting it before him.

'Not really. I know more about men and war.'

Tzuri went to put his hands in the sticky frumenty. Brunetta placed the spoon in his hand, but he wasn't interested in it.

'Do you want to feed him?'

Brunetta held out a spoon to him. Baruch looked at it as if he'd never seen a spoon before, then took it and began to feed

Tzuri. Tzuri seemed to take this new person in his stride. He was hungry and Baruch was finding it hard to keep up with his need for more spoonfuls. Brunetta watched them together. If anyone who didn't know them could see them now, they would think they were a normal family. Man, wife and firstborn.

Douce walked into the kitchen. She took in the scene and her mouth tightened.

'You're up early this morning, Baruch.'

She gave her usual terse nod at Brunetta.

'Morning, *Safta*,' Baruch said, rising from his seat and kissing her on the cheek.

He handed his grandmother the spoon.

'You can take over now.'

CHAPTER

FIFTY-EIGHT

They released Abraham the very next day from his gaol inside the circular turret of Northampton castle. He was cold, bedraggled and unbearably surly. Willem de Buking had only meant to teach him a lesson rather than punish him for which Abraham was most grateful. He now knew how his father felt when the sheriff locked him inside Gloucester Castle. Moses had never seemed quite the same. A sadness overcame him at the thought of how he was not able to protect his father from such an indignity. On the way home, Benjamin tried to engage him in conversation and make light of the situation, but he just grunted.

'It's usually me saying the wrong things about the king. Wait till *Ima* hears what happened to you. She'll be shocked.'

'Just shut up,' he snapped back.

After that, the journey home was long, arduous and silent.

That was some months ago and now they were back in Gloucester and Abraham was back into his routine. Since the *donum*, the king had issued an Ordinance to the Jews that set out the various conditions. It stated:

All the debts, pledges, mortgages, lands, houses, rents, and possessions of the Jews shall be registered. The Jew who shall conceal any of these shall forfeit to the King his body and the thing concealed, and likewise all his possessions and chattels, neither shall it be lawful to the Jew to recover the thing concealed.

When Abraham read this, he flew into a rage. Not only did the king want his money, if he didn't have it the king would take his body. The odds were stacked against him. There was no way out. He would haemorrhage money in the form of legal taxation. He had to do something. He had already paid a substantial sum of money to appease the king at the *donum*, leaving him short. His only course of action was to call in the debts owed to his father.

As predicted at the *donum* a new system of *archa* had been introduced. Only certain towns and cities in England had been chosen to house the chest. One of them was Gloucester.

The chest had arrived in the city a few days ago and was being kept in the castle under the supervision of the sheriff, William Marshal. It was a very large wooden chest, heavily fortified with metal casings and the biggest, most complicated locking mechanism Abraham had ever seen. Not just one lock but three independent metal locks. As it was the first of the chirographs to be placed in the chest under the new system, the chest was accompanied by the king's clerks, William of Sainte-Mère-Église, the Church of St Mary and William de Chimillé. No contract could be drawn up without the presence of these two clerks, two appointed Christians and two appointed Jews.

The idea was that once the contract had been drawn up then it would be torn into two pieces. One piece would remain with the creditor, usually the Jewish moneylender and the other part would remain in the chest. The keys were to be kept by the parties. The Jews, the Christians and the king's clerks.

Abraham could not see how this could possibly work in practical terms as it would require the two clerks to be constantly moving around the British Isles whenever a chirograph had to be drawn up or amended in any way. Nevertheless, they had complied with the new arrangements. Abraham and Elias de Glocestre were the appointed Jews, Abbot Thomas Carbonel and his deputy Henry Blunt had been appointed as the Christian officiants. The contract had to be written out twice on a single parchment which then had through it the Latin word *chirographum* written between the copies. The document was then to be cut in a simple zigzag, through the word *chirographum* and each party was to be given a piece of the original. Later, by aligning the pieces like a simple puzzle, anyone who wished to contest the authenticity of the contract would be able to do so.

Abraham stood in the chamber of the castle staring at the huge chest. He had prepared the parchment chirograph earlier in the quiet of his father's cellar. Writing in Latin, not Hebrew, and using his father's quill and ink he had written in bold capitals:

CHYROGRAPHUM: ABRAHE: FILII: MOSSEI

THE CHIROGRAPH OF ABRAHAM, SON OF MOSES LE RICHE, OF GLOUCESTER

Abraham produced it from the small wooden chest his father had used, unfurled it and placed it on the wooden table in front of the abbot and his scribe. He had written the usual acquittal formula 'From the day the world was created' but instead of using the phrase 'till the end of the world' he had written a precise date, *the seventeenth of Elul 4955*, 17 September 1195. This had given the abbot very little time to get his hands on the money Abraham so desperately needed. No doubt his father would have dealt with matters differently. Moses had always had good relations with the Christians, especially the abbots who were a constant source of good business. But Abraham was beyond the niceties of sound business relations. He was a desperate man. So desperate, he would cross anyone to get what he needed. The desperation was gnawing away at his insides, making him behave irrationally. The chirograph acquittance showed that the abbot and convent of St Peter's Abbey had been released from the debt obligation to Moses by paying it in full. Abraham had no choice but to call in the debt. The abbot was not happy about it as they had suffered great losses themselves as the abbey's sacred chalices and silver vessels had been sold for Richard's ransom. But what else could he do? He had a family to support.

In the final section of his charter, Abraham had written an unusual variation on the standard clause. The standard clause was designed to protect beneficiaries from subsequent claims. However, Abraham changed it, stating that 'he is prepared to defend his chirograph even if the sons and daughters and other Jews come from the four parts of the world carrying the seal of the abbot and convent under my father's name'.

Abraham's hand was shaking as he signed the document, his brow beaded with sweat.

Abbot Carbonel approached the table with an awkward stiffness. He took the quill handed to him by his scribe and signed below Abraham's name. Abraham then produced his father's seal from the chest. He pushed the seal into the melting wax and attached it with a thin strip of parchment on which was written:

Omnibus Christi fidelibus

(To all the faithful of Christ who shall see or hear this present writing.)

CHAPTER

FIFTY-NINE

W hen Abraham returned home, the smell of freshly baked *challah* and *cholent* wafted down the hallway from the kitchen. He heard his mother and sister, Henne, chatting in the kitchen preparing for the start of Shabbat that evening. The sounds and smells in the house brought back happy childhood memories when his father was alive. He saw him sitting at the head of the table, a glass of wine in his hand, a benevolent smile upon his face, his chest swelling with pride as he looked around the table at his family.

What had become of that family? He no longer felt part of it.

The sound of Brunetta's laughter coming from the great hall jarred on his nerves. He wondered what she was so happy about. He couldn't remember the last time he had heard her laugh. Perhaps it was his fault. He should be more like his father and show some affection for his wife. She didn't deserve his sullen moods, nor did his son. He could hear Tzuri chuckling and squealing with delight at something. He decided to go and join them instead of scuttling off to the cellar like he usually did.

When he walked into the hall, he was met with a scene that

looked like a happy family. Tzuri was on Baruch's lap, Brunetta was sewing what looked like a small garment for Tzuri. They were laughing just like a married couple. The words of Isaac of Stamford rang in his ears. *Adulteress.* Baruch's words on his wedding day. *Fidelity.* That he needed to look over his shoulder to constantly check on Brunetta's fidelity. He had dismissed the comment at the time and put it down to Baruch's mischievous character. On reflection he probably dismissed it because he was so blind with love for Brunetta. The love blindness was long gone and so was the love he had for her.

In that instant he knew she had been unfaithful – and with Baruch – right under his nose. How long had it been going on? Years. Now his attention was drawn to his son. Was he actually his? There was a resemblance to Baruch now he looked for it.

'Are you all right, Abraham?' Baruch asked.

Abraham realised he had been staring at them. He noticed Brunetta fumble with the sewing on her lap and her cheeks flush as if she had been caught out.

'Abraham,' she said. 'What's wrong?'

Abraham did not speak. He turned around and left, heading for the cellar.

Once inside his place of sanctuary he tried to clear his head. His heart was racing, and the trembling of his limbs had returned. His palms were clammy, his breath laboured. An uncontrollable hatred for Brunetta was rising from somewhere deep inside him. He loathed her, felt nothing but disgust for her. He was killing himself trying to keep things going to provide for her and that brat wasn't even his. What a fool he had become, cuckolded in his own home, under his own nose. Who knew? Did they all know except him? Surely his mother would have said something if she suspected anything. Perhaps she was in on it too. Perhaps they all were. Laughing at him behind his back.

Abraham spent the rest of the day in the cellar, consumed by dark, murderous thoughts. Only when his mother called down the stone steps did he realise it was time for the Shabbat meal. He made his way up to his bedroom, to the bedroom he shared with his wife. The room was empty. He quickly dressed for Shabbat and went downstairs. A coldness, like hard steel, seeped into his heart as he sat down at the table. Since the death of Moses he had taken the place of his father at the head of the table. Douce still lit the candles and said the blessings like she had done when Moses was alive. The ritual had been performed countless times in that hall with those people. His family. Brunetta sat with Tzuri next to Henne. Baruch sat opposite them. He watched their faces. Would they give themselves away by a look, a smile, a gesture? He was on to them now. They would not get away with it.

Douce concluded the blessing.

'Blessed are You, who sanctifies Shabbat. *Amein.*'

They gave each other the customary greeting of wishing peace on the Sabbath.

'*Shabbat Shalom.*'

Abraham watched Brunetta. As she spoke the greeting to Baruch, she gave him a coy smile and when she saw Abraham watching her, she dropped her gaze, and the smile was replaced by a guilty look. Abraham sat through the meal in silence whilst his family talked, laughed and drank wine. They were all in on it. All of them.

That night, Abraham went to bed determined to have his conjugal rights. He had not bothered Brunetta in that way in such a long time. He could not remember the last time they had been intimate. He made sure he was in bed early, before her. He had taken to staying in the cellar until the family had retired for the night. That way he could avoid them and Brunetta. Tonight would be different.

Tzuri lay asleep in his cot. When Brunetta opened the bedroom door she gasped.

'Surprised to see me?' he said, a sarcastic tone creeping into his voice.

'No. Why would I be?'

She crossed to the window and began to undress. He had not seen her naked for such a long time. She had her back to him, and it was obvious she was trying to hide from him.

'Turn around,' he said. 'I want to see you.'

Brunetta's head swung round, and she gave him a pained look.

'What's the matter? Can't a husband admire his wife's attributes?'

He saw Brunetta squirm, but she didn't reply. She undressed, leaving on her shift.

'Take it off,' Abraham said. 'I want to see you.'

'Don't be silly, you see me every day,' she said, moving with speed to the edge of the bed and lifting the bedclothes. She jumped in beside him, keeping to her side of the bed.

'Goodnight,' she said, turning her back on him and curling into a foetal position.

Abraham was aroused. Half by his boldness with her, half by his jealousy. He turned on his side and pressed himself against her. He was surprised at how hard he had become. He hadn't been able to get an erection since his father died. His sole desire was to take Brunetta and go where another had been. Brunetta pushed him away.

'I'm tired, Abraham. Go to sleep.'

'I'm not tired at all.'

He lifted her shift up and pressed his member in between her buttock cheeks. She squirmed and tried to get away, but Abraham was having none of it. Desire, jealousy and hatred when mixed together was a powerful thing. He turned her over face down and pressed her face to the bed. She struggled. He found that even more erotic. He was like a man possessed with the sinfulness of the devil. When it was over Brunetta was sobbing into the mattress. He lay on his back, sated, with a triumphant smile.

When Abraham woke the next day Brunetta was gone. He lay in bed and thought about his options. Divorce was out of the question. Not in the le Riche family.

He decided to buy a length of thick rope.

CHAPTER

SIXTY

I t seemed rather fitting to Abraham that he should choose the same religious holiday exactly five years ago when Baruch had warned him about his wife.

He had thought about it constantly since Shabbat. The rope had been purchased and was secreted in his cellar. The family would be in the courtyard after the synagogue service and celebrating. There would be noise and chatter, and no one would notice his absence. He would sneak the rope upstairs and later tie it securely to the exposed beams in his bedroom.

In the synagogue he sat with his brothers. As the rabbi droned on, Abraham occasionally threw a glance at the two women in his life. Douce was steadfast, reliable. A small woman with the strength of a lion. Henne was a simple, loving woman. She was happily married to Vives, and they had four children now. He was happy for her. His mother had an air of sadness about her. She was lost without Moses. He had been her rock. He had been his. But now there was to be a new chapter in his life. One that he was in control of.

'The night is far gone, and the day is near. Let's therefore throw off the works of darkness, and let's put on the armour of light.'

That signalled the end of the service and the time to celebrate. September had been unusually warm and sunny this year with calm, balmy evenings. The courtyard looked lovely with the candles in their sconces, the food laid out on the table.

'Play the kinnor for me, Henne,' he said to his sister.

She smiled at him and went over to his grandfather's old stringed instrument. She placed it on her lap and began to pluck at the strings. Bellassez, his mother's friend, joined her and sang along to the haunting tune. He allowed himself to relax. He'd almost forgotten how to. His muscles seemed to be as tight as the strings of the kinnor. It was hard to relax. All his troubles would be over soon. No more worries about money. No more pressure. No nothing. He took another sip of his father's wine. It was the last of the barrel. He hadn't ordered any more.

He looked around the courtyard for Brunetta. She wasn't there. Where was she? With Baruch? The wine and the thought of the end of his troubles were having the right effect on him. He found he didn't care where she was. He had made his plans and in doing so had made peace with himself. He looked down at his hands clasping the goblet of wine. They were not trembling. A strange calmness has descended upon him.

'It's so good to see you joining in and relaxed, Abraham.'

His mother had come to join him. She looked tired and grey. Her slim figure and her fine bone structure belied her age. He gave her a hug and kissed her on the cheek.

'I've had a lot on my mind but it's all coming together now, *Ima*. Everything is going to be fine.'

'I'm relieved to hear that. I've been worried about you.'

'No need to worry about me. I'm fine.'

Abraham gazed ahead of him into the distance.

CHAPTER

SIXTY-ONE

braham remained in the courtyard till everyone left. He helped his mother clear away the food, then kissed her goodnight. Brunetta had already retired for the night. Baruch had not been seen. Perhaps he was back to his old life, whoring in Three Cocks Lane. How would Brunetta feel about that? No emotions of jealousy were stirred by these thoughts. They were just thoughts.

When he opened his bedroom door, the house was quiet. Brunetta was asleep as was Tzuri. Very carefully he set the heavy rope he had retrieved from the cellar on the floor and placed a stool underneath the central rafter. He took one end of the rope and stepped onto the stool. He had already fashioned a noose at the other end. He had only to tie it tightly around the beam, taking care to check the length left hanging. When he thought he had judged it right, Brunetta stirred. Perched on the stool he stood absolutely still. He had slipped a sleeping draught into her wine earlier in the evening so she shouldn't wake. Perhaps she was dreaming. He glanced over at Tzuri. He was fast asleep. He had been a little worried when he slipped a smaller amount of the potion into his milk, but he seemed to be sleeping peacefully.

His next task was to secure the other two nooses.

He had thought about taking his own life and then he thought why should he be the only one to go? If he couldn't have Brunetta no one else was going to have her, least of all Baruch. It was about time he had his comeuppance for all the grief he had caused his family, especially his parents.

This he did quite easily, pulling on all three to make sure they were secure. Then he went downstairs to fetch two more stools. Had he taken them up earlier, Brunetta might have wondered what they were doing in the bedroom. He returned placing Tzuri's high stool underneath the rope with the longer reach.

The next part would be the most difficult.

He took a length of cloth from underneath the bed and tied it tightly across Brunetta's mouth. He couldn't chance that she would wake up and alert the household. He turned her on her side and tied her hands behind her back then lifted her almost lifeless body out of bed and stood her up. Once upright he spoke to her, coaxing her to stand straight. She was surprisingly obliging. He quickly slipped the noose around Brunetta's slim neck and tightened it. The next task would be to tighten the length of rope so that it allowed Brunetta to stand on the stool but when he kicked it away her neck would snap. He needed her co-operation at this point. He gave her a hard slap across the cheek. Brunetta moaned. He slapped her again. This time her eyes opened. When she realised what was happening, she began struggling with the rope around her wrists. As she struggled, the rope tightened around her neck and she started to choke. Her screams were muffled by the cloth across her mouth.

'Baruch warned me about you. Before we got married. I should have listened to him. You've never loved me. That child isn't even mine.'

Brunetta's eyes widened with terror at the mention of her son.

'If I can't have you no one else will.'

Brunetta stopped struggling. The rope was choking the life out of her.

'On the step,' he snapped.

Brunetta glared at him, trying to shake free. Abraham pulled her onto the step. He was beginning to get impatient. This was going to be more difficult than he thought. In his plan he hadn't bargained on Brunetta being obstinate. When he finally forced her onto the step he immediately pulled on the rope. She was then unable to move or step off the stool. She would be committing suicide if she did.

As Abraham crossed over to the cot, Brunetta followed him with her eyes. When she saw the little noose with the high stool positioned below, the tears streamed from her eyes and her muffled screams grew frantic with barely audible cries and pleadings of 'No' and 'please don't' in between sobs.

He woke Tzuri by shaking him. The boy opened his eyes and wiped them, gazing at his father in that sleepy way children do. Abraham turned him away from his mother so the boy could not see her.

'We're going to play a game, Tzuri. I just need to put this around your neck.'

Tzuri giggled in his childhood innocence.

It was just left for him to put the noose around his own neck, but first he must secure a length of rope to each of the stools. They would go together. When he had finished tying the ropes he stepped onto the stool. Brunetta's muffled screams were hysterical. He slid the noose around his neck and tightened it.

Abraham kicked the stool from beneath him whilst at the same time he pulled on the ropes. There was a clatter of stools on the wooden floor. The rope tightened across his throat, then the room went black.

SIXTY-TWO

That night Baruch had spent the evening at the Lich Inn. He hadn't visited in months, but since Abraham's bizarre behaviour he had been feeling the need to leave the house and find some space. He was regretting his decision. His days of bawdy talk, a belly full of ale and a visit to the whorehouse were well out of his system. The company was unedifying and no longer to his liking. All he could think about was how he could spend the rest of his life with Brunetta and Tzuri. His father, Zev, had brought up another man's child – not very successfully, he thought, but as the child on the receiving end of such paternal coldness he was sure he would not make the same mistakes as Zev. Besides, he had virtually convinced himself that Tzuri was his.

He loved spending the odd snatched moment with both of them. His mood changed, his spirits lifted, and an instant fulfilment befell him. It felt so right to be with her even though she was another man's wife. There must be something they could do to sort this all out. Abraham didn't love Brunetta. He was hardly aware of her existence. He even neglected his son although Brunetta had told him that had not always been the case, and that Abraham had once adored Tzuri. Something seemed to have happened when his father died. Something that had changed him as a person.

The drink was making him think creatively. Perhaps he could appeal to Abraham's better nature, have a man-to-man talk with him and explain that he and Brunetta had fallen in love – that it had just happened. Maybe they could come to some amicable agreement. Divorce was not unheard of in the Jewish community. Arlette would understand. She had suffered such things in her life to understand the most important thing was finding happiness. She had found it with Zev. The major obstacle would be Douce. She doted on Abraham, perhaps more so since Moses' death. Still, he could always charm her in the past. It might work. He began to feel optimistic and finishing his drink he made his way back home.

When he arrived, the house was quiet. As he climbed the stairs to his bedroom, he heard a sound. It was coming from Brunetta's bedroom. It sounded like furniture being thrown around. He ran to the door and flung it open. Brunetta, Tzuri and Abraham were swinging from a trio of nooses, their legs wiggling around, their bodies jerking. Baruch's military experience and his sharp fencing skills sprang into action. He ran to Brunetta and holding on to her legs, so the rope had some slack, he took the knife he kept on his belt and cut the rope around her neck. He let her fall to the floor. Next, he grabbed hold of Tzuri and did the same. Tzuri let out a cry. He held on to the child and went over to Brunetta who was still lying on the floor.

Brunetta was choking and spluttering. Her hands were still tied behind her back. He checked on Tzuri then lay him down. He cut through Brunetta's restraints. She immediately put her hands to her throat where the noose had been. Baruch could see a reddening wheal developing around her neck. She was alive.

Next, he checked Tzuri. The lightness of his small body had probably saved his life. The child was crying and frightened, but he was alive.

'Are you all right?'

Brunetta tried to speak but her voice was croaky. She nodded in the direction of Abraham. His legs had stopped swinging, his tongue was swollen and lolling from his mouth. His breeches were wet, and his eyes were bulging. Baruch had seen enough death on the battlefield to know he was dead.

He passed Tzuri to Brunetta who had propped herself against the wall then stood up and went over to the water jug. He poured some water into a cup and gave it to Brunetta to sip. She was rocking Tzuri and telling him he was all right and *Ima* was there to keep him safe, making sure she covered his eyes so he could not see his father dangling from the noose.

'I didn't like that game, *Ima*,' he said in his childish speech.

'No, it was a silly game. *Aba* won't play it again.' She kissed his head and held him tight.

Brunetta looked up when a shrill scream punctured the chaos surrounding them. It came from Douce. She must have heard the commotion and come to see what it was all about. She stood in the doorway, her hand to her mouth, staring at her son's swaying body dangling from the noose.

Baruch put his arm around her and led her to the bed and sat her down. Then he went over to Abraham and cut down his body before anyone else could see him. He righted the stools and took a sheet off the bed to cover Abraham's body.

Douce sprang off the bed.

'We need to prepare the body,' she said, dropping to her knees beside Abraham.

She removed the sheet. Abraham's face had turned a shade of purple and his tongue had become blackened and more

287

swollen, and it lolled to the side of his mouth like a dog's when it's asleep.

Baruch could tell that Douce was in shock. He went to her side.

'I'll help you do that, *Safta*. I think you should keep him covered for now. You don't want Tzuri or Henne to see him like that.'

Douce nodded her head and covered him up.

'But first I need to get Brunetta and Tzuri out of here.'

Douce nodded her head again. She was not crying nor was she questioning what had happened. She seemed to accept her son was dead. The means by which he had met his death seemed unimportant to her. It was not the time to tell her he had tried to take his wife and child with him.

Baruch took Tzuri from Brunetta and helped her to her feet. He shielded them from Abraham's prone body, leaving Douce alone with her son.

SIXTY-THREE

The next morning Baruch rose early. The events of the previous evening lay heavy on his mind.

When he resumed his liaison with Brunetta he never imagined it would lead to this. Abraham's behaviour had become increasingly odd but to murder his wife and son. It was unconscionable.

He decided to go to the castle to see William Marshal. He would be making his preparations to travel to Vaudreuil in France, as the king had asked him to act as ducal justice there. He needed to free his mind of his thoughts and shake off this feeling of dread and foreboding that had been with him since he awoke.

The Marshal was in a fine mood, and this instantly lifted Baruch's mood.

'Where is the king now?' Baruch asked, wanting to know if the Marshal intended to see him.

The king was back in France fighting the French king, retaking Normandy. He had gone back to France only months after his kidnap.

'The last I heard he was at the Chateau de Fréteval, raiding Philippe's entire archive of financial audits and documents.'

'You would think he had had enough of Europe since his kidnap.'

'Never. Richard is noble and brave. Something like that would make him want to conquer his enemies even more.'

'I suppose so,' Baruch said.

'What's the matter with you today? You seem morose.'

Baruch told him about Abraham and what he had done, leaving out his liaison with Brunetta.

'I met him once at Richard's coronation. I carried Moses out of Westminster Hall as he had collapsed. He seemed quite a timid young man.'

'I thought he was.'

'Why don't you come with me to France? A man like you needs the company of men.'

'I don't know. There's a woman I'd like to stay around for,' Baruch said, ruffling his hair and giving William a coy smile.

'Huh,' said William. 'Women. They're more trouble than they're worth.'

'And that's from a married man,' said Baruch as he tossed his head back and let out a belly laugh.

He couldn't remember the last time he had laughed in the company of men. Perhaps he was spending too much time in the company of women. It was making him soft in the head.

'Think about it. We leave tomorrow.'

Baruch said he would give it some thought and left. He returned home, unsure of what his future held. As he opened the door, he heard shouting.

'I never liked her. I knew she would be no good for my son. I felt it.'

Douce was talking to Henne and Arlette in the kitchen, her voice raised in anger.

'You never said anything before about this,' said Arlette.

'But she was Abraham's choice. He loved her,' said Henne.

'Did he though? She never loved him.'

Baruch listened as his grandmother denigrated Brunetta. He began to have grave reservations about mentioning his affections for Brunetta. Douce would never approve. Brunetta would be more of an outcast than she ever was. Douce would never forgive her. And knowing his grandmother, she would claim that she knew all along they were carrying on behind Abraham's back. He could see her now, touching the amulet she always wore around her neck. The Marshal's invitation looked more attractive than ever. There was no future for him and Brunetta. How could there be? He was foolish to think that could ever happen. Brunetta would be better off without him.

He ran upstairs, packed a few things, and came back down. Douce's shrill words were echoing down the hall. He left without saying goodbye and made his way to the castle.

CHAPTER
SIXTY-FOUR

When Arlette realised Baruch had left without saying goodbye, she was heartbroken. They had regained their mother and son relationship, and she was enjoying being in his company. He had changed whilst away. He was more mature, surer of himself. He had even mended the broken relationship with Zev. The household had been happy again. Like it used to be when her uncle Moses was alive. Now there was a gaping, silent void.

Coming to terms with Abraham's suicide had been easier for her than the rest of the family. She had attempted it once, so knew how a person could be so low they would consider it. When she thought of Baruch and Rubin, she shuddered to think she would not have been here to see them grow up. Abraham would not be around to see Tzuri grow up. An emotion, so raw and deep, welled up within her and tears began to spill from her eyes. She let them fall, only wiping them away when she heard footsteps.

Brunetta came into the hall with Tzuri. The boy seemed to have forgotten the awful events of that night. In time, he would probably forget his father.

'How are you feeling today, Brunetta?'

Arlette felt sorry for Brunetta. She didn't have the same resentment as Douce towards her and didn't blame her for one minute for what Abraham did. Of course, Douce believed she had driven her son to suicide. Mothers were like that about their sons.

'I feel all right, I think,' she replied.

'You think?'

'It's hard to tell these days. I don't seem to feel anything at all. Just numbness.'

'It's not surprising given what you've been through.'

Arlette was careful not to talk about what had happened in front of Tzuri. He was only two years old, but he was a bright boy and understood more than they realised. Brunetta slumped onto the chair that had once been Moses'.

'I just don't understand why he did it,' said Brunetta, ruffling her hand through Tzuri's hair.

'We'll never know, I'm afraid.'

'I don't think I'll ever forgive him.'

'You might, one day.'

'I know we weren't particularly happy. We hadn't been for some time. He changed after his father died. There was no getting through to him.'

'He did change. I noticed that. They're together now.'

'I suppose so.'

Arlette was surprised at Brunetta. She rarely engaged in conversation. Perhaps she was feeling particularly lonely today.

'Have you heard from Baruch?' she asked Arlette.

'He's in France. Fighting again with the king.'

'Do you miss him?'

'I do. More this time than before.'

'Why's that?'

'He came back a nicer man. I miss that man.'

'So do I.'

Arlette was not sure what she had just heard. Did Brunetta say she missed Baruch? Was there something between them? Now she thought about it, Baruch did seem overly attentive to Tzuri. Another thought struck her. Was Tzuri his? She studied the boy playing at Brunetta's feet. He could be. There was a resemblance there when you looked for it. But Tzuri had a placid temperament unlike Baruch when he was that age. He was a terror. How ironic, she thought, if Tzuri was his.

'Do you know why he suddenly left?' Brunetta asked her.

'I have no idea. He had no reason to leave. We were all getting on so well.'

'Yes, it was nice to see. I hadn't seen that side of him before. He was always so brash, so selfish.' Then, as an afterthought, 'I'm sorry, Arlette, I didn't mean to be rude.'

'You're not. I know what my son was like.'

'Perhaps he missed that life.'

'The life of a fighter. Maybe. Sometimes it's in the bones of a man. Still, he should have said something before he left. To go without saying anything. That's cruel.'

Brunetta nodded. 'Do you think he'll ever come back?'

'When he's ready. Unless he gets himself killed on the battlefield.'

Brunetta's bottom lip quivered, and she looked like she was about to cry.

'I didn't mean to upset you,' Arlette said, walking towards Brunetta and putting her arm around her to comfort her.

As soon as she did Brunetta started to sob.

'What's the matter, Brunetta? You can tell me.'

'I'm with child,' she blurted out through her sobs.

Ordinarily Arlette would congratulate her, but it seemed indelicate to do so under the circumstances. Her husband not long dead and who knew if the child was his or Baruch's. She was itching to ask but didn't dare. It was Brunetta's business. It would work itself out. These things always did. For now, Brunetta needed her support. She might be carrying her grandson. It seemed a betrayal of Abraham somehow, but life had a strange way of playing out sometimes. She hugged Brunetta.

'We'll get through this. I'll help you.'

'What about Douce?'

'Douce will come around. She's grieving now. She says things she doesn't mean.'

'I don't think she likes me. I don't think she's ever liked me. I was never good enough for her son.' Brunetta's sobs intensified.

'There, there,' Arlette said, comforting Brunetta. 'But you're having another grandchild for her. That'll please her.'

At that, Brunetta howled like she was in pain, her body wracked by sobs. Arlette wondered if she should take that as an admission that the child was not Abraham's.

CHAPTER

SIXTY-FIVE

I t was early evening. Baruch had eaten and was listening to a troubadour play by the campfire. His name was Bertran de Born, a man of middle years who was quite famous in France for writing songs about the King of England. As well as singing he had a market stall in the village of Châlus-Chabrol. Baruch thought he recognised him from the troubadours William Longchamp brought to Gloucester for the legatine council.

He was still listening when the tall figure of the king came into view. Baruch had spent the last five years fighting at his side. The Marshal had been with him most of that time, but the king had sent him to Vaudreuil just south of Rouen to act as ducal justice there. Baruch missed his company. They had become good friends and Baruch looked upon him as the father he never had. Bored with the troubadour's songs Baruch stood up to join him on the battlements of Châlus-Chabrol Castle.

It was a calm evening, the dark sky full of stars. The smell of burning wood filled the night air. The king dressed in casual clothes and appeared to be in an unusually good humour. His trusted Occitan mercenary Mercadier was by his side.

'The men are in good spirits this evening,' he said to Mercadier.

'They have good reason to be. Their king has come to be with them, Your Majesty.'

They walked past a young man who was leaning against the parapet. He was clutching a frying pan in his hand.

'What are you doing with that, young man?' asked the king.

'Fending off the bastard missiles that keep coming at me from over there,' he said and pointed to the dark fields beyond where braziers could be seen glowing in the distance. The king laughed and then addressed a crossbowman standing next to the young man.

'And what about you?'

The crossbowman aimed his crossbow at the king. Mercadier and Baruch stepped forward to shield the king.

'Let him be. He is only showing off,' the king said, pushing them aside and applauding the skill of the crossbowman with a loud clapping of his hands.

Whoosh.

The undeniable sound of an arrow being despatched through the air cut through the laughter. The king staggered, putting his hand to his neck where an arrow had pierced the flesh. Blood pumped rhythmically from the wound. Mercadier shouted for help. Several soldiers came to their aid and helped to carry the king down into the great hall of the castle. Mercadier demanded that his physician, Salvanhac, be fetched.

The king was having difficulty speaking, his words rasping and curiously gargling. He grabbed at the shaft of the arrow and tried to rip it from his neck, but the pain was too much, and he slumped back on the bed. The physician arrived, carrying a wooden box and lost no time in staunching the flow of blood with a square of cloth he carried in there for such purposes. He snapped the wooden shaft of the arrow, ignoring the agonising cries from the king.

'I will have to locate the arrowhead. It may have come dislodged from the shaft. It will have to be removed.'

He looked at Mercadier for permission to carry on.

'Do what you must to save the king's life.'

Salvanhac took a knife from his medical chest and began to sharpen it on a whetstone.

'What are you going to do with that?' asked Mercadier.

'As I said, the arrowhead must be located. I need to make an incision by the entry wound.'

Mercadier nodded, not taking his eyes off the king. Baruch stood close by. Salvanhac called for a flagon of brandy to be brought. The brandy arrived and Salvanhac passed it to Mercadier.

'Make him drink it. It will dull the pain.'

Mercadier took hold of the flagon and put the mouth of it to the king's lips. The king could not speak but drank the brandy offered. Not waiting for the alcohol to take effect, Salvanhac made a long incision close to the wound. Richard howled with pain.

'Hold him down for me, please. I need him to be still.'

Mercadier beckoned Baruch forward and the two men held down the king while Salvanhac pierced the king's flesh. The flesh opened causing more blood to gush. Salvanhac mopped up the worst of it, then slid his finger along the shaft to feel the depth of the wound and to locate the arrowhead which he hoped would still be attached. Salvanhac shook his head. He could not feel the shaft. He pulled his hand from the wound and wiped it on the cloth.

'The shaft has become dislodged. I will need to make a bigger incision to locate it.'

Once again, he checked with Mercadier. Mercadier looked at the king who had almost passed out with the pain.

'Is it really necessary?'

'If you want to keep him alive, yes.'

Mercadier nodded and gave the king more brandy. Salvanhac slid the knife through the king's flesh, opening up the gaping wound further. The king cried out again. He rummaged around, prodding into soft tissue but to no avail.

'The arrowhead must be lodged in the bone, I fear. I cannot locate it but if it has gone into bone, it will be much harder to dislodge.'

'What happens if you don't remove it?' Mercadier asked.

Salvanhac shrugged. Mercadier looked at the mangled mess Salvanhac had made of the king's neck.

'Leave it alone. I don't think he can stand much more. Wait till he gains a little strength,' Mercadier cautioned.

'As you wish,' replied Salvanhac with the professional distance of a surgeon.

SIXTY-SIX

Richard lay for days, febrile and grey, drifting in and out of consciousness. The wound had swelled up and the skin surrounding it had changed to a blackish colour, covered in blisters and pustular sores. A putrescent smell emanated from it, filling the great hall, which did not go away with the bringing of fresh rushes of sweet-smelling herbs. Baruch noticed that when Salvanhac examined the wound, on pressing around the area, it made a wincingly crackling noise.

In one of his more alert awakenings, he demanded the person who fired the arrow to be brought to him. Mercadier had already arrested the perpetrator. His name was Pierre de Basile, and he was no more than a boy. The boy was brought before the ailing king, shackled and with signs of having been tortured.

'You are no more than a boy,' the king said, speaking in a low, almost inaudible, voice.

The boy did not reply.

'Won't you have the decency to tell your king why you did this to him, boy?' Mercadier growled, pushing the boy forward, his chains rattling.

'The king killed my father and my two brothers. It's simple,' the boy said, 'I wanted to kill him in revenge.'

The king did not seem displeased at this confession. He raised his head to take a closer look at the boy.

'I'm dying,' he said to the boy. 'You have your revenge, but I will not take mine.'

As a final act of mercy Richard forgave him. Baruch was astounded. The king was not known for his clemency. It must be the fever.

'Live on, and by my bounty behold the light of day.'

The boy sank to his knees and sobbed.

Richard addressed Mercadier. 'Release him and give him 100 shillings and set him on his way.'

'But, Your Majesty...' began Mercadier.

The king raised his hand to silence his trusted friend.

'It is my dying wish. Go now and leave me.'

SIXTY-SEVEN

Richard's mother, Eleanor of Aquitaine, had been informed of her son's condition. She arrived with her entourage and went to see her son immediately. By this time Richard was gravely ill. He rarely woke from his feverish slumber; his body was covered in a mottled rash of dark purple. Eleanor leaned over to kiss his forehead. His skin was cold and clammy.

'*Je suis ici, mon chér. C'est ta mère.*'

Richard did not respond. Eleanor took him in her arms and cradled him. His breathing was rapid with long periods where he did not breathe at all. Then, without warning, he took his last gentle breath.

'I think he was holding out until you came, Your Majesty,' Mercadier said.

Eleanor did not reply. She drew her son's body close and rocked him.

Mercadier slipped out of the hall and, indicating to Baruch to follow him, left the grieving mother alone. He was making his way to the dungeon where he had taken the young boy Pierre de Basile. Baruch followed behind. Baruch soon realised he had no intention of letting the boy go. As they neared the dungeon Mercadier told him that if the king were to have had all his faculties, he would have wanted revenge. They found the boy huddled in the corner of his fetid cell. He trembled with fear when he saw Mercadier.

'The king is dead. He may have said he did not want revenge, but I will have my revenge for the king's honour. You will suffer for this.' Mercadier raised his boot and stamped on the boy, turning his foot as if he were squashing an insect. 'The king was the most courageous of kings and had the heart of a lion, but sadly he was slain by an ant.' He turned to leave, shouting at his gaolers. 'Flay him alive and then hang him. I never want to see him again.'

Baruch could hear the boy's screams as he left the dungeon. He had seen enough of death and torture and had no desire to look back. When Mercadier and Baruch returned, preparations for the king's burial were already underway by his physician Salvanhac. Richard's heart had been removed and was being embalmed with frankincense, mixed with myrtle, daisy, mint and lime before being wrapped in linen. It was to be buried at the Cathédrale de Notre Dame in Rouen. His entrails and the rest of his body were to be buried at the foot of his father Henry's grave in Fontevraud Abbey. The room no longer smelt of death but had taken on an air of sanctity, fit for a king, who naturally represented the divine on Earth.

A feeling of utter despair descended upon Baruch. The king he had fought with in the Crusades and in France was dead. The Marshal would be equally devastated. Once again Baruch thought of home. It was probably time he went back. Hopefully, the situation between Douce and Brunetta had settled down. He thought of his mother and had an intense desire to see her, to have her ruffle his hair with her delicate, soft hands.

The king's mother, Eleanor, was still in the room, watching

Salvanhac prepare her son's body for burial. She sat at some distance. Mercadier approached her.

'Your Majesty, the king's dying wishes were to appoint his brother John as his heir.'

The queen smiled, a bemused expression appearing. 'So my son John is finally to receive his lands. He will no longer be known as *sans terre.*'

'May he be a wise ruler and a fair king to his loyal subjects, Your Majesty.'

CHAPTER

SIXTY-EIGHT

Baruch stayed in Châlus-Chabrol for a few more days, helping Mercadier in the absence of the Marshal. When he thought he could do no more he left and made the journey back to England. He arrived on the day of the coronation of Prince John at Westminster Abbey.

He wasn't sure how he was going to be received by his family. He had tried to keep in touch with his mother, but it hadn't been easy and after a few months he made no effort. He was curious to see Brunetta and wondered if the old feelings he had for her would surface. He had tried to forget her by lying in the arms of camp followers, but they were working girls and it left him feeling empty.

As he walked through the South Gate into the city, he noticed his heart was beating a little faster than normal. The same feeling he would have at the start of a battle. Why was he feeling so apprehensive? They were mere women. He laughed at himself, but it didn't stop the fluttering which grew stronger the nearer he got to the house. When he reached the High Cross, he saw Brunetta. She was walking in the direction of her mother's house, holding the hand of a pretty little girl who was skipping alongside Brunetta. Walking next to her was Tzuri. He looked very grown up as he walked next to his mother, not holding her hand. Baruch tried to work out how old he would be now. At least seven or eight.

Brunetta had not changed. She still had a voluptuous quality about her. But who was the little girl? She looked to be about four years old. It occurred to him that she might be his. Brunetta had told him that her and Abraham hadn't done it for years. His cold heart softened at the thought of being father to a daughter. Without thinking, he ran towards them, shouting her name. Brunetta turned around and stopped in her tracks. The boy looked from his mother to Baruch. Did he recognise him? By the time he reached them, Brunetta had already turned back around and was dragging both children along with her hurrying down the street.

'Brunetta, stop. Please stop.'

She stopped suddenly. Baruch was out of breath. He took a good look at the girl.

'Is she mine?'

'Yes,' said Brunetta.

Her voice was stern and clipped. Baruch was saddened by her one-word answer. He stood catching his breath and gathering his thoughts and emotions which were whirring around inside him. He had a daughter and very possibly a son.

'Is that all you have to say to me?'

Brunetta was angry at him. The colour had risen in her cheeks and her chest was rising with every breath.

'I'm sorry.'

'Is that it?'

'I didn't know you were with child when I left.'

'You didn't stay around to find out.'

'Who is this man, *Ima*?' said Tzuri, screwing his eyes up and staring at Baruch.

'I'm Baruch. Don't you remember me?'

The boy shook his head. Baruch turned to Brunetta.

'I thought it best I leave, given the circumstances.'

'You thought you'd leave me just when I needed you.'

Baruch realised he had been selfish. He hadn't been thinking of her and how she was feeling. Even though Brunetta was angry with him he knew standing in front of her that he still had feelings for her. He was maddeningly attracted to her. He bent down to the child.

'And what's your name?'

Brunetta answered for her. 'It's Ozanne.'

'So you're not named after *Safta*?'

Ozanne hid behind her mother's skirts.

'She's adorable,' Baruch said, standing up. 'If I'd known I would have come back sooner.'

Brunetta huffed in disbelief. Baruch took hold of both her hands.

'Please forgive me.'

To his surprise she let him hold her hands in his. Her hands were soft. He raised them to his lips and kissed them. Her skin was still an olive shade and smelled of roses. She snatched them away. He couldn't blame her. He had been gone for five long years. He had missed the birth of his child. He had let her down.

'Does anyone know I'm her father?'

'They all have their suspicions.'

More family secrets thought Baruch as he remembered finding out about his real father. History had a habit of repeating itself.

'How are you and Douce getting on?'

'She tolerates me because she adores the children. We muddle along.'

'That's good. Douce can be a formidable enemy.'

'I know. We've been at war ever since my betrothal to Abraham.'

Her voice trailed off. It felt strange to hear his name.

'How is Mother?'

'Just the same. We're all just the same as we were when you left.'

Baruch detected bitterness in her voice. He had a lot of making up to do. He could see that. But for now, he was content to be back in their lives.

'Are you going to see your mother?'

'Yes. She likes to see the children at least once a day.'

'I had better let you go. I want to see Mother.'

'She's missed you. She took your leaving very badly.'

Baruch lowered his gaze. He felt like a complete and utter swine for having abandoned them all.

'Can we talk later, when the children are asleep?'

'If you want,' she said, shrugging her shoulders.

At least she hadn't said no. He took her by the shoulders and kissed her three times in the French way. Her body yielded to his touch. Baruch accepted the small gesture. Perhaps, after all, there would be a future for them.

CHAPTER

SIXTY-NINE

When Baruch walked into his old home in Eastgate Street the first person he saw was his mother, Arlette. She was sitting by the unlit fire embroidering. Alone. The house had an empty feel to it. Much like it did immediately after the death of Moses. Baruch crept up behind her and closed his hands over her eyes. She screamed and tried to escape. Baruch released his hands.

'*Ima*, it's me.'

'Baruch!' she exclaimed, her face draining of colour.

'What are you doing here?'

'I've come home.'

'Just like that. No word. Where have you been?'

'I've been fighting in France with the king.'

'The king is dead.'

'I know that's why I came home. You seem frightened, what's the matter?'

'I'm just on edge. It's been difficult since you left.'

Baruch sat down opposite Arlette. She had aged since he last saw her and was thinner.

'How are Zev and Rubin?'

Arlette winced slightly. He had probably offended her by calling Zev by his name. A reminder that he was not Baruch's father.

'They're very well.'

'Still working together?'

'Yes, the silver business is going well. Rubin is married now. To a lovely girl. They have a child. You have a niece, Baruch.'

Baruch almost corrected his mother and said, 'You mean a half-niece,' when he stopped. His mother was frail, not able to cope with his sarcasm.

'That's great news. What's her name?'

'They named her Damete after Zev's mother.'

'That's nice,' said Baruch unconvincingly.

'Why did you leave?' his mother asked.

Baruch did not have an answer.

'When we all needed you... Not just Brunetta.'

'You know about Brunetta?'

'I didn't then. But after you left, she was so distraught she confided in me.'

'Does Douce know?'

'I haven't told her, but I think she has an inkling. She's not stupid.'

'Anything but. What's been happening, *Ima*, since I left?'

'Douce discovered after Abraham's...' she faltered, 'after his death that he hadn't been managing the family business very well...'

The hall fell silent. Baruch did not fill it.

'It was bad. Douce couldn't help because she'd always kept out of the moneylending business. She'd always left that to Moses.'

'Truth was no one filled Moses' shoes after his death.'

'No one can replace Moses,' she said, her eyes tearing up.

Even after all these years his mother still missed Moses. He drew her to him and hugged her. Arlette buried her head into his chest and sobbed. When the sobs subsided, she pulled away.

'We need you, Baruch.'

'But I know nothing of moneylending. How can I help?'

'Maybe you could use your influence with the king to stop him taking our home.'

'This house?'

Baruch could not believe what he was hearing. No wonder Brunetta had been frosty with him. Not for the first time in his life did Baruch feel like an utter *mamzer*. The irony of it hit him. He was a bastard.

'Why is he taking the house?'

'Because Abraham was so bad at sorting out Moses' death taxes, we may have to relinquish the house to the king to pay the outstanding amounts.'

'This would never have happened when Moses was alive.'

He regretted saying it immediately. Arlette's pained expression made his heart ache.

'Who took over the business after Abraham?'

'No one really. We were all operating in the dark. Like headless chickens lurching from one financial disaster to another.'

'Moses will be turning in his grave.'

Arlette burst into tears at Baruch's careless comment.

'Sorry, *Ima*. I didn't mean to upset you. How can I help?'

'Use your influence with the king...'

She looked at him with pleading eyes full of tears. Her pale face looked thinner than ever. The pain in Baruch's heart intensified and a sickness of conscience overtook him. He was a selfish bastard. No thought for anyone but himself. He should never have left. His mother was suffering. Brunetta hated him. And what had he achieved? A few battle scars. He thought of the new king, John. He barely knew him. His mother's confidence in his ability to influence the new king was sadly misplaced.

'I don't know the new king. My influence was with Richard.'

'What about the Marshal?'

'I could try but I'm well away from all that now. Too much politicking and uncertainty. John is only king by the skin of his teeth. There are many who think Arthur of Brittany should be king.'

'But his coronation is this Thursday.'

'I know. Hopefully that will settle the matter.'

For some reason Baruch remembered the day of Richard's coronation ten years ago when he took Brunetta by the riverside. He was a callous youth back then.

'Let's hope there won't be a repeat of what happened at King Richard's coronation.'

Baruch looked puzzled for a second then remembered the riots and the killing of the Jews and poor Moses caught up in it all.

Arlette's brow furrowed. She was deep in thought.

'How times have changed. Ten years ago Moses and Abraham attended the king's coronation. Both no longer with us and this time Mirabelle will be going with Bonanfaunt.'

Baruch raised an eyebrow, knowing how much acrimony existed between the two families.

'How does Douce feel about that?'

Arlette snickered and a light came into her eyes that hadn't been there before.

'Oh you know those two. Douce will rail against Mirabelle till her dying breath.'

'No love lost then.'

Arlette smiled and stroked Baruch's cheek. 'It's so good to see you.'

Baruch blushed but let his mother's hand linger against his scarred cheek. She fell silent again and looked down at her unfinished embroidery.

'About the house, *Ima*? Will you definitely lose it?'

'I don't know. The old king wanted payment of the death taxes. I can't see that things will change with the new king. The house is all we have left. We've been fighting it but to no avail. Your grandmother is convinced Mirabelle has something to do with it.'

'Knowing Mirabelle I wouldn't put it past her. She's always had it in for this family.'

'Before she was angry with us, now she's positively gloating. All of Moses' wealthy clients have been poached by her and that toad of a husband.'

Baruch had never heard his mother speak in such terms about anyone. She was always such a sweet, mild-mannered woman. She must have suffered a lot to become this embittered. The age-old feelings of guilt hung heavy on his conscience.

'Why didn't you send word? I would have come back.'

Baruch knew as soon as he said it that it was a lie. He would not have come back until he was ready regardless of anyone else.

'We didn't know how to get hold of you. You left without saying goodbye.' Arlette began to tear up.

'Please, *Ima*, please don't cry. I'll try and make it up to you.'

Arlette sniffed, placed her embroidery on the table, then wiped her nose with her apron.

'What's done is done,' she said, taking in a deep breath.

CHAPTER
SEVENTY

The children were in bed and Baruch was eager to speak with Brunetta. She was still avoiding him. He waited in the hall with his mother and Douce for her to join them and when she didn't, he went in search of her. He found her in the courtyard sitting on the bench that was once the favourite spot of Moses. He had a sudden flashback of the family in happier times when he was a boy and everyone around him seemed more cheerful. Or was that just how it was for the young before the outside world soured their view of life?

'Aren't you cold sitting out here?' he asked as he approached.

Brunetta seemed to flinch when she heard his voice. He had hurt her deeply. He must make amends. He sat down next to her and wondered if he should put his arm around her to warm her. Then he thought better of it. She would probably push him away. He had to tread carefully. Think of her this time. Not himself.

'We need to talk.'

Brunetta was silent, staring straight ahead of her, her jaw set.

'I've hurt you. I know that now. I've hurt everyone. Anyone who ever meant anything to me. Anyone who ever showed me love. I was angry with the world, and I never knew why.' Baruch's voice was trembling.

Brunetta turned to look at him. 'Don't you think you're a little too late?'

'I think I may be and that terrifies me.'

Brunetta furrowed her brow and stared at Baruch. Did she believe him? Baruch could not tell.

'Why are you telling me this now?'

'I don't know. I–'

'You can't just breeze back into our lives and think you can pick up where you left off. Life doesn't work like that.'

'I'm finding that out. Please, Brunetta. Give me one more chance. I promise you I'll never leave you and the children again.' He paused. 'They are my children, aren't they?'

Brunetta faced away from him, her face set in anger, her hands twisted together in a fist on her lap. Even in anger she was beautiful. He wanted to kiss her. Not lustfully like in the past but tenderly. Lovingly. He placed his hand on hers. He felt her try to pull away then stop. Did she still have some feelings for him? Was her anger a sign of love for him? Like waking from a dream and feeling a heightened sense of clarity he knew that all along he had loved her.

'I've treated you abysmally, but in my own strange way, I have always loved you, Brunetta. I know that now.'

Baruch's voice broke. He removed his hand from hers and placing his elbows on his knees he buried his head in his hands and began to sob. Gentle sobs. Brunetta swung round. She stared at him for a moment and then her own tears began to flow.

'I loved you from that first moment when you took me by the river but later, I convinced myself it was just lust. I never loved Abraham. It was always you, but you made it hard for me to express that love.'

Baruch looked up. His face was wrought with torment, the tears falling down his sun browned cheeks.

'Marry me.'

SEVENTY-ONE

The wedding was a low-key affair. Just close friends and family. Abigail, now infirm and unsteady on her feet, walked with Brunetta to the *chuppah*, the wedding canopy, where the rest of the family waited for them. Then afterwards a small celebration in the courtyard.

Baruch was in a thoughtful mood as he sat in the courtyard listening to his cousin, Henne, play the kinnor and the sound of Bellassez's pure voice. He was staring at the steps leading to the *scola* and remembered how he had seduced Brunetta on her wedding day and taunted Abraham afterwards. The sex had been impassioned. Brunetta wanton. His gaze switched to her. She sat with Ozanne on her knee. Tzuri was chasing his cousins around the courtyard, screeching excitedly. Would she be as wanton tonight? Would it be as exciting as it was in the past? Baruch swept his hair from his forehead, agitated with himself. What did it matter? They were married and he loved her. He was going to be a good father to his children and a good husband to his wife. No more whores; no drinking in taverns. He had even renewed his belief in the Jewish faith by attending synagogue regularly. He let out a snort of laughter. He could hardly believe he was the same man.

'What are you finding so amusing?'

Baruch smiled at Douce. She had been a constant in his life. Never judging him as others had. He had often wondered what secret she and Moses had spoken of that day he overheard them. The day Moses died. Douce had said she would take whatever it was to her grave. It had something to do with his father. He looked at the lines around her eyes, her aquiline nose, her prominent cheekbones. She was imperious.

'I was just thinking of the past.'

'It never does any good to dwell on the past. On this day of days you should be looking to the future.'

'I'm actually looking forward to the future for once in my life, *Safta*. I really think I have a chance at happiness.'

'You've changed so much since you came back to us. I am so proud of you.'

A hard lump formed in Baruch's throat. Douce had never told him she was proud of him. He hadn't given her much to be proud of.

'I tried to save him.'

Douce shifted on the bench. They had never spoken of Abraham's death. He had left before those awkward conversations could take place. Running away again.

'Brunetta told me you did your best.'

'I'm sorry it wasn't more.'

'You have nothing to be sorry for. I loved my son, but he did a wicked thing.'

'He wasn't in his right mind. He would never have done anything to hurt anyone. He must have been in a dark place.'

'I am just thankful your grandfather wasn't around to witness it.' She stood up. 'Come, let's join the dancing. This is not a day to be maudlin.'

Baruch made his way over to Brunetta. He picked up Ozanne and set her on the floor and took Brunetta's hand and pulled her up from her chair. He slipped his arm around her waist and led her to the group of dancers.

'I don't think I've ever danced with you,' he said, brushing his lips across her cheek.

Brunetta nuzzled into his cheek and whispered, 'You've never made love to me as my husband either.'

Baruch held her at arm's length. There was a coquettish smile upon her lips and a twinkle in her eye. His stomach flipped and the long-held desire for her engulfed him.

'Don't say those things or I may have to take you to bed now.'

Brunetta gave him an inviting look. She wanted him.

'Would that be such a bad thing?'

Baruch slipped his arm around her waist and pulled her to him.

'Not at all.'

THE END

Historical Notes

1. For the account of the riots and massacre at Westminster I have relied loosely upon Roger Hovedon's account.
2. For the account of the massacre at York I have relied loosely upon Ephraim of Bonn's account.
3. Abraham's chirograph of 1194 is in the archives of the Dean and Chapter of Hereford Cathedral.
4. Journey times have been calculated using the ORBIS online tool.
5. Dates have been calculated using HebCal.
6. It is a tradition in the Jewish community to have historically used Hebrew patronymic names. We know Moses le Riche had another son whom they named Samuel, presumably to honour little Samuel, who died. To avoid confusion for the reader, as there are several Samuels, I have called him Benjamin.
7. In order to distinguish between Christian and Jewish characters I have used some Jewish words which I acknowledge may sound anachronistic for some readers.

8. For descriptions of Jewish culture and religious services I have relied on Rabinowitz's book: *The Social Life of the Jews of Northern France in the XII-XIV Centuries*, L. Rabinowitz, M.A. 1938.

A NOTE FROM THE PUBLISHER

Thank you for reading this book. If you enjoyed it please do consider leaving a review on Amazon to help others find it too.

We hate typos. All of our books have been rigorously edited and proofread, but sometimes mistakes do slip through. If you have spotted a typo, please do let us know and we can get it amended within hours.

info@bloodhoundbooks.com

GLOSSARY

Aba: Father

Alaichem shalom: A greeting

Amein: Amen

Archa: An official chest, provided with three locks and seals, in which a counterpart of all deeds and contracts involving Jews was to be deposited in order to preserve the records

Ba'al tokeah: One who blows the shofar

Baruch HaShem: Thank God

Bet Din: Means house of judgment. Jewish tribunal empowered to adjudicate cases involving criminal, civil, or religious law

Birkat HaMazon: Grace after meals

Brit milah: Circumcision ceremony

Challah: Egg baked bread served on the Sabbath

Chametz: Unleavened substances, such as wheat, barley, oats, spelt, rye

Chevra kaddisha: A group of volunteers who help prepare the body for burial

Cholent: Slow cooked beef stew served on the Sabbath

Chuppah: Wedding canopy

Elohim: One of the words in Hebrew for God

Erusin: Betrothal

Eschet chayil: Woman of worth

Fiancée: Engaged woman

Haggadah: The Haggadah is a Jewish text that sets forth the order of the Passover Seder

Hag Pesach Sameach: Happy Passover

Hashem: Literal translation: The Name. Used as a name for God

Havdalah: Ritual to mark end of Sabbath

Ima: Mother

Ketubah: Marriage contract

Kiddush: A special prayer for the Sabbath or other special religious occasion, recited over wine

Kosher: Food sold, cooked, or eaten and satisfying the requirements of Jewish law

L'chaim: A toast

Ma chérie: My darling (to a female)

GLOSSARY

Mamzer: Bastard

Mazel tov: Congratulations

Mikveh: Sunken bath for ritual cleansing

Mon chér: My darling (to a male)

Niddah: A Hebrew term describing a woman during menstruation or bleeding after childbirth

Nissuin: The second part of the Jewish wedding process. Marriage

Olam Ha-Ba: The afterlife

Oy lanu: Woe is us

Paschal: Relating to Easter

Perutah: An ancient Jewish coin of small value

Pesach: Passover: a Jewish religious festival commemorating the emancipation of the Israelites from slavery in ancient Egypt

Sabba: Grandfather

Safta: Grandmother

Scola: School

Seder: The Passover meal

Shabbat: Jewish Sabbath

Shalom Alaichem: To you be peace

Shanah tovah: A common Jewish greeting on Rosh Hashanah

Shechinah: Divine presence

Shehecheyanu: A blessing, the first time you do something each Jewish calendar year

Shevarim: The second of the shofar blasts. The word literally means: break or fracture

Shofar: An ancient musical horn typically made of a ram's horn

Shokeling: The ritual swaying of worshippers during Jewish prayer

Shomerim: A person who sits with the dead body out of respect, literally a guard

Tallage: Tax

Urchatz: Ritual hand washing

Yahrzeit: The anniversary of someone's death

Yichud: The prohibition of seclusion in a private area of a man and a woman who are not married to each other

Zonah: Prostitute

Printed in Great Britain
by Amazon

22104935R00192